Renowned throughout Canada and the world as a poet, playwright, and novelist, Anne Hébert devoted her life to writing.

Born on August 1, 1916, in Sainte-Catherine-de-Fossambault, a tiny village 40 kilometres northeast of Quebec City, Anne Hébert was encouraged to write at an early age by her father, Maurice Lang-Hébert, a respected poet and literary critic and her cousin, the poet Hector de Saint-Denys Garneau.

Anne Hébert published her first volume of poetry, *Les Songes en équilibre*, in 1942. The book garnered strong critical praise and won the Prix David in 1943. Despite this success, Quebec publishers refused to publish her subsequent dark and violent works, *Le Torrent* and *Le Tombeau des rois*. As a result, the former was published in 1950 and the latter in 1952 at the expense of Hébert and her friend Roger Lemelin. In 1954, with the help of a grant from the Royal Society of Canada, Anne Hébert left for Paris, a city she believed would embrace her style and subject matter. Although Paris's provocative cityscapes and mysterious underground later set the scene for four of her novels, Hébert remained fascinated and inspired by Quebec, and became revered as one of French Canada's literary treasures.

During a career that spanned nearly sixty years, Anne Hébert was honoured with many prestigious awards. She won the Prix France-Canada and the Prix Duvernay in 1958 for *Les Chambres de bois*, the Governor General's Award in 1960 for *Poèmes*, the Molson Prize in 1967, a second Governor General's Award in 1975 for *Les Enfants du sabbat*, the Prix Femina in 1982 for *Les Fous de Bassan*, and a third Governor General's Award in 1992 for *L'Enfant chargé de songes*. Sheila Fischman's translation of *Le Premier jardin*, *The First Garden*, won the Félix Antoine-Savard Prize for translation and *Am I disturbing you?* (her translation of *Est ce que je te dérange?*) was a finalist for the Giller Prize in 1999.

Anne Hébert's work has been widely translated and has sold throughout the world. Two volumes of her poetry, *Anne Hébert: Selected Poems* and *Day Has No Equal but the Night*, and her novels *In the Shadow of the Wind*, *The First Garden*, *Kamouraska*, and the four included in this extraordinary collection have been published in English by House of Anansi Press to stellar reviews.

Anne Hébert passed away in Montreal on January 22, 2000. She continues to be celebrated for her literary genius and for her enrichment of Canadian literature.

Anne Hébert
Collected Later Novels

ANNE HÉBERT
COLLECTED LATER NOVELS

Translated by
Sheila Fischman

Introduction by
Mavis Gallant

ANANSI

Published in 2003 by
House of Anansi Press Inc.
110 Spadina Avenue, Suite 801
Toronto, ON, M5V 2K4
Tel. 416-363-4343
Fax 416-363-1017
www.anansi.ca

Distributed in Canada by
Publishers Group Canada
250A Carlton Street
Toronto, ON, M5A 2L1
Tel. 416-934-9900
Toll free order numbers:
Tel. 800-663-5714 Fax 800-565-3770

These books were first published by Éditions du Seuil as *L'enfant chargé
de songes* (1992), *Aurélien, Clara, Mademoiselle et le Lieutenant anglais* (1995),
Est-ce que je te dérange? (1998), and *Un Habit de lumière* (1999).

07   06   05   04   03   1   2   3   4   5

Canadian Cataloguing in Publication Data

Hébert, Anne, 1916–2000.
[Novels. Selections]
Collected later novels
Translation of: Aurélien, Clara, Mademoiselle et le Lieutenant anglais, Un habit
de lumière, Est-ce que je te dérange? and L'enfant chargé de songes.
ISBN 0-88784-671-8

I. Fischman, Sheila II. Title.

PS8515.E16A24 2001   C843'.54   C2001-901822-3
PQ3919.H37A24 2001

Cover Design: Angel Guerra
Page Design & Composition: Kevin Cockburn / PageWave Graphics Inc.

THE CANADA COUNCIL | LE CONSEIL DES ARTS
FOR THE ARTS | DU CANADA
SINCE 1957 | DEPUIS 1957

*We acknowledge for their financial support of our publishing program the Canada Council
for the Arts, the Ontario Arts Council, and the Government of Canada through the Book
Publishing Industry Development Program (BPIDP). This book was made possible in
part through the Canada Council's translation grants program.*

Printed and bound in Canada

CONTENTS

Introduction

by
Mavis Gallant

The French author Marguerite Yourcenar believed it was impossible to write anything about women, because their lives were so full of secrets. A woman's life, she said, was like one of those old-fashioned sewing machines with a multitude of small drawers meant to hold thread and buttons and miniature scissors. Every drawer contains a different secret. Yourcenar said nothing about men and their secrets or about artists in general or writers in particular or the profound split between life imagined and lives lived. All this is to say that a friend may be allowed a glimpse of a drawer opened and feel entitled to suppose it reveals an autobiography. Years later it can turn out that the revelations were elements of a creation, or of things that actually happened, but to different people. In short, the writer is quite correctly taking for granted that the work produced out of these fragments is a whole continent while daily life is a piece of land so small one could drive past it in a minute. If real life has any meaning or even makes any sense, it is because the artist's view of it is reality in essence and a plain truth undimmed.

I met Anne Hébert in 1955, in Menton, a large town on the Mediterranean coast, the last train stop before the border between France and Italy. I knew only that she had moved to Paris from Quebec to live and write. All I had read of hers was a short volume of poetry, *Le Tombeau des rois*, which a friend had sent me from Montreal. It was elegant, haunting, and filled with death — the Quebec imagination of that period — and composed with calm self-assurance, well beyond the tone of a beginning poet. Jean Paul Lemieux, the Quebec painter, and his wife Madeleine Desrosiers, also a painter, had asked me to call on Anne at her hotel, the Aiglon. I had rented a small house in Menton. Anne knew no one.

They forgot to tell me that she was paralyzingly shy and suffered from acute myopia. We remained standing at that first meeting in the lobby of Hôtel Aiglon, because she was too diffident to ask me to sit down. I wondered why she wore blue-tinted glasses indoors, unaware that her eyes were painfully sensitive to light. When, groping for conversation, I asked if she was missing Quebec, she said yes, she missed the smell of breakfast toast. I thought she was dismissing the question or perhaps Quebec itself. Years later, I discovered it was all she could think of to say. An invitation to come and see my rented house, with its garden and the olive trees and wide view over the sea, and stay to lunch, produced a long silence I took to mean no.

In fact, she was silenced by the tumult of possibilities that can assail someone in a strange place, confronted with a strange person, offered an invitation that seemed dangerous in itself. What if she couldn't find the house? How was she supposed to get there? What if I invited the British neighbours I had mentioned, and all conversation turned to English? What if I served food that didn't agree with her? (Raised by devoted but anxious parents, she had grown up believing that harm was generated by quite ordinary meals — a fear that would evaporate as she continued to live in France.) Moreover, what could she possibly have in common with me?

As it turned out, there was a great deal. We were both from Quebec, though from dissimilar backgrounds, hers in Quebec City, mine in Montreal. We had been to convent schools run by the same order of nuns. We had both worked at the National Film Board, when it was still in Ottawa. We had both moved to Paris to live and to write. We had both decided to live for and on our writing, and we did. As a result, we both got to know what it was like to be broke in postwar Europe. We both survived. (She was a few months short of her eighty-fourth birthday when she died, in Montreal, in January 2000.) For some forty-odd years after that odd meeting we talked, on and off, sometimes with long gaps between conversations. I spent half the year in Menton; she went often to Quebec. One or the other might be immersed in work and not seeing anybody. We discussed our work, which is something writers don't often do — at least, in my experience. The fact that we did not write in the same language somehow made us feel free. We could pick up a broken-off conversation almost in mid-sentence. I remember a lunch in a restaurant called La Bûcherie where we talked on and on, sharing a bottle and a half of champagne, until a waiter asked if we were keeping the table for dinner. It was now half-past eight and we had not noticed the restaurant had emptied and was now filling up again and that outside it was night.

I have a record of one of those long meals. It was in Montparnasse, at a small fish place, Le Bistrot du Dôme, in rue Delambre. It belongs to the more famous Dôme but is less formal and less expensive. The novel Anne describes and is working on is *Am I disturbing you?*

13 January 1996

It is just past eight and the place has already filled with noise and people and a thin blue haze of smoke. Anne doesn't seem to mind. Looking around at the tiled walls and cheerful lights she says, "Il y a tellement longtemps que je ne suis pas allée au restaurant…" (It has been such a long time since I've been in a restaurant…) She does nothing but work on the novel she began last summer; months of writing by hand, pages and pages covered with the back-slanted script that looks like a shower of rain, typed and corrected and typed again on the rackety manual machine.

She went all over Paris, she tells me, looking at places she lived in in the fifties. Says that at one point, when she was living in a shabby hotel on rue Jules Chaplain, three minutes from where we are this minute, but miles away in time, she had bronchitis and a badly sprained ankle, and the hotel would not bring food up to her room, "not even a piece of bread." She depended on friends, but most of them were out of town. It must have been summer, probably August. There were visitors from Canada, who brought her the only thing she wanted, a thin slice of lean ham, which she ate from the paper it had been wrapped in. Finally one of the visitors [Jeanne Lapointe, professor of contemporary literature at Université Laval] found her a room in a hotel catering to the elderly. (A. must have been in her late thirties, early forties at most.) It was very cheap but she had to pay a whole month in advance. She recalls it with horror. During that month her sheets and the one towel they gave her were never changed and the room was never cleaned. But there was room service. Three times a day the only maid — the only one she ever saw — staggered upstairs with a heavy tray holding more food than A. was ever likely to eat.

When her bronchitis cleared up and when she could walk she had her meals downstairs in the dining room, and she tried to clean the room. She found an old broom and a decayed-looking sponge, but the only thing that seemed like scouring powder turned out to be DDT — the flea-and-louse killer of postwar Paris, liberally sprinkled in restaurant kitchens and in theatres and bought by flea-ridden tourists in pharmacies. The hotel owner, Anne says, was an elderly woman who seemed never to leave her office between the lobby and the dining room. Anne saw her just once. The door was ajar. Anne was on her way to lunch or dinner. The old woman was screaming at the maid. The maid suddenly screamed back, and was instantly fired. Anne never saw her again.

Something about the place, as Anne describes it — above all the mysterious owner — makes me think of *Hotel Savoy* but Anne has never heard of the novel or even of Joseph Roth. When she went back to look at the street and the hotel last year she was surprised to find an attractive building on a pretty street and Parc de Monceau nearby, all in bloom and very green. The hotel quite obviously had changed hands and there was nothing to show it ever had been a hotel at all. She did not try to find out what it had become or to go inside, for she needed to keep her memories intact for the novel.

She seems to think this may be her last book. She will be eighty this summer. Her sight is failing fast. She says quite casually that she is "nearly blind." Her hands are knotted with writers' rheumatism. Says the novel is important to her, about something she wants to set down before it is too late, i.e. before she dies. Works all day, every day. Never leaves her apartment except to shop for food for herself and the cat. Says the thick wild carpet of ivy that covered the ground in that sinister courtyard behind her apartment building has been cleaned out. The rat colonies that lived under the ivy have been chased away. (I say "sinister," but I should say "sinister to me," not to Anne.) I always contrive to sit with my back to the window when I visit. Whereas she writes all her first drafts — novels, poems — facing the big window, sometimes at the big round table, sometimes in the chintz armchair, with her feet on the hassock.

Now that the rats have left she no longer speaks of trying to find another place. I notice she says nothing about the new idea of moving to Montreal. I'm just as glad, for all we do (about Montreal) is weigh up the arguments, for or against — yes, no, yes, no.

A year later she no longer mentioned *Am I disturbing you?* or indeed any work at all. Her mind was on the move to Montreal: it seemed still to be yes, no, yes, no. In fact, she must have begun her final work, *A Suit of Light*, the essence of her particular Paris, and my favourite of her novels. But she said nothing about it and, of course, I didn't ask.

3 January 1997

Yesterday tea with Anne, whose apartment is ice cold. There's been a flood in the kitchen. The plumber says he can do nothing until he gets a green light from the building management. He has with him a little boy, to whom he hands the tip Anne has given him. Then the husband of the concierge arrives, Portuguese, looks so young I think he must be the concierge's son. He says nothing can be done about her cold stopped-up radiators unless…I forget what.

Her eyes are painful to see, the skin around them thick and red. She has been told there is nothing to be done about that either. No wonder she thinks she'd be better off in Montreal.

She tells me about a dream she had the night before. She is a patient in a French hospital, so inefficient and overcrowded that she has to share a bed with another patient, a large stout woman who seems to be important and takes up most of the bed. She turns out to be Simone Veil. [A well-known and very popular political figure, a former Cabinet minister and president of the European Parliament.] Simone Veil has a great number of visitors who swarm all over the room and the bed. Some climb over A. in order to see the famous Mme. Veil. One is a priest wearing a soutane and carrying a bowl filled with champagne. In the dream, A. tells herself that this is what French hospitals are like.

I say that the dream is an argument in the Paris vs. Montreal debate, with A.'s sleeping mind taking sides. She brings up another argument, not out of a dream: the absurdly high rent she pays and the exorbitant utility charges that come due at the end of every year. For years now she has been soaked for things that do not work or do not even exist.

It is now pitch dark outside. I wish A. would draw the curtains. Light from windows on that side of the house shines on the courtyard. It looks more than ever like an abandoned graveyard. I wonder if she has finished last year's novel. [*Am I disturbing you?* would be published in France one year later, in 1998.] All our conversation now is about apartments and catastrophes and the comparative cost of living here and in Montreal, with plenty of black marks against Paris. I have not lived in Montreal, except in hotels, for forty-seven years, so I have nothing to say. If she goes it will be this spring. If she stays she will have to find a new apartment. This one has become unliveable. To find a place in Paris now is about as it was in Montreal during the war. One has to "know someone," and I'm not sure whether or not she does.

There was another reason I had decided not to interfere, or even to have an opinion. I had believed her to be happy in Paris. I had never known her to say anything else — at least, not in my hearing. It had been a shock to discover, the previous year, that she had been dissatisfied and thinking of leaving for a long time. All our conversations now were about nothing much. I had been shown the wrong drawer of the sewing machine or hadn't known how to draw the right conclusion about what was on display. Probably I should have taken as definite her announcement just two months before that she had actually found an apartment in Montreal.

13 November 1996

Anne calls in the afternoon and says straight off, "Ça y est! Je retourne au Canada!" She has informed her friends in Canada. She will finish her novel this winter, in Paris, and leave next April. It is true that 1996 has been a wretched year. The courtyard is filled with garbage the tenants on that side throw out their kitchen windows now. There was her accident, the broken shoulder bone [owing to her worsening eyesight, she had failed to notice a tree root jutting above ground in her own street, rue de Pontoise, and had tripped and fallen, fracturing a bone in her right shoulder], her need to depend on other people, the breaking off of her novel, and her feelings of solitude.

Rather, an unexpected attitude to solitude. It was something she liked and wanted and even cherished. So I thought. So I believed. What happened? She tells me that last summer she visited an apartment in Montreal and took an option on sight. It is on the seventh floor, very bright, in the Côte des Neiges–Queen Mary area, with a *vue sur la montagne*, two bathrooms and an extra bedroom. There is a swimming pool in the building and everything she needs at hand: a restaurant, a salon de coiffure.

I say, "C'est la fin de toute une vie," meaning the end of her long Paris adventure.

She says, "C'est la fin de LA vie," meaning that she is eighty and that life has to stop.

She tells me that her accident (when she fell in the street) made her realize she was alone in Paris. In Montreal she has deep, old friendships. I am too shocked to reply. She was alone because she wanted to be. Could I have misheard her for decades on end?

Did she say one thing and mean another? A writer's need for solitude was something we often talked about. Perhaps I didn't know how to listen. Once she said, "I don't know if I'd want the same life again. A writer's life is marginal." I said, "What else did you expect?" We left it there. It was unmapped territory. I didn't know if I wanted to explore it much. I think I didn't even bother to make a note of it. Probably I couldn't take it seriously. I should have been more careful. She must have thought I was being impatient. I was worse than impatient. I was disappointed and I think it showed.

Something else: the Montreal apartment will cost exactly half the amount she has been paying in Paris. With her savings, she says, she will spend every winter in Menton, in her room — always the same one — at Hôtel Aiglon. She thinks it unlikely she will ever come back to Paris again.

A Suit of Light appeared, in French, in the spring of 1999, and the splendid English translation by Sheila Fischman a year later. Anne Hébert had died that January. In the last conversation we were able to have, Montreal-Paris, she said, "I have a new novel in mind. I hope they'll let me up soon, so that I can work."

— Mavis Gallant
Paris, January 2003

BURDEN OF DREAMS

I

At the end of his first day in Paris, his large frame still swaying from the rolling of the ship, an exhausted Julien gave in almost at once to the apparitions of night.

Suddenly she was there, in the darkness of his room, becoming clearer and more precise as he realized who she was. Soon the unmoving, weighty giant began to radiate bad temper, and Julien knew his mother had not forgiven him for crossing the Atlantic and leaving his native land.

She was seated on her immense rump as on a throne, her presence spreading into the untidy room. Tufts of short hair were sticking up on her head, giving her the prickly look of a pale Venetian thistle. Her turned-up nose, the extreme pallor that made her brownish freckles seem even darker, a pair of men's trousers cinched at the waist by a metal-buckled leather belt, the lighted cigarette held awkwardly in nicotine-stained fingers — everything was there to identify her to the eyes of her son.

He watched her as he lay motionless under the covers. He breathed in the smoke that escaped through every pore in the skin of this all-powerful creature, who had settled there in his hotel room as if she were at home, the one person in the world who possessed any rights over him.

The smoke filled the room, clung to the green plush curtains, moved to the fake mahogany armoire, drifted onto the imitation paisley sateen comforter and inside Julien's pyjama jacket, it brushed his face and hands, and slipped onto his neck in suffocating swirls of blue. Second by second the smell of Virginia tobacco in which he had grown up seemed about to grasp him again in its thick clouds and return him to a childhood he only wanted to be over.

Fearing suffocation, he tries to pull himself up on his elbows. But no movement is possible in this dream state that persists and threatens to annihilate him.

He cannot help reasoning as if he was awake and in full control of his powers. How could she have got in here, inside this locked room? A profound sorrow catches at his throat. He remembers that his mother is dead. Abruptly, he wakens in a strange dark room.

After taking care to switch on a light, he finally goes back to sleep.

In the morning he is roused by the chambermaid bringing the breakfast he'd ordered the previous night. She waves the key Julien had left in the door outside the room.

The wide-open window frames the city Julien has dreamed of for so long — the Quai Voltaire, the Seine, the Louvre — and over it all the filtered light, like an uncertain softness. The hotel had been chosen out of dozens of others because of its location, here in the very heart of Paris. And this morning, instead of rushing to the window, whose shutters the chambermaid has flung open, Julien stays curled up in his bed and does not stir. Everything that is happening now suggests he has no right to look at Paris, to sense it living under his gaze and find it delectable, for someone extremely powerful has come to him in a dream and forbidden him any pleasure, any joy, outside the strict enclosure of his childhood.

The chambermaid's angular silhouette lingers, backlit against the window, tense and concentrating. She says "Zut" and returns to the room. Very slowly, even reluctantly it seems, she swipes at the table with a rag, declaring abruptly:

"There's another one's had his last swim!"

Now Julien goes to the window. He does not see the drowned man, only the crowd surrounding the body, which has just been fished up. The endless wave of cars along the quay, like the serried ranks of an army, covers everything with its deafening racket.

"All hail my first morning in Paris!" Julien croons at his mirror a minute later, recalling a melody from *Faust,* as he tries to groom his thick, curly hair in which a few silver threads are tangled.

◆ ◆ ◆

During the first days in Paris he was like a sleepwalker, gazing wide-eyed but unseeing. Notre Dame, Place de l'Etoile, the Invalides, Place de la Concorde — the usual tourist itinerary files past, but Julien has no hold on anything. Is the real city beyond his reach? he wonders as he endlessly compares the Paris of his dreams with the reality before him. A grey filter covers the monuments he has seen before, so clear and pure, in artbook reproductions. Crowds of people around him hamper him at every step. It's like being in a museum, so pushed and jostled on all sides that he cannot stand alone at any painting. Too many people. Too much noise. Too many cars. Though he pricks up his ears, he can hear neither the light breath of Paris nor the muffled voices, so eagerly anticipated, of his favourite poets.

There is something like a screen between the city and himself, a translucent window behind which stand strange closed dwellings and inaccessible creatures.

Disdaining tourist buses and guided tours, Julien wanders from morning to night through the streets of a city that eludes him as soon as he draws near.

He strolls along the Grands Boulevards, slowly, cautiously, like a cat walking along a wall. The space reserved for his long, slightly hunched silhouette seems measured, tightly limited, amid passersby dressed in black, beige, grey. He remembers the garish colours of his native continent. He thinks about the red shoes of his sweetheart, Aline, recalls the surprising brightness they would bring to the surrounding dullness.

Little by little he can feel in his legs, his arms, in all his weary muscles that something is adapting itself and taking on a rhythm. And now the alien crowd is carrying him along just as the sea grasps a boat and holds it as it travels across the water.

At the end of every day, tired from walking, he collapses onto the bed in his hotel room, feeling the movement of the living crowd spread through his body like intoxication as he falls asleep.

Julien discovers the terraces and cafés. At times when he is too thirsty or too hungry, when fatigue makes him drag his feet, he escapes from the mass of strollers that is sweeping him along the streets he knows not where. Then he finds himself all alone, leaning at one of the small tables and shyly ordering:

"A coffee, please."

He sips black coffee from a tiny cup for hours. Sometimes familiar ghosts, come from his native land, accompany him along the streets, sit with him on the terraces and in the cafés.

At other times it may happen that Julien forgets his past life, even his painful status as a stranger in this city. Certain cafés bring him luck. In them, he calmly breathes the same smoky air as the people at the tables all around him. And if he lights a cigarette, he enjoys watching the blue smoke drift up to the ceiling and disappear into an opaque cloud, as if his entire life were joining the life he shares with all the world, in one ephemeral eddy.

But it is only after the concert at Les Billettes that the city will truly begin to be tamed.

◆ ◆ ◆

At length he decides to go to a concert in the church of Les Billettes, on rue des Archives. As soon as the decision is made, the air around him seems more breathable, as if the music has already begun its healing work. For has not music, ever since his childhood, had the power to make him happy in spite of everything?

From deep in the past the buried sounds and images arise. He hears Mozart and Schubert anew. Sees the music light up Lydie's animated features. Savours the bliss on her beautiful face before it is given over to her passion for life.

Adrift in memories, Julien crosses the Pont d'Arcole without seeing the greenish Seine as it moves in the sun. Only when he arrives at the cloister of the church of Les Billettes is he aware of the cloudless summer sky.

Here begin the lamentations of Jeremiah.

First, the lead tenor's voice, a cappella — only the voice, for the singer cannot be seen.

There is no preamble or introduction; from the first note it is the song that rises from the shadows of the earth, neither avoiding nor bypassing them but, rather, taking possession of them to give them a form and a face in the light.

The lead tenor makes his way into the plain, bare choir.

The great cross behind the altar, the wooden railings of the galleries.

Another tenor, a harpsichord, a viola da gamba.

Julien abandons himself to the music, his own dislodged darkness part of the night that radiates with the *Lesson of Darkness,* now being celebrated in the little church of Les Billettes. Nothing in the world, it seems, can distract Julien from his contemplation.

Twice, though, his gaze alights on the shoulders of a woman dressed in black who sits two rows in front of him.

Jerusalem, Jerusalem, come back to the Lord thy God.

It's not that she is unfamiliar with the music of Couperin or with Julien's fervour; on the contrary, it is Julien who is troubled by the lack of distance between the woman and himself. He has the impression of being shut away with a stranger (who suddenly stands out against the crowd of the faithful) in an enclosed place, reduced to the same breathing, the same shared delight.

His gaze lingers on the shoulders draped in black. He observes the chignon, low, at the back of her long neck.

When the concert is over he sees her walk slowly down the cloister, look up towards the intersecting ribs. He watches her intently. The narrow face, the coils of her black hair. She turns on her high heels, stretches as if she were alone in the world, a dark presence in this summer light, and arches her back, throws out her chest, her red lips smiling vaguely. How she resembles Lydie, Julien thinks, and suddenly all he wants to do is to check the unknown woman's face for the little mole, the black beauty spot that adorned Lydie's right cheekbone. Julien takes a step in her direction. She is looking at him, a broad smile showing all her teeth. Caught unawares by that too easy smile, those lips too thickly painted, and suddenly feeling terribly strange, Julien lowers his gaze, then turns and strides away from the cloister.

He walks briskly down the rue des Archives as far as the rue de Rivoli. Just as he is about to cross the Seine he slows down, imbued with the fine weather that prevails on the water and in the sky. All at once he stops comparing a troubled adolescent from the past with the unknown woman from the church of Les Billettes.

He leans on the parapet, looks at the water that flows beneath the bridge, first dark green, then pale blue because of the changing sky filled with fraying clouds.

Still, Julien wished he knew if the woman from Les Billettes had a tiny black-velvet beauty spot on her right cheekbone. For a long time he looks at the moving water until he no longer sees it at all, for his eyes are blurred with dreams.

◆ ◆ ◆

Most nights, despite the heat, Julien dresses in a three-piece suit, with a white shirt and tie, in honour of the music. Like someone without hearth or home, he goes from concert to concert. Solo recitals, chamber groups, symphony orchestras. Julien joins his hands, gathers his thoughts, laughs and cries, trembles from head to foot. His lean frame in its Sunday best, his dishevelled hair, stand out in the top tiers of the concert halls, where men in shirt sleeves and women in bright dresses perch. The gallery and the gods. Julien spends his meager

savings without keeping track. Spends intermissions spying
on the wave of listeners who pass slowly, then stop, talk,
and gesticulate in little groups. As time goes by, the hope
of seeing the woman from Les Billettes turns out to be
more and more absurd.

Late Sunday afternoon finds Julien at Notre Dame for an
organ recital.

Perched on a straw-bottomed chair he listens with his
whole body, his mind as taut as a drum under the onslaught
of the great organ.

And now the organ falls silent, the huge vessel continuing
to vibrate with diminishing waves of sound beneath the vault.
The stained-glass windows are tinged with glowing light.
Julien takes cover behind Paul Claudel's pillar. He closes his
eyes. Pleads for grace and revelation.

Little by little the cathedral empties. The silence of God
fills the space. You could touch it with both hands, as if you
were making your way through damp, dense fog. It is from
the depths of this silence that Lydie suddenly appears, beneath
Julien's closed eyelids. She shows herself both full-face and
in profile, her long black hair in wild disarray on her shoulders
and her back. She is sitting astride a dapple-grey plough
horse, showing off, endlessly. A little more and she will pass
into Julien's memory like Eve emerging from Adam's ribs,
she will escape into full daylight, she will enter the nave and
cry out at the top of her lungs beneath the vaults of Notre
Dame, "Dear little Julien." The faithful gathered there will
be startled, and Julien, lurking behind his pillar, seeking wonder and miracle, will be like a man succumbing to a dream.

If only he opens his eyes, his solitude and the soothing shadows all around will be restored to him. The straw-bottomed
chairs are lined up neatly. Small flames flicker in the side aisles

like frightened breaths. Julien feels only an immense fatigue.

Now he can clearly distinguish the confused trampling inside the church. All these people come and go, meet and vanish, look all around but see nothing; they could pass through fire and water unharmed.

Standing still as if carved there against the wall of the porch, a nun holds out a little basket. A woman's hand drops in a banknote. Julien looks at the hand as if it were the only one in the world and has suddenly broken away from the crowd to be looked at by him. He studies the bare arm, the shoulder draped in black.

The woman from Les Billettes has come here most likely to pay her share for the organ recital — or does she intend it for God's poor, to solicit some secular favour? Julien drops in his offering. The foreign banknotes in his fingers seem false to him, like stage money.

Soon they are both in the square outside the church, part of the wave of tourists, standing face to face like two individuals waiting to be introduced.

◆ ◆ ◆

There is no beauty spot on her cheek. The woman from Les Billettes bears less and less resemblance to Lydie. Julien persists in seeking a likeness.

"You remind me of someone . . ." he says, across the round table on which she is resting her elbows.

"You don't remind me of anyone, dressed up like that in this heat."

She laughs. There is some red on her white teeth.

"There's no one in the world like you, I'm sure of that. Where do you come from?"

He feels like answering that he comes from nowhere, that he'd like to go back there and not be asked any questions. Across from this woman who is full of life and laughter he feels like a convalescent, barely recovered from a strange illness with no precise name, a kind of dreadful aridity that has taken hold of him since his arrival in Paris.

He is silent amid the noise all around them, this confused world where unkempt people slump on cane chairs and lean on the little fake marble tables lined up on the sidewalk.

She eats her sherbet with a long, icy spoon. You can see the tip of her catlike tongue between her teeth. You might even think it's the only thing in the world she has to do — to eat ices in the bright summer sun not far from Notre Dame, lost in the wave of tourists, while scraps of sentences in foreign languages pass over her head.

A little more and she will get to her feet in her close-fitting dress, resume her stroll through the city, sit at other terraces, opposite other men, eat more ices, laugh and make appointments for a tomorrow of little importance.

She has finished her ice and now she is looking at Julien as she leans across the table, her face very close to his, waiting for a sign from him that doesn't come.

"How sullen you look. Is your bow tie making you uncomfortable. Or is it me?"

This woman has agate eyes, with veins of brown and green. She is so close to him he can see the matte texture of her skin.

He hears himself say very clearly, each syllable quite distinct, as if he was making some irrevocable disclosure:

"Lydie's eyes were perfectly green, like grapes!"

She laughs so hard that he jumps to his feet, furious, and flings at her all the belligerence held back since his arrival in Paris, getting it off his chest.

"Everything here is too old, too ancient, the past is suffocating, and most of all everything's too small. Your Seine is
more like a stream, your forests are like well-groomed parks,
and the salt's not salty, the sugar's not sweet, there are too
many people, too many cars, too much pollution . . ."

She chokes with laughter.

"How I adore your accent! What a treat! Please don't be
angry. You remind me of the deep dark countryside. Go on,
please go on."

She has stopped laughing. She closes her eyes as if in med-
itation while anticipating some new delight.

He rose so abruptly he almost knocked over the little table
where his glass and the metal sherbet dish collide.

She gets up, too, perfectly erect in her narrow dress. Not
young enough for such a dress, he thinks. Lydie's image
rises once more between him and the woman facing him.
Against the image of Lydie at seventeen, a long slim body
and endless legs.

He speaks clearly so she won't notice his accent and mock
him further:

"Goodbye. I have to go home now."

She stammers, afraid of losing him and of being alone:

"How uncouth you are. I'd have liked to go for a walk with
you in the Jardin du Luxembourg. It's not polluted at all
there, I swear."

He has already turned his back and now is walking
towards the quays. She stays there for a moment, motionless
and infinitely idle. She straightens her little purse with its
gold chain and reluctantly begins to walk. Soon she has
resumed her nonchalant step, alert for the slightest encounter
with another human. Only after she sees Julien's long, narrow
silhouette disappear into a hotel on the Quai Voltaire does
she realize she has followed him all the way from the café.

So I'm uncouth, Julien thinks as he crosses the threshold of his hotel.

◆ ◆ ◆

He likely doesn't hear the hum of traffic on the quay, nor the vibration of the windowpanes. Julien makes an effort to tally up his expenses for the day, the way someone else might examine his conscience. Coins and bills are scattered over the bottle-green bedspread. Julien frowns. Isn't a thousand-franc bill missing from his wallet?

He thinks of the woman from Les Billettes and frets, certain he will never see her again. For he doesn't know her address or even her name.

Julien shuts himself in for the night. Creates a void within himself and around himself. Makes a secret wish. That the woman from Les Billettes will remain inaccessible, stay outside in the shadows of night, an eternal stranger completely absorbed in eating lemon sherbet on the terrace of an unfamiliar café. *Amen.*

All the precautions seem to have been taken: shutters and curtains carefully closed, key turned twice in the lock and left conspicuously inside the room. Only the night light on the bedside table casts its little yellow glow into the darkness. The room's four corners are filled with softly moving shadows.

Safe from both the dead and the living, Julien stretches out on his bed. The French money seems real to him now that he thinks he has lost a banknote. His meagre savings are shrinking before his very eyes and soon he'll have to go home, poorer than a church mouse.

Julien flings aside the bolster that makes his neck ache.

Lying perfectly flat on the bed, arms crossed above his head, he goes over the state of his finances which strike him as catastrophic. Even though he grasps at concrete problems, when sleep comes to blunt his vigilance, images submerge him.

A tall girl with long black hair appears briefly, calls him by name, "Dear little Julien," laughs and laughs, then flies into the shadows of the room, only to reappear with the features of the woman from Les Billettes. While his mother, huge and sacred and surrounded by clouds of smoke, takes up all the space next to his bed, leans forward and sends spirals of Virginia tobacco smoke out her nose and mouth. She maintains that Lydie is cursed and that he must avoid her like the plague — and any other creature who resembles her.

He is an old adolescent falling asleep in a strange city. Soon, in his sleep, he turns towards his early childhood, that blessed time before Lydie first appeared. He wraps himself in his sheet and hides his face. Already he can hear quite clearly, from the other side of the world, the sound of the evening angelus in the church at Duchesnay.

II

It is the hour for bringing the cows in from the fields for milking. Whole herds are ambling down the sandy roads in single file, while barefoot children with sticks and with long green poles covered with leaves follow behind the cows, crying:

"Ke-bossy, ke . . ."

Julien is eight years old. He is holding the hand of his little sister, who is six. Here they are on this road, as they are every evening, charged by their mother with fetching the mail from the post office in the railway station. Both are very frightened by this procession of ruminants, pure white or russet or spotted rust and white, that pour onto the road, herd upon herd, with a stirring of bells. At the risk of ruining their white sandals, the two children stand by the side of the road, their feet in the stream, waiting for the herds to pass.

They particularly fear cows that jump fences and those with yokes around their necks that may at any moment charge like bulls, amid a savage lowing and a cloud of dust.

They have spied her in the distance, walking briskly down the road to meet them, her long navy cape unfurled around her, and their panicky hearts are calmed at once.

She leads them away at a run, turning her back on the station, pulling them firmly by the hand without slowing her pace. They can hear her powerful breathing, feel the warmth of her kindled by running; the woolen cape brushes their cheeks and they inhale its smell.

Pauline, winded, says once again that those piggish farmers are bringing their cows in later and later, that now they'll have to wait and fetch the mail long after six o'clock.

She is travelling so fast they have trouble following her. Her only thought is to make herself and her children safe once and for all from these cattle that stream through the countryside night after night, on the stroke of six.

From the ground where his mother let it fall, Julien has picked up the navy wool cape with its big collar of grey angora. It's a habit he has developed — to pick up whatever she drops anywhere in the house. He hangs the cape behind the bedroom door among the masses of garments and linen flung onto nails in the wall. There are no closets or cupboards in the house. This was at the blessed time when Pauline still wore dresses, skirts, petticoats.

The little boy takes an inventory of the clothes behind the door. Both hands press the calico faded from washing and the sun. He recognizes the skirts and blouses and buries his face in their folds and gathers. With eyes closed as if he was sleeping, he savours the smell of his mother's soap and perfume. He can vaguely hear Pauline in the kitchen, working the pump and grumbling because the water won't come at her bidding.

Behind the bedroom door, piles of sundry objects are strewn across the floor. Usually this disorder is hidden because Pauline keeps the door firmly shut. Sometimes you have to push quite hard to squeeze everything inside. Open it too fast and everything comes tumbling out, as if a dam has given way.

She has no control over the things around her. Anything that can be touched, taken, moved, washed, put away gradually escapes her, like stubborn weeds that spring up where they will. Clumsy hands. Her heart is elsewhere. She breaks things, is impatient and awkward. Her relationships with objects are marked by suspicion and testiness. Only her two children seem to guarantee her a certain hold over the hostile and elusive earth. Not until Julien's birth did she begin to wield some power, not over the rebellious objects in her house or her runaway husband, but over a human being who was well and truly hers, who had emerged from her womb.

Two years later, Hélène was born. Pauline, confirmed in grace, now held in her arms a second creature, warm with her own heat. Breaking free of the vague and misty universe that had been hers since childhood, she was suddenly like a pauper who moves from utter destitution to the undivided wealth of the world.

Pauline, her two children huddled in her skirts, declared quite freely to anyone who would listen:

"I cram them with affection, they can't defend themselves."

She says "Julien," she says "Hélène," with something like childish arrogance. The pleasure she derives from naming her two children brings a gleam to her small grey eyes, between pale lashes. But the rest of the world, herself included, remains for Pauline a kind of formless magma to be designated by a vague "somebody." She says:

"There's somebody who came and barked under my window this morning . . . There's somebody who took off for who knows where and left their wallet on the chest of drawers . . . There's somebody who backed the wrong party — as usual."

Whether she is talking about the neighbour's dog, her own husband, or a well-known political figure, the only identification she needs is that one word. One day she cut her finger on a broken bottle and the blood ran onto her dress. She said in her muted voice, barely audible:

"Somebody's cut their finger."

◆　◆　◆

From the very beginning, Julien was loved more than anyone in the world. He experienced that overwhelming happiness from his first breath.

One day he was the child taken from the mother's darkness who cries for the first time. It happened in a little village called Duchesnay, on the shore of a river of the same name. His mother's name was Pauline Lacoste and she had been married one year before to Henri Vallières, a minor official at the city hall in Quebec.

The child had been born by the glow of an oil lamp, in a tiny frame house at the edge of a sandy road, just next to the bakery. Tall poplars, their silver leaves in constant motion, isolated the house and provided it with a kind of rustling shelter filled with the aroma of fresh-baked bread. An Irishman named Pat Karl rented his little house to Julien's parents. Penny by penny, Pauline had saved twenty-five dollars — the rental fee for the summer months.

The young woman wanted to provide her firstborn with pure country air from his very first breath. She who knew only the city was terrified of mosquitoes, ants, wasps, spiders, caterpillars, potato beetles, and all the insects the country is teeming with. At that time, though, when the threat of tuberculosis made mothers tremble, she thought it was the best way to offer her child a good start in life. The first air he breathed should protect him from all the germs to come.

However, despite her vain attempts to "get a grip on herself," as she put it, the least moth sputtering above the lamp before it dropped into the fire filled her with disgust and terror. The utter lack of comfort, the cold water, the absence of electricity or a bathroom, the pump in the kitchen, the wood stove, the stench of the outhouse hidden in the trees behind the house, tempted her sorely, every day, to return to Quebec City with her child in her arms, wanting to share a tranquil urban life with him until the end of her days.

There was no doctor serving the village. But Pauline's doctor had promised to come from Quebec as soon as they phoned him from the general store.

The road from Quebec City to Duchesnay was long and arduous in those days, covered with sand and pebbles and often flooded when the river overflowed its banks. Not knowing if he should be more concerned about the sand and pebbles or the river in spate, Doctor Fortin listened closely to the engine of his highly polished black Ford as if he was sounding a human heart in great danger of sudden death. All the way there he grumbled at that stubborn little bourgeois, Pauline Vallières, and her ludicrous insistence on giving birth in the middle of nowhere, like some poor farmer's wife.

"It's a boy!"

She looks at him and despite her weakness and her broken body she has never looked so intensely at anything or anyone. It's a tiny creature, red and creased, that the doctor holds out to her, yet Pauline recognizes at once her most precious possession, flesh of her flesh, delivered and brought into the world at last. The confused feeling that swells her eyelids and makes her cry seems like an odd mixture of love and dread.

That night she had a dream. A blind kitten, still sticky from its birth, was lying in her hand, no bigger than a mouse. She alone had the power to drown it or to let it live.

Two years later, amid the same pain and sorrow, Pauline gave birth to a second child in Pat Karl's little house that she'd rented for the summer.

While the doctor still held the howling, naked little Hélène in his arms, against his white smock, Pauline knew that she now possessed her full share of life and the plenitude of her heart. Of what importance to her now were the inadequacies of the poor pale man who stood with arms dangling, planted like a fence post on the little wooden stoop, ears pricked up and waiting patiently until the noises of birth had abated so he could finally learn the sex and the weight of his child?

Bending over Julien's cradle and Hélène's in turn, Pauline watches at the bedside of her own childhood. Everything between her and her children takes place as if the goal was to right the wrong done in another life to a little girl named Pauline Lacoste. That little girl has been shunted from town to town, from one boarding school to another, summer and winter, school holidays or not, her parents having little time between moves for more than a stormy tête-à-tête and a brief reconciliation between the sheets.

If Henri sometimes tries to approach his son or his daughter, Pauline shoos him away like a troublesome fly. It's never the right time and besides, she tells herself, he doesn't know how to go about it.

Summer faithfully brings the Vallières family back to the river. They have already moved several times, Pat Karl's house having proven too small. The children are growing so quickly. But Pauline seems not to notice. She cannot see her son and her daughter being gradually transformed before her eyes. All of Pauline's efforts are aimed at maintaining the utmost transparency between her children and herself.

"Tell me always where you are going, what you are doing, what you are thinking, and I'll listen to you and ask you questions till the sun comes up, if need be. I must know what interests you, what bothers you. I'm there to listen and to hear whatever goes through your minds."

For her part, she would tell them about the father who got on her nerves till she could kill him, the pink crétonne fabric she'd just bought in the village, the jam she would make tomorrow, and the small cyst that had appeared on her left breast.

They in return had no peace until they'd opened their hearts to her satisfaction; having no real secrets yet, they willingly went along with the apparently innocuous game. It only made her love them more and she was grateful to them.

The world that the three of them lived in, with the father increasingly in the background, more and more interested in cards and dice, kept them isolated from the world at large. It might have seemed that real life was just that — an endless childhood, a kind of hanging garden, suspended between earth and sky, where mother and children played, safe from pain and sorrow and from death.

It was Pauline, however, who committed the first transgression against the customs of childhood. Giving up skirts and petticoats, she now only wore men's trousers, somewhat shapeless after her husband's long use. These coarse cotton garments, Henri's castoffs softened by frequent washings, now clothed her all summer, supposedly to protect her from mosquitoes and blackflies. If by any chance her husband wrapped a tired arm around her waist and looked longingly at her, she would offer as excuse that it was a nuisance having to unfasten the firmly buckled belt.

To the horror of the local farmers, she travelled down roads and across fields dressed snugly in her husband's trousers, the two children dogging her footsteps, and she was growing fatter by the day. For some time now she had been smoking Players, inhaling greedily, and she reeked of tobacco.

At night before going to sleep, after one last cigarette, it seemed to her that the smell of tobacco wrapped her in a soft shroud, a kind of diaphanous armour that protected her from her husband's advances. Had he not told her one day, turning away in disgust:

"You stink of tobacco like a man!"

After that, Pauline had her hair shorn like a little boy who drives the cattle out to pasture, and her husband realized that he'd made a bad marriage to this woman who went out of her way to displease him.

Henri Vallières consoles himself with beer and cards. In the dark, noisy tavern he knows he's alive, half dissolved in an alcoholic haze, but alive: he can feel his arms and legs and tells himself again and again, I can walk wherever I want, go where I want, I can put my arms around whatever unknown woman I want.

When he had been so hopelessly offended that he had to leave his wife and children, Henri saddled himself with suitcases and a big wicker basket in which he transported the family cat. He left a note for Pauline. She didn't seem surprised.

Perhaps she'd even been expecting this farewell message since the early days of her marriage.

Wife, I'm leaving you. You probably won't even notice, you've got so good at managing without me except when it comes time to do the accounts. Send me the bills as they come in, I'll deal with them. Be happy. I'm going away. You can live your life now as if I didn't exist. I'm taking the cat.

Love,
Henri

She sent him the bills and she waited for payments. The wait grew longer and longer until, three years later, there was no longer any answer from Henri at all. Pauline's letters were returned, marked "Unknown at this address." Then she got the idea of baking cakes and selling them. But she ruined half of them and wasted quantities of eggs and flour. She'd just been considering hiring herself out body and soul to scrub floors and scour sinks, to get rid of other people's grime, when she came into a small inheritance. A forgotten aunt who had died in St. Bridgid's Home had bequeathed her the meagre fortune of a stingy old maid.

At night it sometimes happened, in the solitude of her double bed, that she had a dream, always the same one, which she'd forget by the time she wakened. All that remained was a sensation of infinite pity, for herself and for the poor man who had left her.

◆ ◆ ◆

One day Hélène and Julien were fourteen and sixteen years old. It was the year of the big polio epidemic.

When the opening of school in Quebec City was postponed because of the epidemic, Pauline kept the children in the country as long as possible, so great was her fear.

Every day after school the teacher came to the house to give Hélène and Julien private lessons.

Pauline boiled the water and the milk and she forbade her children to eat any high-bush cranberries, bitter berries that thicken the mouth and tongue. Rumour had it that the disease could be spread by the little wild fruits that grow at summer's end in the hedges lining the fields.

At first it was as if the holidays would go on forever. The air you breathed was still clear, but every now and then some mist crept into it. Soon she would have to light the oil lamp above the supper table.

Hélène and Julien were well aware that in spite of the violent brilliance of sunlight on trees that sometimes made them light up like fires, a new season was insidiously establishing its reign all around them. Some mornings were cottony with mist, with frost as white as sugar on the flattened grass and the dark ploughed fields.

It was at the time of year when the earth was damp that fresh hoof prints were discovered one morning in the fields around the village and all the way to the little cemetery by the river, close to the church. Great amazement, then superstitious fear clutched at the throats of farmers who lived on the back roads, when some of them discovered at dawn that their horse was in his stall as usual, but exhausted and covered with foam as if after a long run.

The curé began to bless the stables and the horses, accompanying his benedictions with the appropriate prayers. The mayor recommended that stables be barricaded for the night. The men stood watch, relieving one another in the black autumn night. But there were no more strange occurrences, and it was as if the entire matter of the horses had been only a dream by the inhabitants of Duchesnay.

◆ ◆ ◆

It was in full daylight that she was seen for the first time, astride a dappled horse that belonged to Zoël Ouellet, at whose house she'd been staying for a while now. The weather was splendid, with a hard blue sky of the kind you sometimes see during Indian summer, and lots of little fleecy white clouds that chased each other in the blue air. The horse was trotting along the street that led to the church, and the bare legs of the girl riding it bareback were spread far apart over the plough-horse's tremendous girth.

She might have been doing it deliberately, parading slowly in order to be seen, so people would know who she was — horse thief and the village's queen of the night. Men, women, children, anyone not busy in the fields watched her cross the village like an apparition. A little farther and she would be free of them. Already the horse's steps rang out, heavier, faster, across the hardened earth.

That was when they got the idea of blocking her path to stop her from getting away. Alexis Boilard parked his truck across the road.

Julien was there with his sister, on the sidewalk across from the general store. He took Hélène's hand in his own and held his breath.

The big horse reared up before the truck, and the girl's long legs were unable to hold him back, nor could her long hands, which clung to his mane. She was thrown to the ground. For a moment she lay there, huddled motionless on the ground, as if she were dead. When the men approached her, cautiously, fearing one of her tricks, she got to her feet like a sleepwalker, her blue shorts streaked with dust, knees covered with dirt and blood. She looked around, seeing no one, stunned to be there, thrown by the horse, defenceless and surrounded by strangers. She said "Damn animal" and walked away, very stiff, in the direction of the river, displaying indifference to the horse Alexis was now trying to capture. She walked so gingerly that she seemed about to stop at every step. All her efforts were intended to keep herself from limping in front of all these people assembled on both sides of the street to watch her pass.

No one dared to go after the girl. The villagers were unsure, in fact, what accusations they could make to the authorities. Neither the mayor nor the curé was alerted. And then she had seemed so strange and proud on her grey horse, as if she were riding in glory, elusive as a vision they might all have seen together in full sunlight on the main street that afternoon around three o'clock. Every one of these people, captives of an austere, monotonous life, were now suddenly living an amazing adventure that glued them to the spot with surprise and satisfaction.

"Please God, don't let this incredible drama end too soon," a fat woman murmured, one thumb rapidly making the sign of the cross on her vast bosom.

Their attention soon turned away from the long silhouette moving stiffly, almost imperceptibly, down the road. They turned to the horse, because of its neighing and the sound its hooves made as they scraped the earth. Clutching its mane, Alexis stroked the horse's neck and tried to climb onto its back. He talked to the animal, fierce words proffered with a kind of stubborn, hypocritical sweetness. The man looked very small, like a gnome hanging onto the mane, and the horse rose on its hind legs, shimmering grey and bluish white, as if its quivering coat were reflecting the sky and the restless clouds.

Once he was on the horse's back, Alexis had no need at all to drive him, so eager was the animal to return to the stable.

As he was about to cross the bridge that spanned the river, Alexis spied the girl two steps ahead of him, limping terribly along the ringing planks of the bridge, thinking herself safe from any eyes. He invited her to ride behind him so he could take her to Zoël Ouellet's, but she shook her head, glaring at him. Her eyes seemed to be pure white in her face smeared with blood and dirt. A lock of black hair was plastered against her cheek, like seaweed on a drowned man's face. Alexis couldn't tell if she was truly beautiful or simply strange. But he remembered her long thighs spread wide across the horse.

◆ ◆ ◆

Once they were back at the house, Julien and Hélène began to describe, with a good many gestures and details, the ride across the village by an unknown girl astride Zoël Ouellet's dappled horse. They omitted nothing, neither the truck parked across the road, nor the girl's brutal fall in the dust, nor her departure along the main road, nor the silvery brightness of the horse as he reared up against the sky. As they talked and Pauline, frowning, listened, mute and icy, they had the impression they were committing some bad deed, betraying themselves or divulging something precious that should have remained secret.

In the long low room with its rough walls, Pauline's silence lingered on. It seemed as if she was grabbing hold of every word her children uttered so as to silence them, to enfold them in her lap again as if they had never existed, neither they nor the stranger who had come to Duchesnay to change their life, which had been good and without complication.

Soon there was nothing alive and palpable left in the stifling and thickening air of the room, nothing that was expressed or spoken between mother and children, only a tremendous refusal on her part and theirs.

Pauline was the first to speak, her voice hardly louder than a muffled breath, snatching each word from the silence as if it was difficult for speech to emerge from her throat:

"That girl is nothing but an outsider come here from who knows where; she's a horse thief, a crackpot, a lunatic. Watch out, and if you ever run into her, above all don't speak to her."

That night Hélène and Julien went to bed in their adjoining rooms under the eaves with walls of darkened fir, briefly saddened that Pauline wanted to rob them of even the memory of their marvellous afternoon in the village. They were consoled almost at once, though, for in their still fresh memories that persisted into sleep rose up time and time again a stunt horse and the fabulous creature who rode it.

◆ ◆ ◆

She entered the Ouellet house through the small side door so no one would see her in such a sorry state. She went directly upstairs to her room, pulling the door shut behind her. Now she is standing naked on a newspaper spread on the floor as a bathmat. The flowered basin, the ewer filled with cold water. She sponges herself from head to foot. The water in the basin turns red. Her knees and legs are covered with scrapes and scratches. She weeps as if she had never wept before, suddenly discovering that the salt of her tears scalds her slender face. She weeps because she has been humiliated and insulted. And she is ashamed because Alexis Boilard caught her limping across the bridge that spans the river.

"Supper's all ready, Mademoiselle Lydie, it's on the table."
Madame Ouellet calls to her through the closed door.
Lydie pulls on silk stockings and her longest dress so nobody can see her scrapes and scratches. She combs her wet

29

hair and carefully ties it at her neck with a black velvet ribbon.

She remains silent all through supper, afraid her animosity will get away from her in angry words dropped into the Ouellets' big bright kitchen.

"You're pouting, Mademoiselle Lydie. That's not nice!"

Only when dessert is served, when she sees the hot apple pie on her plate, does she feel life becoming good again, and light. She declares:

"This is the best apple pie I've ever eaten!"

Madame Ouellet smiles with contentment.

And that was when Zoël Ouellet, encouraged by his wife's smile, stood up very straight across from Lydie and forbade her to ride his horses in the future. His muffled voice trembled a little between his tobacco-stained teeth.

"My horses aren't made for the circus, and anyway it's not fitting for a young girl like you."

She finishes her apple pie, not so happy now, and the words "not fitting" stick in her throat.

◆ ◆ ◆

False summer breezes, the sun beating fiercely on the brown ploughed fields. These brief flamboyant days, these bright red leaves — there is nothing in the world more beautiful, and evening is quick to return all this splendour to the deep darkness that is like a foreboding of endless winter.

Pauline has already begun to examine every one of them, without seeming to, as if merely asking about the weather. Madame Jobin at the general store, the dressmaker Mélanie Richard, the Pruneau twins — young ladies who play the harmonium in church, each taking her turn, Jean-Baptiste Dumont, the schoolteacher from Pont-Rouge, Réjeanne Cloutier, the curé's fierce and garrulous housekeeper who has eyes in the back of her head.

I shall turn this village upside down, Pauline tells herself, I'll shake it up as hard as I can. Information must fly through the air like the dust when you shake a carpet.

They have told her everything they know about the young woman boarding at the Ouellets — which is, in fact, very little: Lydie Bruneau, aged seventeen, a horse thief brought to Duchesnay by her parents and entrusted to the Ouellets, who rent out rooms in the summer.

Julien and Hélène walk across the roads and through the fields all the way to the little woods at Les Ours, in the hope of seeing Lydie again.

The countryside is full of the smells of soaking leaves and damp earth. Most of the time the river is blue, with glittering waves. Julien and Hélène climb and descend endlessly. The country is covered with hills, and with hollows between the hills. It is rather as if every person lived in a compartment of his own. A valley, a rise, a rise, a valley: the country is full of secret places, of landscapes buried or spread out. A land on many levels. There is the village proper, with the church, the graveyard, the presbytery, the high school, a few frame houses, the bridge that straddles the river. It is all flat and hollow, level with the river, made for holding in the mist and dampness. To escape, you must climb Savard's hill, which takes you to a flat expanse that extends all the way to the little violet-coloured railway station. Moïse's hill takes you in the opposite direction, towards Pont-Rouge, along the sandy road that skirts the broad flat fields hemmed in by the squat, slate-coloured mountain. Seen from there, the river runs deep and grows agitated, bristling with white rapids amid a haze of water and a savage roar, and divided in two by an island.

The Zoël Ouellets built their house on this steep hill, shielded from the river and its heady sound, in the middle of fields lying at the end of a long lane that's hard to keep up in winter because of the snow. Three silvery poplars rustle above the house.

Lydie treats her scrapes and chomps at the bit, under the poplars, wondering how she can get herself a horse and ride it without provoking the whole village. While she waits she struggles to string delicate beads of multicoloured glass on a nearly invisible thread.

◆　◆　◆

Faithful to the promise he'd made himself to see Lydie again, Alexis Boilard came to the Ouellet house one fine Sunday afternoon before Lydie's wounds were fully healed.

She was sitting in the grass under the poplars when she saw him approaching, his truck speeding down the lane in a cloud of dust.

He asks how she's getting along, then immediately offers to take her for a ride in his truck. She shakes her head as if she were mute, and at the same time gives him a mocking look, her slanting eyes half shut against the brilliant light. He asks "Why?" in a bewildered way. She is still looking at him from between her eyelids. He sees a little glimmer of blinking green.

He stands there before her, with his sun-reddened face, his hair glistening with brilliantine, a white shirt unbuttoned on his pale chest. He has gone to some trouble for her and here she is refusing to get in his truck. Stubbornly he asks again, "Why?" A shrug and she goes back to her beads, creasing her brow. In the silence one can hear a delicate little sound as glass beads clink together in a tin box.

He turns on his heel very quickly, ready to flee, takes a few steps in the direction of the truck parked by the kitchen door, then retraces his steps. For a moment Alexis looks in silence at Lydie, who is zealously stringing her beads. He says very quietly, weighing each of his words:

"It could be that somebody my family knows very well has got some horses for hire. If you want, I could ask that person one of these days . . ."

She echoes, without looking up:

"One of these days . . ."

For the first time he hears her voice, somewhat hoarse and pitched low, and he finds it inexplicably overwhelming.

Since he's just standing there, she gets up abruptly and drops a string of beads around his neck.

"In the meantime, wear this day and night, in memory of me."

He still has not moved, looks crestfallen and glum, his ears red, the beads around his neck. She sends him away with an imperious wave of her hand.

"Bye now, Alexis Boilard, one of these days . . ."

And now, in a flash, he regains the image he has always invented for himself — a virile man and quick to take offence. A village rooster with his hackles up, a flamboyant cockscomb, his heart filled with violence and rancour. He rips the necklace from his neck, breaking the string, scattering the beads, and they sparkle here and there in the grass. His voice trembles with rage.

"Horse thief, outsider, cripple . . ."

With one leap he is back at his truck, starts it up with the grating sound of stripped gears.

◆ ◆ ◆

In the meantime, Hélène and Julien run through the countryside as soon as they can get away, hoping to catch a glimpse of Lydie. Evenings, bent over their schoolbooks, they grow distracted, dream in silence about the runaway rider astride Zoël Ouellet's dappled horse.

The rain has come all at once, settling over the landscape day and night, draping it in a grey and barely transparent curtain. Its steady sound drips inside the frame houses, already made airtight for winter. From the shingled roofs comes a sound like the stamping feet of a patient, stubborn crowd, countless, endless. The wind rises quickly and the glorious leaves of Indian summer become dull then fall in close-packed swirls. The smell of damp earth is so strong now it permeates the animals and people who breathe it in, sniffing it as if it was their own odour.

There is a long bench in the general store, a plank resting on kegs that hold nails of all sizes, from tacks to six inches long. Julien and Hélène are sitting on the bench, engulfed in the leather aroma of the harness hanging on the wall above their heads. Their feet in rubber boots are flat on the knotty wood floor, making puddles and rivulets. They sit there in their yellow oilskins, bags of groceries on their laps, waiting for the rain to let up so they can go home. They can see nothing through the screen door silver with rain, but they can hear the gusts of rain falling on the countryside all around them.

She has come inside, streaming wet, the door slamming behind her. Everyone who is in there waiting for a respite stares at her. In her grating voice she says, almost softly, as if it was a secret:

"I'd give my soul for a chocolate bar!"

As soon as she is served she sits on the bench next to Julien and Hélène and munches the chocolate without looking at them. She is so wet, she's dripping onto the floor, even onto the bench near Julien and Hélène who can breathe in her odour of wet wool. Her hair plastered against her skull gives her the look of a Buddhist priest with shaven head. Julien would see her like that much later, in his dreams, when she would have a little death's head.

She laughs with her mouth full, and her teeth are smeared with chocolate. The two youngsters next to her as if frozen in their glistening raincoats dream of being beyond her reach, and they cannot move, like spellbound birds.

She speaks without turning around, addressing no one in particular. Everybody in the store is looking at her, listening to her. She does not raise her voice, and her low, rough inflections overwhelm them as they sit there killing time, stripping their defences, putting them at her mercy, from the first word she utters.

She chatters about this and that, about sunny days and dull ones, about horses, those magnificent creatures, about her parents who live in Quebec City, at the Claridge, about how boredom lingers in the rain, about her tremendous yearning for life, which possesses her like a fever. She seems to be speaking only to herself, and her last words are barely audible. Unanimous silence follows her remarks. The others dare not move for fear of being suddenly, brutally thrown back into their everyday lives.

Just then Alexis comes in, slamming the door behind him. Checked shirt, leather boots, a mulish look on his face. He spotted her on the bench right away and now he looks at her impudently while conversations in the store pick up again *sotto voce*.

As soon as she recognized Alexis she turned towards Julien and Hélène.

"Look at these little dears sitting beside me, all yellow like baby chicks! Cheep, cheep!"

Alexis laughs very loud. He thinks he is back in Lydie's

good graces because she is mocking others in his place. A kind of transference that gladdens him and makes him swagger. He leans on the counter, sends great gusts of cigarette smoke to the ceiling and never takes his eyes off Lydie.

People have been looking at her for so long, she should be used to it. When she was hardly more than one or two years old, when her parents entertained they would display her naked on the table, like a centrepiece surrounded by flowers. The white cloth, the silver, the china and crystal gleamed before her like an entire city with all its wonders in a row. There were little flashes of strange rapture in the eyes of the men in tuxedos, the women in long dresses, who loudly applauded the naked child in the middle of the table where they sat. The torrential sound pouring over her is one she will hear forever.

Lydie grew up under those same gazes of idle men and women avid for pleasure. Her father's friends would introduce her very early to scotch, cigarettes, and flirtation. The desire of some was at times so urgent that they coveted more than her nascent beauty, desired even that which was sacred and lay at the heart of her beauty. She would insult them with all her might, ridicule them with a skill at mockery that stunned them.

And now she is here, unable to bear any longer the stale air inside the store or all those eyes staring at her. She turns towards Julien and Hélène.

"Let's go, chicks, quickly now. We're going outside. It's stifling in here. Hurry up. We're going out."

They stand up, clumsy in their bewilderment. They follow Lydie without protesting, so much do they long to be with her in the open air and away from all these people who have sought refuge in the store. At once they are out in the rain, the same rain that was drenching her, while she pulls them onto the road, holding each one by the hand and shouting:

"Ah, the rain! I love it, I love it, I love it!"

Very quickly she noticed that the rain couldn't penetrate Julien's thick curls but settled there like hoarfrost on a bush. Of Hélène she sees nothing but two long braids of hair and a childlike profile, all pink now in the rain.

She speaks quickly as if she has very little time to tell the story of her life to these youngsters who already expect everything from her. She says that on the pretext of protecting her from the polio epidemic in Quebec City, her parents have sent her to board with the Ouellets. And they've taken advantage of her absence to go on a trip to New York.

"I'm sick of this! I won't hang around here very long, that's for sure. One of these days I'll just pack up and go. Today it's hello my chicks, tomorrow it will be bye-bye forever."

She chants these last words, almost sings them.

To his amazement Julien hears himself say, his changing voice beyond his control, cavernous, then suddenly flutelike in the wet air:

"Don't go away yet!"

Bolstered by her brother, Hélène ventures to say very quietly:

"But we've only just met . . ."

Lydie walks with them to the Michauds' house by the river, the one Pauline has rented for the summer.

Pauline lifts the cheesecloth curtain that covers the small windowpane and sees three wet figures standing at the door, in the rain, for a moment until Lydie goes down the road and disappears.

That night, for the first time, Pauline makes a scene, railing and weeping at Julien and Hélène.

"I forbid you to see that girl again. Nobody knows where she comes from. She's an adventurer, a schemer, a . . ."

As usual, her voice was so feeble and so monotonous, though furious, they had to prick up their ears to grasp the extent of her wrath.

While Lydie, alone on the road, hands in her pockets, soaking wet and shivering, mutters to herself. "I'll set them free, those little chicks. I'll be their evil genius."

A ground swell surges from the darkest part of her, though she thinks she's just obeying her own free will to relieve her boredom.

Life pretends to be as it was before, when we know perfectly well that never again will anything be as it was. Julien and Hélène do what they can to avoid another confrontation with their mother, while the memory of the day of the rainstorm lingers in their minds, along with the picture of Lydie soaking wet and holding them by the hand, like children being taken away to the end of the world.

Pauline's vigilance is resourceful and discreet. She showers them with kindness and gentle caresses. The slightest delay in coming home from a walk is seen as an offence, a knife that gives them pleasure to drive into her heart.

"It's past six, I've been worried sick. Where have you been this time?"

"You know very well, at the blacksmith shop watching Monsieur Thibault shoe the horses. I told you before we went out."

Most of the time she goes with them, down the roads and across the fields, indefatigable. Nothing discourages her. Neither the hills nor the ruts in the road. They despair of ever being alone, of being left in the countryside like two lean wolfhounds without collars.

At night in the lamplight, when their dreams become too

great a burden, she approaches them stealthily, softly kisses their foreheads and their hair, gently murmurs the magic words, saying them twice — first to the son and then to the daughter:

"My love."

It's not that Lydie has disappeared altogether from the autumn landscape. Often they catch sight of her at a turn in the road, bending over her bicycle, pedalling lightheartedly. She waves to them, greets them tauntingly, calls out:

"Hi, little chicks!"

Julien and Hélène just have enough time to note Pauline's sudden pallor when Lydie is already on her way down the road.

"Above all don't look at her. Pretend you don't see her."

Pauline's voice grows faint, is barely audible.

◆ ◆ ◆

One fine October afternoon around four o'clock she was with them again, in the suffocating heat of the blacksmith shop, the fire's glow, the horses' powerful scent. She seems at home there, absolute mistress of the forge, reigning over the fire and reeking of horse and burned hoof.

Gripped by fear, they look at her as if she was part of a fearsome mystery being celebrated before their eyes, amid showers of sparks and the untamed stamping of hooves.

Lydie appears not to see them. All that matters to her is the young chestnut horse that is struggling and refusing to be shod.

The blacksmith, bare-chested, emerges from the glow and the din. He raises one huge arm covered with red and blue tattoos. A cavernous voice comes from his toothless mouth.

"Out of here, you kids, scram! We're too busy for your silliness and getting under foot. Out!"

Once again, the three find themselves on the road, hearing the horse inside the blacksmith shop neighing and struggling, the men swearing very loud.

"Hi there, chicks! You children aren't very polite. I keep running into you on the road, the least you can do is say hello."

She repeats her greeting and each time raises her arm and waves.

They try to respond, rather like robots with rundown mechanisms, unable to complete their gestures. They raise their arms no higher than their shoulders, then let them drop.

Her mocking laughter rings out in the cold, echoing air.

She talks about autumn, her favourite season, about hunters who poison the air with their smoke and lethal gunshots, about brown-haired children who could be mistaken for deer.

"Be careful, chicks, watch out for hunters . . . and huntresses . . ."

Loud laughter comes from her throat. She stuffs her hands in the pockets of her blue wool jacket. A long red scarf trails behind her.

They listen to her talk and laugh, are under her spell, offer no word or gesture that might betray their pleasure at being with her.

Soon Lydie's voice changes, becomes hoarser, more aggressive.

"What funny chicks you are, standing there like statues and never opening your mouths. Did somebody swallow your tongues? I bet it was the mother fox who panicked and started the job. It's common knowledge: at the slightest alarm a mother fox will devour her young, to protect them. So watch out, children, that mother of yours has long teeth, and today's the day the alarm will sound. I'm the alarm. I'm standing here before you in the flesh. I'm the public danger, the witch. Beware of going home. She'll punish you, I guarantee it. She'll make mincemeat of you just because you ran into me at the blacksmith shop."

Again her cascading laughter.

Julien turns to his sister.

"Come on, Hélène, let's go."

Abruptly Lydie stops laughing, as if exhausted from so much laughter. Suddenly, surprisingly, she oozes sweetness. Her voice is captivating again, is surrounded with silence between the words, touching them, wounding them, again and again.

"No need to be afraid of me, my chicks. Take a good look at me. My name is Lydie Bruneau, I'm seventeen years old and I'm bored. About the same age as you, only not quite so wet behind the ears . . ."

She comes very close to them, looks at them scornfully, says again:

"Take a good look at me."

Hélène turns away, tugs at her brother's sleeve. Her voice is quivering, she's on the verge of tears:

"Come on, Julien, Mama's waiting for us."

Julien does not lower his gaze, despite the blinding sun. He stares at Lydie without blinking. Lydie's image is trembling before him. He cannot distinguish the green eyes or the swollen mouth. And now, suddenly, he can clearly see the strong white neck that contrasts with the red scarf with a strange sharpness, an insistence, that disturbs him. He could simply put his hands around Lydie's neck and squeeze a little, and nothing of what he both desires and fears would occur between them. That strange notion only brushes against him, briefly, while the sun dazzles him like a mirage.

Now Lydie has had enough of being a moving target, standing before this boy who stares at her without seeing her, it seems. She stirs, stretches in the light. Julien and Hélène make a show of going away. She slips between them, takes their hands — to stop them. She points to an old forked birch tree beside the river, not far from the blacksmith shop, in a little field lying fallow that belongs to no one.

"Why don't we write each other love letters, my chicks? Surely the mother fox hasn't forbidden us to write? I bet she hasn't even thought of it. There's the mailbox, in the fork of the old birch tree. Understand? I'll go first, to encourage you. Just a short little note to begin with, what you might call an introduction to me and my personal history. After that we'll see. We might even move on to epistles and poems. It depends on you. On your answers to my letters. You'll see, it will be lots of fun. Till tomorrow, my chicks. The mail comes in at ten."

She has already straddled her bicycle and the red scarf floats behind her like a banner.

◆　◆　◆

Julien is taken up in a kind of drawing frenzy. India ink drawings, very black, in his schoolboy's copy books. Whole pages of minuscule flowers, insects, dots, lines, squares, an entire dark petit point background where in several places the bright shape of a horse ablaze with sunlight stands out.

"Is that what you call working?"

Pauline stands before him, looking at the drawings.

She sets on the table in front of Julien a slice of freshly baked cake still warm from the oven. Pauline's kindness exasperates him. She wants to buy me, he thinks. She is frightening and she's my mother.

While she studies his drawings intensely, he uses red ink to trace a broad scarlet band that is wrapped around the horse's neck. He extends the band down the length of the page, turning it back on itself several times, as if he was crumpling and smoothing Lydie's scarf in his hands.

Pauline says:

"For heaven's sake, Julien, that's your French book!"

Pauline doesn't see that as the red scarf fills in the page of the copy book, it renders unreadable her son's first poem that is scrawled across the same page. A scant few lines Julien dreams of offering to Lydie as a strange and priceless gift.

We shall enter splendid cities
Stripped to the skin
astride steeds of horror.

After prying everywhere, Julien has discovered, under a stack of linen on a bathroom shelf, an old razor that was once his father's. Relinquishing his mother's tweezers, Julien shaves like a man for the first time, looking into the half-mirror that hangs over the sink. While Hélène grows impatient and pounds on the door, he gazes at length at his face, red from razor burn. He tries to guess what will become of this face that is still childlike and uncertain, and that he wishes were virile and rough, with a beard as curly as his unruly hair.

◆　◆　◆

The next day the old white birch looked pink in the rain. All that Julien can think of is to run to the old tree and look in the fork for Lydie's promised note. Twice he tries to shake off Hélène, who is dogging his footsteps.

"Wait up, Julien! Wait for me!"

"Hélène, you're as sticky as glue!"

Two letters on blue paper have been left in the hollow of the birch, protected from the rain in an empty tin of English biscuits.

"It smells good!" Hélène sniffs her letter greedily.

"Bah, that's childish!"

Casually, Julien crumples his letter and shoves it into his pocket, then strides off down the road.

Hélène wanted to read her letter right away. She sat on some stones by the river, the waves coming to her feet, the rain falling down on her. She unbuttoned her wool jacket so she could hide her face inside and read her letter safe from the rain.

On it there is a long line of Xs followed by:

Hélène, you're as lovely as a tiny flower bud that's still wrinkled, not yet opened out, all bubbling with nectar and good to bite into. Your pigtails like a model little girl's should be undone and brushed to their full length and spread out in the daylight. I'll teach you to ride a bike if you want.

XXX
Lydie

When Hélène looked up, after committing her letter to memory, she chewed it for a long time, then gulped great mouthfuls of river water, dipped up in her joined hands, to help her swallow the blue paper that was now reduced to a pulp.

Hélène returned home by herself. Pauline sniffed her thoroughly, like a mother cat.

"Where have you been, child? You smell so strongly of rain and dead leaves it's quite amazing. What got into you, going out on a day like this without a raincoat? And where's your brother?"

Pauline takes her daughter's jacket and shakes it vigorously, after emptying out the pockets.

Saved, thinks Hélène, I've been saved. My mother picked up nothing with her terrible sense of smell, neither the blue paper nor the English biscuits nor the lines of Xs, nor my lie nor my betrayal: only an autumn smell that inexplicably breaks my heart.

Pauline hangs Hélène's jacket by the kitchen stove to dry. She repeats her question:

"Where's your brother?"

Hélène shrugs, stops herself from uttering a ready-made reply from Sacred History:

"Am I my brother's keeper?"

♦ ♦ ♦

He strides along the road beside the river, hands in his pockets, chin buried in the turned-up collar of the jacket that he's outgrown.

The little field with its old forked birch tree is far behind him now. He is still walking. His whole body feels as if it's burning under the wet clothes. He walks beside the river, suddenly loses sight of it, and then a space filled with grass and brush appears between him and the river. Sometimes an entire field appears, while the running water of the distant river, invisible now, persists in its murmur. Then he sees once more, from very close, the arm of black water between the island and terra firma where the blacksmith's little boy drowned last year. The flat tip of the island, covered with logs, sandy as a beach, becomes blurred in the rain.

He hears the noon angelus ringing, oddly clear in this landscape drowned in mist. He knows Pauline expects him home for lunch, but all he wants to do is put as much space as possible between himself and his mother so he can read his letter in peace.

The rain has stopped. The island is far behind him now. The roar of the rapids in his ears has been muffled for some time. The mist lingers, white and insubstantial; it rises from the river, soaks his face, his hands, his dripping clothes. He shivers. Dreams of getting warm, of holding in his hands and bringing to his lips a blazing glass of the alcohol he has never tasted.

An abandoned barn, half ruined, low and lopsided, next to the road. Thrusting his knee into the worm-eaten door, Julien tumbles onto dry hay that smells of dust.

His hard-earned solitude spreads out around him into the shadows. His heart pounds in his chest. I'm just tired from walking so far, he thinks to reassure himself. Nothing's really bothering me. I still love nothing and no one. His wet clothes cling to his skin. Icy sweat trickles between his shoulder blades. His numb fingers are unable to take Lydie's letter from his pocket. A strange dread makes him tremble. He fears more than anything in the world the insults and scorn that might come from Lydie.

Dear little Julien: You mustn't be afraid of me, you sweet silly child. It is wrong for the woman who rules your life to require you to be silent. Forbidden to speak to me. But I'm there watching out for you. I can hear your confession, my angel, and your little sister's too. You're enduring violence, my curly little lamb. Surrender. I shall teach you the work of damned and dangerous poets, and you'll see how you resemble them deep in your innocent little heart.

Lydie

Julien peers for a long time at the skinny wrist emerging from his too-short sleeve. I'm growing by the minute, he thinks, my mother keeps telling me so. Soon I'll have reached my full height and then I'll pit myself against that girl who mocks me. What a pretentious letter, from a person who likes the sound of her own voice. Here's what I'll do with it. He goes through the motions of tearing it up, then he stops, carefully folds the blue paper, and puts it back in his pocket as if afraid of damaging it. "Lydie, Lydie, Lydie," he says aloud in the silence of the barn.

The hay crackles under his weight. Julien turns and turns again, gradually overcome by a reverie at once cruel and sweet, so close to fever that he cannot ward it off. Soon he sinks into a half-sleep from which he escapes by fits and starts, tries to bring into the daylight some fragments of fabulous poems half-glimpsed in his dream, offered to Lydie and at once swallowed up by the night.

He stands up, buttons his jacket, teeth chattering, afraid he has caught cold. Dreams of getting back as soon as possible to the warm house that waits for him in the village.

But before he gets there he still has a good way to walk, and his legs are giving way beneath him. He must, without fail, go past the blacksmith shop.

♦　♦　♦

At first, standing in the fog alongside the road, he sees only a glow, as from an old lantern, a comforting beacon in the submerged landscape. He goes towards that glow like someone who is lost. Lightheaded with fatigue, he is drawn to the flame of the forge like a moth to a lamp. He tells himself stories for reassurance. A stop, just a brief stop on the way home, he tells himself, only long enough to warm my hands and the rest of my body before I continue on my way home. The hope of seeing Lydie again brings him, powerless, weak, and defenceless, to the threshold of the blacksmith shop.

He is here in the suffocating heat. He breathes in an odour of stable and hell. His wet clothes steam on his body. Only with effort can he make out Lydie among the children sitting on the floor, side by side in the shadows, fascinated by the spectacle of fire and horses.

She stands and approaches him, smiling ecstatically, as if she was about to disclose her whole life. Comes very close to him, murmurs:

"I have a passion for horses."

Julien hears himself say, his voice barely passing through his tight throat, as if he, too, was confessing a formidable truth:

"I have a passion for you."

Pausing long enough to hear the fierce laughter that shakes the blacksmith like a storm, Julien races outside.

While Pauline won't leave the bedside of her son who is burning with fever, little Hélène takes advantage of his illness to get closer to Lydie.

Meetings at the blacksmith shop, long walks through the countryside, blue letters exchanged in the hollow of the old birch tree.

You darling androgynous creature with your little breasts, your narrow hips, your indescribable candour, your beautiful hair. I want you to be trusting and shameless in my hands, as if I were everything and you nothing. I want you to be obedient from the start. A single quiver of my eyebrows should bring you to the brink of tears, and I'll be your queen and mistress till I disappear on the horizon, like a day that has run its course. If you want, I'll take you to the gates of death. Should you escape, nothing will ever be for you as it was. You will be queen and mistress in your turn. But before that you must submit to the trials, all the trials I'll suggest to you. Only then will you become strong, independent, and cunning enough to face your mother who dreams of stifling you in her bosom. I shall rid you of your childhood before I leave. That's a promise. And then you'll be so lonely, you'll miss me forever.

Lydie

The two of them are sitting on a pile of beams behind the Ouellet house.

"In my letters I play at being a creature from Hell, like my favourite poets. It amuses me. Relieves my boredom. And it's fun. Pay no attention, Hélène dear. Writing letters makes me drunk, it goes to my head. Till I don't even know where I am."

Lydie laughs. Hélène, her little face tilted up towards Lydie, is filled with a sense of helplessness and fear.

"How you're trembling, and how silly you look with your pale eyes as wide as saucers."

What Hélène fears most in the world is that Lydie will do what she did the other day: shift one of the heavy beams lying on the ground and uncover the monsters that hide underneath and swarm across the yellow flattened grass — earthworms, a toad, a thin grey snake . . .

"You're afraid of your own shadow, Hélène dear! We have to tame you. Come here, let me fix your hair."

Hélène's hair covers her shoulders, her back, falls to her hips. Lydie works with the comb and brush, makes Hélène's hair froth in the light.

"What hair you have! It's a pity to braid it like that, tight as rope."

Hélène grabs the comb and brush from Lydie's hands.

"My turn now. I'll fix your hair. You're so dark, Lydie, and your hair feels cold."

"Turtledove, sweet turtledove," says Lydie.

"Crow, beautiful crow," says Hélène.

They cluck, each louder than the other, like little girls.

Soon they are coiffed identically, hair pulled back on the neck and tied there with a black velvet ribbon.

Now Hélène mounts the bicycle while Lydie runs behind, encouraging her.

"Faster, Hélène dear, faster. Now straighten out, you're swerving all over the road."

◆ ◆ ◆

In the half-light of the little bedroom under the eaves, with its walls of darkened fir planks, Pauline's ailing son has been restored to her, delivered into her care. She helps him drink by raising his head, she turns him over in his bed, changes his sheets and pillowcases, lets her cool hand rest on his brow for long moments, listens for the incoherent words of his delirium, despairs at his confused remarks, records every one of the extravagant words that break like bubbles on the surface of a deep, dark pond. A single word stands out from this magma, detested above all others — the name of Lydie, which he utters several times. From what strange illness does Julien suffer, and what business does that girl have at the most secret moment of his suffering?

The doctor summoned from Quebec City talks about the persistent ache in his side, about the lingering fever. He prescribes calm and rest.

As she's done every morning since he took sick, she bathes him from head to foot with a sponge soaked in soapy water.

Now the fever has broken. Already he has ceased to be that child, inert and burning with fever, who let himself be tucked in and turned over in his bed. He opens his eyes wide, is astonished to see himself so thin and so naked, lying full-length on the narrow iron bed while Pauline bends over him with her sponge and soap suds. Abruptly, he pulls the sheet over his nakedness.

"Never mind, Mama, I can manage perfectly well by myself now. I don't need you, honestly. You ought to get some rest."

Now that she has been dismissed, she goes into the corridor for a smoke, stands leaning against the wall. Her first cigarette in ten days. She barely has enough time to take a few good deep drags, to watch the blue swirls rise to the ceiling, when already she must see to her daughter, Hélène.

◆ ◆ ◆

The girl stands before her, inexplicably triumphant in her torn and dirty dress, with bloody knees and a big lump on her forehead.

"I was coming back from the lake and I fell on the stones. Lydie's bicycle is all twisted but Lydie says it doesn't matter. The important thing is, I pedalled all the way to the lake by myself. Lydie says that's very good."

This child is beyond lying. She didn't think it necessary to invent a story to explain her cuts and bruises. Shamelessly and with perverse pride, she flaunts her deed and defies me.

Pauline bandages her daughter in silence, swallows her misfortune, grits her teeth, promises herself to return to Quebec City as quickly as possible, to get away from the stealer of children who is wreaking havoc on the shores of the Duchesnay.

There are odours nearly as strong as those of spring, but poignantly sharp, like freshly turned earth. At times a semblance of summer floats in the air, then disintegrates at the end of day with the freshly fallen leaves.

The polio epidemic is subsiding with the arrival of the cold. Pauline packs her bags. Negligently tosses into trunks and cartons armloads of clothing and sundry objects, seeing nothing, it would seem, so anxious is she to be gone.

Little by little a strange kind of peace comes to her, while an astonishing thought was forming that leaves her disarmed and saps her strength. To end in triumph. Invite Lydie here to the house. To unmask her, uncover her true face. To stop struggling against a ghost. To confound her. Have the girl at her mercy. Look her in the eye as if she was a real person who can be touched, seen, heard. Make her lower her gaze. Let her know this is the first time, and the last, she'll ever set foot in this house. After, it will be too late. Julien and Hélène will be far away, safely out of Lydie's reach.

Soon Pauline's desire to know Lydie becomes so urgent, it is virtually the same as Julien and Hélène's fascination that first time they saw Lydie riding Zoël Ouellet's horse.

◆　◆　◆

She has unwound her long red scarf, taken off her coat, and now she is standing among them in her sleeveless white summer dress, her tennis shoes, her long bare legs, with that insolent little beauty spot on her right cheekbone, her mocking manner, and the pride at being alive that illuminates each of her deeds and even her immobility and silence.

"Hello. It was so nice of you to invite me."

Her voice is low and deep.

She replaces her scarf, winds it twice around her neck. She sits down calmly, is as familiar and agreeable as any ordinary guest — a relative, a cousin, a sister — suddenly very real in their everyday life, in this low room with its darkened beams.

Hélène already regrets having to share Lydie's presence with her brother and her mother. She stares obstinately at the toes of her shoes. Seems embarrassed and uncomfortable.

Julien shields himself behind his convalescence. Shuts himself inside a state of languor where all considerations are due him. Waits for someone to draw him from his solitude and console him. Listens to the heartbeats at his wrist. Is distressed to be so tall and thin, barely recovered from his fever and released into the world, frail and flayed and as breakable as glass. He looks surreptitiously at Lydie, is sad to see her beautiful face offered to everyone, and bitterly but very softly reproaches her.

Everything that happens now is between Pauline and Lydie. The teapot and thick china cups rented for the season with the house, the freshly baked galette and the strawberry preserves. Lydie bending over her bread and jam. Pauline facing her.

"I've never eaten such delicious preserves."

They play at having tea. Hide their evil designs under equally stubborn brows. Exchange of rapid glances, strong impressions retained. Both profoundly occupied with efforts to avoid a settling of scores.

"How are your parents?"

"Very well, thank you. They're coming to get me in a few days."

"We leave next Thursday. We've already booked the truck."

"What a beautiful autumn! I'll remember it for a long time."

"I'd rather forget it, like a dead leaf that's rotting in the ground."

"That's up to you. I'm very glad to be leaving for my school in the States, on Staten Island . . ."

Suddenly they are very close to one another, leaning across the table, their faces almost touching, like two fighters ready to exchange blows.

Pauline tries to stand up to her, her imposing stature now huddling on her chair, her entire being reduced to a thin, fierce voice:

"The sooner you go the better it will be."

Lydie takes the scarf from her neck, pulls it around her

53

shoulders as if she was cold. Her moves are exaggeratedly slow and precise, her voice excessively cautious and polite.

"My own parents are very broad-minded. They've never forbidden me to see anyone, not even the Vallières children . . ."

Pauline remains motionless, content to exude her fury in silence, through every pore of her skin. She is surrounded by clouds of cigarette smoke like a cuttlefish by its ink.

Lydie springs from her chair, strikes her forehead.

"But this is our day for goodbyes! We mustn't let bad tempers ruin what time we have left. Julien, dear, don't look so grim. Get that look off your face for heaven's sake. Cheer up! And you, Hélène, you look like a little girl paying a visit. Come and sit beside me. Shall we put on some music to clear our minds?"

Everyone's attention is so keen, so strained, they can hear, magnified tenfold, the needle as it moves across the record in silence. Pauline has all the time she needs to fear the music before it even begins.

The long low room whose wood bears the patina of time serves as a resonance chamber. Woodwinds and strings reverberate off the darkened beams, while the piano's voice flows limpid as a spring between one's fingers.

It is a concerto by Mozart that suddenly emerges in the untamed New World landscape to the delight of three grave and silent children.

Once again Pauline wants nothing to do with it, for she fears music, has dreaded it since her own childhood. But Lydie is there, listening so attentively you can see the music move across her animated face in jubilant waves. Pauline looks away. The girl is indecent, she thinks.

And now Lydie jumps to her feet, approaches Hélène, pulls her with both hands as if inviting her to dance, forces her to stand.

"Listen carefully to those little piano notes, my angel. They're so much like you. They're Hélène personified. I'll never be able to hear that rondo again without thinking of you."

Facing her mother and brother who are staring at her, Hélène restrains herself from dancing. She merely blushes with pleasure, while her little face is creased with suppressed laughter.

It is while listening to Schubert that this solitude develops for each of them, this isolation inside a poignant secret. Here is the heart-rending *andante*. Too concerned with his own torment, Julien doesn't see a veil of shadow fall over Lydie's face. Soon she turns towards him, grave and dreamy, is astonished to find him so remote, a prisoner of himself. She calls out gently, very softly, for him alone to hear; names him *the Sombre one, the Widower unconsoled*.

She is on her feet in the middle of the room. Her eyes cold cinders, her hair bristling in sturdy tufts on her head, all her height, all her being offended. Pauline feels deprived of her children, she watches them move about as if they were behind glass while the music enfolds them inside an enchanted circle, ruled over by the stranger she has invited here herself, at her own risk.

On the gallery, when the time has come for Lydie to leave, Hélène clutches Lydie's scarf, throws her arms around her neck, whispers something in her ear. Then Julien approaches, says very low, as if he was choking:

"I'm going to write to you, we can't say anything to each other here."

Pauline stands in the doorway gazing silently at the scene, fretting because these two children who are her whole life have suddenly been caught in an act of betrayal.

◆ ◆ ◆

Strangely at ease now that he is alone and no longer facing
the person who causes him to stammer or fall silent, he writes
her a long letter, as if he were slashing his wrists. For the first
time he calls her "tu."

*This is my first letter and probably my last, in other words my
one and only letter. It's as if I'm a man with just one word to say,
who suddenly throws it in the face of anyone who'll listen, an all-
inclusive word that contains everything and spares nothing and
no one. The other day at the blacksmith shop I told you I had a
passion for you, and saying that was better than all the letters in
the world. It was more condensed, closer to a cry or, more surprising,
a truth that probably shouldn't be said aloud, like all the truths
we hold back because we're well brought-up and on our guard, for
fear of betraying ourselves. I did betray myself at the blacksmith
shop the other day and I'm prepared to do it again in this letter,
so that you'll answer me as directly, as truthfully as I'm speaking
to you, this time with you across from me and forced to answer, to
tell me clearly it's not just horses or the people in the village who
matter to you. I'm here, too, I'm truer than the horses, the trees,
and the river, more alive than all the villagers assembled at the
blacksmith shop or the general store, more real than the entire
countryside rolled out at your feet like a carpet, I, Julien Vallières,
with the strength of all my years, promoted to the state of mature
man thanks to you, Lydie Bruneau, from the first time I saw you
riding Zoël Ouellet's dappled horse, I existed so strongly beside
you that my heart pounded between my ribs like a captive beast,
screaming with more life than Alexis Boilard who looks at you
with rotten eyes. See me and know me, as I do you. I must have
your answer to what I said at the blacksmith shop the other day,*

and to this letter today, which is the same thing, the same confession, only longer and more urgent, because time is passing and soon we'll be apart, you and I, as you go to your American college and I to Quebec with my mother and sister. Above all, don't think I don't know that appearances are against me, my little boy's manner that makes you laugh. Brought up under the mother, as they say about an unweaned calf, I may seem like a child gone to seed, yet I love you as a man loves a woman. You who are full of experience, don't see this as negligible, a boy who is in love for the first time and refuses himself nothing. My ignorance is equalled only by my love. Watch out for the traps set by Pauline, my mother. Those social get-togethers where I die of loneliness, with the music, the cakes and preserves, under her vigilant eye, such occasions exist the better for her to keep her eye on us and prevent us from seeing each other unless she is there. Poetry and music illuminate my life, enlarge it endlessly, bring me closer to you at the speed of light, let me be there with you in the same brightness. Tell me quickly where I can see you alone before we leave, day or night. I'll do anything to be with you, no matter where you are.

Julien

◆ ◆ ◆

Hoarfrost covers the fields, the grass by the side of the ditches, the trees and bushes. If you would make your way along the road at dawn, you must pass through banks of fog that unravel as the sun climbs higher in the sky. The Ouellets wait till mealtime before they light a fire in the kitchen stove. Lydie has decided to stay in bed and wait for her parents, now home from New York, to come and fetch her. Twice already Alexis Boilard has come to the Ouellets amid the din and clatter of his old truck. He asked for Lydie and was told she didn't want to see anyone.

She is shivering in her bed, under the woolen blankets. She reads Julien's letter. That child is out of his mind, she thinks. His demands are unreasonable, they kill me. He begs me for everything. *He will have my soul in his beak* if I let him have his way. I must defend myself. His letter drives me to despair. But if I'm weeping now it's from anger.

She wipes her eyes. Crumples Julien's letter, closes her fist like someone smothering a bird, while Alexis's truck circles the house with an infernal roar.

The order is given to her in the obscurity of her heart to take revenge, at once, for a slight she experienced in the mists of time, at the very sources of her own life. She writes:

Julien, dear, you read too much. You write too much too, roman-tic letters that are far too long. I like my poets in books, not in life. In real life I prefer boys like Alexis who don't beat around the bush, who expect from me only what I can give, which is very little, as I'm stingy with the gifts that nature gave me and I fear love as I fear my own death, and the death of my freedom.

Lydie

She hears the truck driving crazily, turning sharply around the house. She covers her ears with her pillow. She feels a very strong desire to roll in the mud and to do crude things with Alexis, to fling herself headlong into disgrace.

Lydie plants herself in the very middle of the lane, waves her arms above her head. Alexis stops his truck. His angry head appears out of the cab.

"Are you getting in, yes or no?"

She says in a feeble voice like a sick child's:

"Yes, yes, I'm coming, you don't have to make such a racket!"

◆ ◆ ◆

She swears very softly that she will impose her law on Alexis and bring him to pleasure according to limits she has chosen.

Her father's friends smelled of after-shave and scotch. Alexis reeks of beer and sweat. But it's still the same face, ravaged as if by illness. She looks at the profile of the boy hunched over the wheel, at his mulish expression. As she is accustomed to hasty, inconsequential caresses in cars and other unsuitable places, she refuses to worry for another few moments.

The truck bumps along a bad road, a shortcut that Lydie doesn't know. Alexis hasn't raised his head. Driving his truck seems to demand maniacal attention. When the road begins to resemble a path about to disappear through the spruce trees and the leafless birches, Alexis cuts the engine. He turns to Lydie, meekly, like a pet begging to be stroked. Says, over and over again, "Lydie." Lets his head fall onto her lap. She feels the wet warmth of his mouth, his puppy's teeth, through her skirt.

He nibbles at her skirt, her underwear. Spreads her thighs with his head. Buries his head under her skirt.

Soon it will be done, she thinks, I'll still be unscathed, I'll pull down my skirt, go back to the Ouellets, and eat supper with the family, as usual.

She tries to sit up.

"I'm the one who decides, Alexis Boilard: let go of me."

He grabs her around the waist and drags her out of the truck. She struggles and falls to the ground, onto the grass, full-length. She is momentarily stunned and sees the sky above her, white and chalky. The metallic dazzle blinds her briefly until Alexis's heavy body drops onto her and blots out all the light.

He pleads with her, insults her, calls her "Little slut" and "Sweetheart." She insults him and derides him. Calls him "Clumsy ox." And now an unfamiliar little voice is emerging from her, demanding its pleasure and giving precise instructions.

◆ ◆ ◆

He has donned a navy blazer with his school crest, he has put his head under the pump, run a comb through his streaming hair again and again, and left the house. When his mother asks where he's going so late, he shouts hoarsely:

"Leave me alone and let me live my life!"

A vast prairie sky at sunset, flat land with stubby hills on the horizon. Here is the lane of poplars, their leaves still green and curled by the wind. Julien makes his way amid the sound of trembling leaves and he trembles along with the leaves.

From her bedroom window she has seen him coming. She tells herself that nothing will ever be the same again between them, that she is a woman now and has no need for this child with his burden of dreams who is coming towards her down the lane.

Lydie's face is creased with worry and dread. She believes she can feel, moving in her bruised belly, small brick-coloured hands with diminutive black nails, a whole creature, white as lard, taking root, strangely resembling Alexis.

Before Julien can knock at the door she is there on the threshold, her mood foul and grim.

"Did you want to see me, Julien dear? You can call me

'Madame' now, you know, I earned it yesterday, while you, you're just a little brat still wet behind the ears!"

What is strange is that Julien doesn't hear what Lydie says to him. He repeats in a mechanical voice that doesn't seem to belong to him:

"I have to know. I want to know. Alexis Boilard and you, in the truck — is it true? The whole village is talking about it."

An icy silence filled with menace nails him to the spot for a long moment.

"Do you really want to know, Julien dear? Too bad for you. But first we have to find a quiet spot so I can tell you everything, so you can hear everything, since you want to so badly."

She has thought of nothing better than to take him to where the fox cages are, abandoned now for a long time.

They walk down the narrow path one behind the other, Julien following Lydie, like birds lost in the wake of a ship they depend on for their sustenance and their lives. He expects everything from her, the revelation that has already broken his heart, the knife and the wound.

On either side of the path the crickets' last song before winter crackles in the cold air. Lydie becomes voluble, starts to explain that fox farms are always far from houses because of the smell and the yelping that sounds so mournful, especially at night. She turns to Julien.

"Besides, if the mother foxes are disturbed they eat their young, to protect them."

She bursts into great cracked laughter that breaks.

Julien's voice again, still just as strange, as if detached from his body, sounds dry and mechanical:

"You already told me that. You're repeating yourself, Lydie. You're talking for the sake of talking."

Here are the ramshackle cages, the wooden shed where

they used to kill the foxes. Julien wonders how they were able to slit the foxes' throats without damaging the fur. How could they take the lives of russet or silvery animals and have nothing of their torture show on the lovely pelts destined for lovely ladies?

Lydie walks around the shed, looks in vain for a window, spies a small plank door with a rusty padlock, tries to open it, thrusting with her shoulder.

The door gives way at last, while Julien pleads:

"Let's get out of here, Lydie. It feels so eerie."

"What are you afraid of, Julien dear . . . Of me or of any foxes that might have escaped the massacre?"

The light is gradually dwindling. The grey shed, the rusty bars of the cages seem to be dissolving in the autumn dusk. There is no pity in the livid sky as its light is extinguished.

Animated and light, she leads him into the shed, bumps into the furniture and objects piled in the shadows.

"What a lot of junk! Like a beggars' auction!"

Striking match after match, they make out an old eviscerated horsehair sofa, a rickety table, quantities of rusty, battered utensils, a handleless rake, a pitchfork missing half its teeth. Here and there on the floor are dusty straw and quantities of field-mouse droppings. On the table, a lantern with blackened glass. The candle inside is almost intact. Lydie lights it at once.

The silence catches at their throats, impresses them as if someone infinitely fearsome, the worm-eaten genius of the place, were hiding in the big footless armoire, or behind the little straw-bottomed chair that's half eaten away.

Their shadows shift on the wall and on the piles of furniture. They have to come very close to the lantern that sits on the table if they're to remain visible one to the other, one opposite the other, all smeared with night, as the candle flame flickers between them.

Julien is astonished to find Lydie intact before him. Smooth and hard as usual. Not a trace of her disgraceful behaviour with Alexis. He persists but looks in vain for signs on her face. Stares wide-eyed. Is like a blind man; his whole life is before him to be grasped, yet he sees nothing.

Lydie is the first to look away.

"Don't stare at me like that, shooting daggers with your eyes."

With no rifle or knife, I'm unarmed, thinks Julien, and he presses his long bare hands together as if he was testing the fineness of his bones.

She goes and sits on the little horsehair sofa at the back of the shed, in the shadow zone, as if she wants to burrow into it.

Her voice seems to emerge from the gloom of night.

"Have you ever seen the sun come up, Julien dear? What if we stayed quietly inside here, you and I, until dawn? You'll see how sad and beautiful it is when the night slowly gives way and is filled with light."

She seems moved by the fate of the night to die in the first hours of dawn.

"Come closer. Stop looking at me with those eyes like pistols aimed at me. Come."

He collapses at her feet with a muffled growl, like a wounded beast. Hugs her legs with his trembling hands. Raises distraught eyes to her.

She shrinks from him. Good Lord, what is he doing at her feet, this boy who demands everything of her, even the secret part of herself that she persists in refusing, her child-like innocence.

"Julien dear, let me go, you're frightening me."

She buries her head in a cushion that is split and smells of mildew. She laughs because her mouth is full of horsehair. She chokes and spits.

"You're so funny, little Julien, with half your hair plastered down and the rest standing up on your head. You look like a kingfisher that's been in the water! And so curly, Julien dear, it's quite amazing."

She runs her hands through his hair again and again.

"You're too late, Julien dear. How I would have loved you only yesterday, and you'd have been the first and maybe the last. But today it's too late. My day of kindness has already passed. I'd be too afraid of becoming pregnant twice at once. Can't you see it: twins pressed close together in my womb, one all red and smelly, the other as curly as a lamb!"

She buries her face in the cushion, chokes with laughter again.

He has got to his feet and is speaking now into the door, his hand on the panel, ready to go out.

"You're cruel, Lydie, and I wish I'd never met you."

"I'm neither cruel nor kind, little Julien, I'm possessed, that's all, which isn't the same thing. Don't go right away, please don't go."

He turns and comes back. Again he kneels close to her. He speaks in a muffled murmur, his head on Lydie's lap.

"I love you so much."

"What are you complaining about, Julien dear? You wanted to become a man and now it's done. You have your disappointment in love, your broken heart. At least you have that."

Julien can't hear Lydie, he is so busy savouring the warmth of her knees against his cheek, his forehead.

"You're a beautiful boy, Julien dear, very beautiful. I think that tomorrow I'll be madly in love with you and I'll shed every tear in my body because of it. For the time being, though, I've other things to do. This is the day after my wedding and I have ordinary things to look after. My parents are coming for me in two days. I'm going to a college on Staten Island, in New York, by the ocean, where all the fishermen are Portuguese. I'll be there till the end of the school year. But before I leave, I must take care of your little sister, Hélène. I have a date with her tomorrow."

She speaks as if to herself, choosing her words, seems unaware of Julien's warmth against her legs, the weight of his head on her knees.

For some time now a little field mouse atop the footless armoire has been gazing at Lydie with its beady eyes. How he looks at me and how I look at him. She is fascinated. It seems to her that the image of the field mouse on the armoire is being engraved in her with strange precision, as if later, in the normal course of time, any other memory of her night with Julien would be taken away from her.

They have waited for the sun to rise, Julien huddled against Lydie's legs, Lydie running her fingers through Julien's hair. Between them, quantities of things both childlike and childish. He speaks of his *primitive state as a child of the Sun.* She says it's the same for her, though she's a girl. Julien swears that it's till the end of life, till death; Lydie pulls his hair by the handful, assures him she's as old as the earth and the sea together, and that it's pointless to think of tomorrow.

"Between us, Julien dear, the order is reversed, for in the proper order of things it's the man who is older and the woman who's as artless as a yellow-centred daisy in a field."

Again, her cascading laughter.

All around the shed, birds have begun their quiet chatter before even a vague glimmer of light appears in the sky. When he kisses her, like a boy bestowing his first kiss, she tells him to start again and to pay close attention. The second time, she pretends to be asleep. She is like a dead woman who is about to fall to the ground.

The day dawns slowly, on all sides at once, seeping into the sky second by second, like liquid spreading underground, far from its source, its bleeding heart hidden behind the trees.

It is she who kisses him, who puts her tongue into his mouth, who bites him fiercely. Here she is, now on her feet, tidying her dishevelled hair, smoothing her dress.

"Hurry, Julien dear, it's morning. If you don't go now you'll be scolded. Don't complain. You've had your wedding night. Goodbye. I'm going now. My holidays are over."

He stands before her, stunned and helpless, like a traveller who is lost in an unfamiliar station.

He speaks softly, tonelessly, as if the words that come from his mouth do not concern him.

"Goodbye, Lydie Bruneau. I'm leaving, too. Right now. It's morning. I have to go home. I won't see you again. You're the devil, Lydie Bruneau."

As Julien walks away, down the path that grows brighter as the sun climbs higher in the sky, he doesn't know that Lydie, behind him in the shed, her face in the split cushion to muffle her wailing, is saying his name again and again:

"Julien, Julien, Julien . . ."

◆　◆　◆

No cries, no insults, no reproaches. She has no thorns or barbs. Is exhausted. Bereft. Turned away from her life. She stands before her son and asks where he's been.

"Lydie and I wanted to see the sun come up . . ."

She waited all night for his return, standing at the window in the hall, pressed against the cold glass.

Pauline is silent. There are no words available to her to express her grief and fatigue. Strange phrases form in her head that will never see the light of day: I loved you first, I am the first woman in your life, like Eve beneath the tree of good and evil, in the lost Paradise; remember, that was your childhood.

He puts his hand over his mouth to hide the lip that was bruised by Lydie's bite. As if he was suffering from a toothache.

◆ ◆ ◆

Already Hélène obeys her every command. I whistle and she comes, Lydie thinks, as she drinks cup after cup of coffee in the Ouellets' big kitchen so as not to succumb to the urge for sleep. Forget her sleepless night in the fox shed. Forget Julien. Wash herself clean of her night with Julien. Turn her attention to Hélène. Make her undergo the final test. The brother first and then the sister. Each one in turn. Has she not sworn to set them both free? Tomorrow it will be too late. Today.

She lights a cigarette. Blows the smoke up to the ceiling. She likes the mixture of coffee and nicotine. Her eyes are half-closed, she is resting. Madame Ouellet is bustling about the table. She has seen that Lydie's bed wasn't slept in and looks at the young girl surreptitiously, suspiciously.

Concentrating on her coffee cup, Lydie has caught a glimpse of Madame Ouellet watching her. Lydie's green eyes are utterly blank above the cup. Madame Ouellet goes back to her cooking. At once Lydie calls to her, bows low to her.

"Good morning, Madame Ouellet. Consider yourself greeted by me, Madame Ouellet. Morning has come. I have a busy day ahead of me. I'll tell you about it tonight. Till then, think of me. Make a cross over your heart when you think of me, Madame Ouellet. Tell yourself no one can paddle down the river like me. I've been doing it since childhood. It's been decided. I'm going now. And little Hélène Vallières is coming with me."

Lydie asks for the key to the boathouse. She doesn't say that she wants to shoot the rapids. Quietly overcomes her apprehensions. There is only the savage heart of the river to be crossed.

◆ ◆ ◆

Soon Hélène is there in her yellow oilskin, her hair knotted at the neck like Lydie's.

"I'm scared, Lydie, I'm so scared."

"You have to get beyond your fear, pass through it as if it was a ring of fire in the circus: you know that. Afterwards you'll feel strong and tall, your mother's equal, and you'll be able to look her in the eye and tell her to mind her own business. No one will dare to pit themselves against you, you'll be a grown-up person forever, as free as me, Lydie Bruneau. And it's not complicated. You'll just sit in the canoe without moving, while I paddle. There's nothing in the world like shooting rapids, dear Hélène. Tempting God and the Devil at once. Quite a feat! You'll remember it for the rest of your life. Do you have a heavy sweater on under your raincoat? You'll need one. Here, let me fix your clothes a little better."

She tugs at Hélène's turtleneck, pulls it over the collar of her raincoat, brushes Hélène's cheek with her fingers.

"You're so sweet, Hélène, so lovely."

Hélène melts like a Christmas candle under Lydie's caress.

"You're the lovely one, Lydie, and I'd die for you."

Lydie has only to smile at little Hélène to be sure of herself beyond life and death, even though she knows she'll hurt Pauline.

"Your mother will be worried sick!"

Hélène lowers her head. For the second time, Lydie runs her fingers gently over Hélène's cheek.

The Ouellets' canvas canoe has been freshly caulked and painted. For a long moment the red of the canoe, the yellow of Hélène's oilskin, the blue of Lydie's jacket, the red of her scarf — all these bright colours gliding along the river are visible from the shore, at high noon.

When the river brought them in sight of the flat village, several recognized the red canoe and its passengers.

As she sits motionless in the canoe, Hélène can feel with her whole body the shock of the waves pounding against the canoe harder and harder as they approach the rapids. Now she has surrendered entirely to the terrifying force of the water. Now she is utterly obedient to the canoe's mistress, who paddles on the right, then the left, constantly restoring their balance. Already long white trails of foam, like spittle, run through the water as the churning grows and the roar becomes deafening. Here, there, rocks covered with green moss loom before them. Soon the water's bland smell, its supreme fury, replace all the breathable air, all earthly life. The red canoe dances and creaks, at the mercy of the waves. Together, Lydie and Hélène enter the seclusion of death.

◆ ◆ ◆

For a long moment she was like a drowned woman, streaming water and mud as she lay full length on the blacksmith's dock. The current had flung her onto the pebble beach and men gathered her up, not knowing if she was dead or alive, not knowing what to do with her because she had no relatives here or anyone to care for her. She spat water through her mouth and nose. The whole village, assembled on the dock and all around as far as the road, watched her choke and vomit. Her ears are filled with tumult, her face is streaked with mud and grass. She looks, unseeing, all these people gathered around her.

It was Alexis who wrapped her in a blanket and took her home in his truck.

A tiny log cabin stands in a treeless field. An enormous garage with a tin roof that gleams brightly in the light of the cold sun. Alexis Boilard's domain has no fence, is surrounded by a scrubby hedge.

She is feverish. Her head is filled with sound and fury. The waves crashing against the rocks pound endlessly at her temples. The water's din sounds to her like deafening applause, while an earthly and indifferent voice counts off the seconds, to calculate how long she can go without breathing, at the bottom of the river, and stay alive. She calls Hélène. Tries to extricate her from the green, sticky moss that slowly, gradually, is covering her like a second skin. The king of the mud hides in the deepest part of the river. His voice makes bubbles the colour of café au lait amid the hurly-burly of death, and with dense gurgling he declares: So much for the earthly life of Hélène Vallières.

Lydie cries out in Alexis's cabin. She calls Hélène. Shivers and doesn't stop vomiting in Alexis's bed. Thinks she must spit out the whole river, and her life, in a wave of bile.

Alexis has lit a fire in the wood stove and heated some water. He tells Lydie to take off her wet clothes. She can hear nothing he says, for any human voice is alien to her now and ricochets vainly off the sound of water in her head. Her teeth are chattering.

He undresses her as if extricating her from a slimy mass of seaweed. Holds her in his arms for a moment, naked, absent, icy cold. He swathes her in sweaters and blankets, places bottles filled with hot water at her feet and along the length of her body. There's no shortage of bottles in Alexis's cabin, either empty or full. The boy tries in vain to lift Lydie's head and make her drink, but the gin trickles from the corners of her tight-pressed lips.

He sits on a chair he's pulled up to the bed and studies Lydie, who lies there twitching among the bottles of hot water. Little by little she calms down and falls asleep, curled up as she was in her mother's womb. The air in the room thickens. The light is dwindling. Alexis's hand brushes against Lydie's on the grey wool blanket. He speaks to her aloud, calls her "Sweetheart" and "My pretty owl." He begins conscientiously to drain the bottle of gin.

Long before darkness has fallen completely, Alexis has collapsed onto the bed, at Lydie's feet. The empty bottle rolls along the floor from one end of the room to the other, then comes to a standstill against the stove.

The sound of a motor, the dazzle of headlights in the window without shutters or curtains, confused trampling around the cabin, loud knocking on the plank door were not enough to wrest them both from the deep sleep that protects them from the sounds of the earth.

A vigorous push opens the unlocked door. Now they are huddled here in this room, clear and precise like responsible adults who know what has to be done and have only enough time to do it.

Madame Ouellet has brought dry clothes. She shields Lydie with her massive body while the girl puts them on in the cabin's one room, now full of people. Madame Ouellet talks about little Hélène Vallières who died in the rapids when her head was shattered against the rocks.

Lydie's parents are there, cowering against the door, gasping the stuffy air inside the cabin. They are waiting for their daughter to be returned to them so they can take her away to college, where she will be safe.

The father in his long belted coat and holding his velvety fedora walks stiffly towards Alexis. He extends a hand half-closed around some crumpled banknotes. He mutters between his teeth:

"For taking such good care of my little girl."

Carefully Alexis unfolds them for everyone in the cabin to see — one twenty-dollar and one five-dollar bill. He takes them disgustedly by one corner, as if holding a dead mouse by its tail, then lifts the stove lid and drops the bills into the fire. He closes the lid, then turns around, yawning:

"I don't need anybody here now. Don't bother hanging around. I've got things to do early tomorrow morning, three cords of wood to deliver. I need a good night's sleep. So goodnight, everybody."

Without even glancing at Lydie he sets to work tidying the bed.

It is Lydie now who approaches Alexis, breaking free from the hands of her mother who had grasped her arm and is pushing her towards the door. Her pallor is extreme. She is walking as if about to fall at every step. But a bright flame lights up her icy face again. She speaks softly into Alexis's ear.

"Do it for me, please do it. You must. You must. Before I disappear from here forever. Set the horses free in the municipal field. You know the one, the field beside the river. Set them free in the village. Then I'll be able to leave here with my mind at rest, and I'll have all my time to think about you, Alexis Boilard, when I'm in my American college, between classes in moral philosophy or lengths of the pool."

Again she has an urge to laugh, as if she was in good health and everything was normal.

Lydie's mother has lifted the veil that covered her eyes like a small black grate and with her large and very red mouth she says:

"Come along, child. Quickly now."

Lydie crosses the village one last time, comfortably ensconced in her parents' long car. She tries to engrave in her memory the houses, the trees, the river, the hills, the entire familiar landscape that moves away at dizzying speed with every turn of the wheels.

She will not hear the huge confused stamping of the heavy plough-horses, set free on the main street after her departure with great lashes of Alexis Boilard's whip. She will not see the frame houses light up, one after another, wakened by the galloping of the horses. Only the Vallières house, glimpsed through her tears along the way, will continue to blaze in Lydie's memory, like a mortuary chapel lit by candles.

◆ ◆ ◆

Pauline, incredulous, held her daughter's body, saturated with water and sand, as if she was alive. She bandaged the cut on her head, gently brushing aside the blonde hair. She washed and dressed and laid out her sleeping daughter on her own bed. She crossed her hands on her breast. All night she sat at her side, as though beside a sick child.

Not until the early hours when the first glimmers of dawn have appeared in the windowpanes does Pauline begin to howl, like a she-wolf caught in a trap. Then collapsed with her face against the ground.

III

Henceforth Julien learns to live alone with a woman whose white freckled face is immobile, like wax, its expression frozen, whose massive body refuses to move. Deliberate refusal or genuine paralysis? The days pass and Pauline regains neither speech nor movement. Abandoning his studies, her son devotes all his time to her. He carries her from bed to chair, from chair to bed, fixes her meals and feeds her, washes her and brings the bedpan.

From studying the impassive face in the hope of noting the slightest reaction, the slightest sign of life, he realized that his mother's features were being transformed, were hardening little by little to become more virile, the bridge of the nose more prominent, the jaw more protuberant, the mouth more bitter. Soon he became so skilful at detecting the smallest shudder on his mother's face that he realized there were certain moments when Pauline's lips moved imperceptibly. He applied himself to reading his mother's lips. Eventually he was able to distinguish two words, chewed at in silence, always the same ones, depending on Pauline's mood: "Goddamn" or "My love."

Julien was careful not to tell the doctor of his discovery, for he wanted to keep to himself this secret he shared with Pauline.

If the image of Lydie came back to him sometimes with violence, he immediately pushed it away, forcing himself to do all sorts of household tasks, however finicky and all-absorbing. His resentment of Lydie was very great.

The silence in the apartment on rue Cartier grew heavier day by day, and Julien's youth adapted to it as to a misfortune. Soon the only thing he wanted to do was make his mother speak, drag her out of her muteness. He would take her in his arms, speak to her very softly, saying into her stony face and as close as possible to her vacant eyes, her silent mouth:

"Just say hello, how are you? Please, just hello, how are you?"

And he would shake her by the shoulders.

"Hello, hello, say hello. There's nothing to it. Just try. I talk to you the whole blessed day. I'm your son, Julien. Little Hélène is dead. Lydie is cursed. But I, I'm right here. Just say hello. It's me, Julien."

Three years after the death of Hélène, when Pauline herself was very close to death, she dropped her head onto his shoulder, her whole body tilted to one side as if she was about to fall out of bed, and said aloud and very distinctly:

"I'm slipping."

Only her son Julien heard the last words of Pauline Vallières, who passed away on April 5, 1937, at the age of forty-five, from the aftereffects of an intolerable sorrow.

Having abandoned his studies to care for his mother, after her death Julien went to work for the post office, at the main branch on rue Saint-Paul.

It didn't take him long to get his bearings in his new territory. A few rooms in the apartment on rue Cartier, a few city streets. Never again would he go to Duchesnay, either the river or the village, or to the Claridge Hotel on the Grande-Allée. By thus avoiding certain streets, certain parts of the countryside, he felt as if he was consoling his mother, being faithful to her beyond death.

It sometimes happened in his dreams that he sensed, acutely, Lydie's kiss on his lips, in his mouth, felt her teeth and her bite which awakened him brutally. On those mornings he escaped from his uneasy happiness only by accusing Lydie aloud of all the wrongs on earth.

Sitting in the same wing chair evening after evening, when his work at the post office was done, walking down the long corridor to stretch his legs, dressing in the morning and undressing at night, shaving at the same hour before the same old pitted mirror, unaware of the aging of his youthful face, sorting letters all day long, eating quick snacks, curling up for sleep, living without making a sound, from rue Saint-Paul to rue Cartier, rue Cartier to rue Saint-Paul — thus did the unhurried days of Julien Vallières unfold.

The apartment, cluttered with Victorian furniture, its red rep upholstery faded by wear and the sun, and heavy with accumulated silence and with memories that lurked in the shadows, hemmed him in like a prison. He broke free of it only to go back to the mailbags and to the small grey wood boxes into which he deposited letters at the pace of a silent, well-oiled machine. He rarely spoke to his colleagues. Did not distinguish one from another.

Gradually, furtively, like someone concealing objects on the sly, Julien began to rid the parlour of the things that had been his mother's or his sister's. He brought in his own books and his record player, arranged the big wing chair to suit himself. On winter evenings he would draw the faded curtains over the frosty windows, then read poetry or listen to music until late at night.

The days pass, and the months and years. Julien does not read the papers. Doesn't listen to the radio. He seems unaware that the war is establishing its reign upon the world a little more every day, tipping countries into horror one by one.

But Julien's strange peace was becoming more and more fragile, like the skin that forms over boiling milk.

◆ ◆ ◆

Her name is Aline Boudreau. She is childlike and plump. Her diligent little hands go past Julien all day long, completely engaged in their daily drudgery, among the letters at the main post office.

One day Julien got the idea of capturing one of those little hands in midair to feel its warmth on his own hand. When he did so he saw a face overwhelmed with happiness suddenly appear, for the first time, in this familiar place where he recognized no one. Pale eyes were raised towards him, regarded him as if they were looking at the apparition of a saint. Julien immediately thought that this girl's power of adoration must be boundless. This long, lanky man who was already beginning to stoop suddenly felt an insane urge to be swaddled like a newborn and loved without limits by a woman who resembled neither his mother nor Lydie.

For a week he courted her, giving her flowers and a tortoiseshell comb, walking her home every night to rue Latourelle, to a house made of yellow bricks that were blackened as if by a fire.

When Sunday came he went up to her room, which smelled of polish and lye. She was his, when he wanted her, as he wanted her. She said over and over, delighted:

"I'm risking damnation for you, you handsome man."

And she hid her face in her hands.

Julien's pride was so great that he'd have liked her to hang his big white bloodstained handkerchief at the window — the way Arab brides hang out their bedsheets on the morrow of their wedding day. At the same time, though, he was ashamed of what he'd done and afraid he had hurt Aline.

They lay for a long time snuggled close together in the shadowy light of the room and the warmth of the bed. When Julien thought he detected a vague glow through the flowered curtains he got up hastily, like Cinderella on the first stroke of midnight.

"I have to go now! I have to go!"

By way of farewell she gave him two full pages of her ration book, one for sugar, the other for coffee.

"You're far too thin and too sad. Eat. You have to eat. It's good for you."

"I have to go now! It's morning!"

◆ ◆ ◆

"Have you ever seen the sun rise, Julien dear?"

For the first time since the fox shed, he is outside in the dew of early morning. He must not linger in Aline's bed when the sun is climbing slowly in the sky. This uncertain hour between day and night belongs to the light spirit of

Lydie. The act of love with Aline has only wakened Lydie's memory.

"You'll see how sad and beautiful it is when the night gives way gradually and is filled with light."

Her throaty voice in Julien's ear like a vibration in the air around him.

Julien has a rendezvous with Lydie in the dead city, at the hour when only ghosts are abroad, in full freedom.

With a beard smudging his cheeks like dirt, hands in his pockets, and chin enclosed by his turned-up collar, he turns onto the Grande-Allée. He stops outside the Claridge, carefully studies the blind windows, wonders in what secret room, behind what drawn curtains, Lydie might be resting in all her sleeping glory.

Now the day has returned like a great warm wind that spreads across the rooftops; it runs breathlessly down the longest avenues, slips into the labyrinth of little streets, stretches endlessly over the Plains and along the river.

Julien crosses the threshold of the Claridge. Speaks to the porter. Asks for the number of Lydie's apartment.

"Monsieur and Madame Bruneau, their daughter and all their belongings, enough to fill two Baillargeon trucks, moved to the States some years ago and left no forwarding address."

While all those years were passing I was asleep on rue Cartier, shut inside with my records and books. During that time Lydie disappeared.

I was like a dead man in his shroud. Aline had to appear before I half-wakened, like someone supporting himself on one elbow to greet the day from his bed. It was enough that Aline appeared, that I touch her as a man touches a woman. To hell with Aline. She just has to avoid doing things by halves. It's not enough to love me like a god. I wish she were supernatural, Lydie's equal, her magic double. Aline is unworthy of Lydie. I won't see her again.

◆ ◆ ◆

After Julien had gone, Aline stretched, naked, at the window, forgetting that only the night before she never had clothes enough to hide her from the eyes of the world. From her window she looks down on the houses, the streets, cars, small individuals walking along the sidewalks, the line of mountains in the distance. It's high time for her to dress and go to the post office, but she lingers there, looking at the city as if taking possession of it. Though she has just one room on rue Latourelle at her disposal, she feels as if she now has title to the entire city teeming with life, spread out at her feet. Somewhere, in a house unknown to her, Julien, too, is preparing to go out; soon he will come to her along the still-cool streets.

Aline hurries. Her red shoes trip lightheartedly along the sidewalk. She sees everything, hears everything along the way, as if everything was being offered and given to her. Streets, houses, the small lots in front of houses, the children playing, the barking dogs. The entire city has been tamed. Aline herself could define the city's boundaries, organize it in her own way, locate its secret heart, and lodge in her own breast the city's radiant heart that so enchants her.

All day, Julien's place at the post office stayed empty, surrounded by piled-up bags of mail.

Aline has neither his phone number nor his address.

◆ ◆ ◆

His head filled with romantic models, Julien revels in his solitude. Ensconced in his armchair he reads poems, listens to records. He seeks accomplices and brothers. Wishes he could unite his voice with the most hopeless songs on earth. Having put off mourning Lydie for so long, now he would like to celebrate her in a great dirge of a poem, like a poisonous flower wrenched from his heart. He is swallowed up in dreams.

Soon he hears nothing in the silent red room, sees nothing, feels nothing but a vast weariness. Books closed, records still, the reasons why his soul is lost are no longer apparent to him. Julien falls asleep in the threadbare old chair that smells of dust.

On wakening he is not quite sure if it is the end of a day or its beginning. Pale sunlight filters in through the windowpane. Time can no longer be measured. All that is left for him to do is drag himself like a sleepwalker, walk endlessly down the long corridor, knock at the closed doors of Pauline's room, and of Hélène's.

Julien's life is filled with dead women. Where does the idea come from, suddenly, to hurl abuse at Lydie as if she was alive?

◆　◆　◆

Aline thinks she'll never see Julien again. She continues to look out her window. The wrong side of the city is there before her eyes, after the good side — the one she knew first and that will not return. The sick, the crippled, the humiliated, the injured, the old, the prisoners, the battered child, the woman gravely offended — all are there beneath her window, assuring her that a disappointment in love is a mere drop in the ocean of the world's pain. Now she need only take her place like everyone else in this city that has belonged to her for just a short time, go back into the rank that was intended for her for all eternity. Here is the share that is just for her, the bundle of her belongings she must shoulder at any moment. More than the city where she was born, the entire world is there before her, round as an orange she could hold in her hand. Invisible creatures are born, then they die. Their cries are lost in the boundless emptiness. Now Aline is simply a dot that is erased from the map of the world while a gigantic shadow hovers over the land and the seas, tracing there the shape of a cross.

Aline has no tears. A sharp burning stabs at her eyes, dries her lips.

On the evening of the third day she has gone to bed, as usual. Sleepless for a long time, she looks at the ceiling, at the glow of headlights from the cars that pass along the street.

◆ ◆ ◆

We shall enter splendid cities
Stripped to the skin
Astride steeds of horror.

His one and only poem. Again and again, Julien repeats those words from another time. It was autumn on the shore of the Duchesnay. A scant three lines in honour of Lydie Bruneau. Julien sits at the kitchen table. He drinks coffee. Pleads for grace. He hopes a poem will come. He darkens entire pages, then immediately tears them up. Dead letters no one will ever read.

Once only, it was autumn on the shore of the Duchesnay, there was love and in his poem the steeds of horror turned loose against his heart. The splendid creature who was driving them has fled out of this world to the sound of clattering hooves.

Here is the apartment on rue Cartier. In the kitchen, torn scraps of paper on the floor and around the deal table. The red room with books, records, clothing, empty cups, and the coffeepot overturned on the carpet in the stuffy air.

Julien throws the window open, breathes deeply like someone recovering his breath after running for too long. He is hungry and thirsty.

In the kitchen, not a grain of coffee nor the smallest crust of bread. Julien leans out the window, listens to the rumours of night rising towards him. Aline's slight body is resting somewhere in the night. Julien has only enough time to go to rue Latourelle. He is afraid of losing Aline. He showers, shaves, rushes out into the sweltering summer night. He will kneel before Aline, beseech her forgiveness. He will beg a cup of coffee and a piece of bread.

◆　◆　◆

She heats water. Brews coffee. Now she takes pure white slices of bread from a brown paper bag. You can hear the water sing in the kettle. She turns around slowly, she is barefoot, wrapped in her flowered housecoat. Her tangled hair foams across her forehead and down to her nose. Her voice is different. A feeble thread, barely audible:

"Do you want sugar for your coffee?"

She crosses and recrosses her housecoat over her breasts. He eats and drinks. Holds a tray on his knees. He avoids looking at Aline but can feel her gaze fixed on him. She stands before him, unmoving, and studies him endlessly, as if she is amazed to see him here, in her room.

Again her voice, half stifled:

"I think I nearly died."

She laughs, embarrassed, as though she's just said something very stupid.

"Never mind me. I'm just being silly."

Aline is so tired that Julien takes off her dressing gown and gently, with infinite care, puts her to bed. Now she is lying on the narrow sofa. She shuts her eyes, exhausted from holding back so many tears. Whispers:

"Good night, sleep well, see you tomorrow."

"Yes, see you tomorrow," replies Julien, already sorry to have committed himself a full day in advance.

He stuffs his hand in his pocket, touches the cold metal of his own apartment key, as if he had access to his full freedom as a man.

◆ ◆ ◆

Julien sees Aline home every evening after work. Sometimes he goes up with her to the room under the eaves. She fixes him spaghetti or French toast, instant coffee and cheese with cherries. They make love together, without extravagance and without forgetting to take precautions. She is crazy about him. He is as reasonable as a model student.

As soon as he leaves Aline, Julien returns to the solitude of his red room. Sometimes he writes poems, then tears them up. He plays records, listens to Bach, Mozart, Beethoven, to Schubert, Ravel, and Stravinsky. He reads poems and novels. He is transported to a world without limits, one where strange sensations and astonishing characters abound. A second existence doubles the little life he leads as ideal employee and well-behaved lover. Fabulous cities appear between the lines of his books, allowing him to glimpse a labyrinth of strange streets and lanes, while great sacred squares loom up before cathedrals like huge standing stones, filled with carved saints and demons.

Anywhere out of this world. The domes of St. Petersburg, Raskolnikov and Stavrogin, the smog of London streets and the debtors' prisons of Dickens, Esmeralda dancing on the square outside Notre Dame, the blue of Chartres (as seen in costly picture books), so many images that appear to

Julien's eyes like scattered elements of the promised land of his dreams.

Following in Baudelaire's footsteps he tastes the spleen of Paris, breathes the noxious air, wanders endlessly through the haunted streets, while the cry of the evil glazier splits his ears and Mademoiselle Bistouri dogs his footsteps, asking endlessly:

"Are you a doctor?"

When the war is over and he has saved enough money, Julien will leave. He will board a ship and cross the Atlantic. Over the course of days and nights he will come to know the sea.

Julien goes more and more often to Aline's. He climbs the stairs, breathless. Calls Aline "My sweet," "My pearl," "My marvel," though he doesn't like her checked or flowered dresses.

◆　◆　◆

When Julien is with her it seems that nothing can violate Aline's peace. With her face buried in Julien's neck, she sometimes thinks of eternity, without fear or dread. When the earth no longer exists, she thinks, and when Julien, reduced to his volatile soul, is cast alive into God's burning bush, like a brief candle flame at sea in an ocean of fire, I shall turn to him out of all the rest, and warm my hands and heart there, world without end.

Sometimes Julien ventures to read Aline a poem of his rescued from the wastebasket, sharing it with her like a formidable secret.

She listens, knitting her brow, utterly attentive, fascinated by the strange language that she understands no more than she did the Church Latin that lulled her childhood. Can it be that all these fantasies Julien has written are, like Latin, only some obscure signs of the word of God?

She hides her face in her hands. Julien's mystery embarrasses her and frightens her as if it was sacred. She stammers:

"Where on earth does all that come from, for the love of God!"

Often when Julien raps at her door — three short knocks, following the signal they've agreed on — Aline is startled because she has been hunched over her crackling radio, listening to news of the war. Softly she laments refugees, prisoners, those who are tortured or killed under a rain of fire. She retains the names of countries, imagines the tears and the blood. As time passes and the horror advances, she says: "The poor little Poles, poor little Belgians, poor little French, poor little Canadians, poor little Russians, poor little English." One night when Julien showed up after a week of silence, she switched off her radio and in a voice filled with infinite compassion, murmured:

"Poor little me."

Giggling, she makes small talk. Again and again, she repeats the same trivial details of her everyday life as if they were affairs of state. But when it's a question of what matters to her most in the world — her love for Julien — every word must be torn from her mouth, as if she was afraid she'd have to spit out her heart and die on the spot.

She mutters, seems to mock both herself and Julien:

"When we're together it's paradise, you handsome man!"

Never, not at the sweetest moments, nor at the bitterest ones, does she ask Julien:

"Do you love me?"

Does she not know in the hollow of her bones that Julien has no answer to such a question?

◆　◆　◆

He is like a childish Don Quixote, crammed full of reading and music, who accumulates treasures before going out to explore the vast world. One day Julien will set sail for Europe, having stocked up on marvels in a closed room.

Sometimes he takes Aline to Anse aux Foulons, where they look across the immense river to the Lévis shore. Soon he plays at pretending it's the Seine. He tries to fit the St. Lawrence River into the scale of his desire, finding it inordinate, vertiginous. He gazes at the water and waves through a small circle formed by his thumb and forefinger. I believe what I want to believe, he tells himself. Here is the Seine between my fingers, flowing and returning to the sun. At any moment Baudelaire may appear upon the rocky shore, with his green hair and his stovepipe hat over one ear.

Aline touches Julien's shoulder as if he was a child who must be wakened softly, without shaking him or frightening him too much.

"Come, quickly. Time to go home now."

◆　◆　◆

When the war was over, Julien, torn for a moment from the world of his imagination, felt something like a shiver pass over his skin. The harsh reality of the earth was counting its dead and its survivors. He asked Aline to arrange a little party to celebrate the victory.

Aline set up the card table and there was no room left to move around it. She set the table with a white cloth with cross-stitch embroidery, blue plates with yellow figures, carefully washed cream-cheese glasses that sparkled like crystal, a lighted red candle. The small size of Aline's room seemed not to hamper her precise gestures in the least. She turns and turns, from the table to the tiny electric hot plate, from the hot plate to the table, like someone dancing on the spot. On the sofa bed, hulled strawberries in a blue bowl. A stew is simmering on the hot plate, the aluminum lid bobbling up and down amid gusts of aroma.

On the windowsill there is the pink rose Julien gave her and put in a glass.

If Aline takes a step towards the window, it is to smell Julien's rose, to feel it soft and cool against her cheek.

When they had finished eating, after each of them had smoked a cigarette, Julien kissed Aline. He told her that with the war over now, all he wanted to do was leave for France as soon as possible. He continued kissing Aline, who sat there as still as the dead.

It was then that Aline realized that along with Julien's mysterious reveries, she too possessed a secret of her own. A vast room with tall windows, a long table with a cloth upon it white as snow and reaching to the floor, a huge oven where three-layered cakes were baking, air to breathe deeply all around, like at the seashore, a big bed to lie in with Julien and make love without precautions, to start a family in full peace of mind.

◆   ◆   ◆

Julien waits for things in France to calm down: the settling of scores, the trials, the girls with shaved heads. He reads newspapers and magazines. He is learning about the world in the days when it was cursed.

Julien scrimps and saves to prepare for his journey overseas. He does without socks and movies, no longer buys flowers for Aline. He pinches pennies, pinches dollars, too. He counts the months, the weeks, the days that separate him from his Atlantic crossing. He writes poems and immediately discards them.

One night Julien gave Aline the keys to his apartment. He

asked if she wanted to live there while he was away. Two rooms were off limits, however: Pauline's bedroom and Hélène's. Aline looked around the apartment. She saw two blocked-up doors in the long hallway. Dead women whispered dimly behind them. Aline was as sure of it as is someone who hears a mosquito buzzing unseen in the dark.

Aline looks at the bunch of keys in her hand. She thinks of *Bluebeard* and refuses to enter into a tale that is so cruel. She tells Julien she'd rather stay in her own room on rue Latourelle.

She insisted on seeing his ticket with the number of his cabin. Promised to write.

Two days later, Julien bids Aline farewell. He kisses her on the mouth, the eyes, the nose, the brow, he drinks the tears all down her cheeks.

"I'll come back. You know perfectly well I'll come back."

The *Mauritania* slowly pulls away from the wharf, leaves long thick trails of oil and tar. Aline measures the space that is growing imperceptibly between the ship and the wharf. She watches the deck where Julien's white handkerchief is waved, then gradually disappears.

When there was nothing to see on the horizon but the grey of the water, the grey of the sky, Aline felt very cold — on her back, her bare arms, to the very roots of her hair — despite the vast warm June day all around her.

IV

Here they are sitting side by side on a wooden bench, in an *allée* of the Jardin du Luxembourg. Julien is no longer alone and at sea in a strange city. A woman is with him here beneath the placid, orderly trees, in the hot air of July.

He bows his head, stares at the sand at his feet, digs at it with his shoe. Real life is not here, he thinks, with this unknown woman at his side and this overly manicured garden around him. He is all stubborn, testy silence.

"Oh là là, what a grump you are!"

Her laughter is light and she looks at Julien with amazement.

He is thinking about the trees he knew in Duchesnay, that grew there untidily, the dead ones mixed in with the living. He looks up but no longer sees anything around him, neither the garden nor the woman at his side. Inside his chest a savage and taciturn land is wringing his heart.

"Good God, this garden is so tame and tidy!"

She laughs very loud, sure of the satisfactory beauty of her garden and of the fullness of her life.

He bows his head again, peers closely at the sand and gravel at his feet. He wishes he had neither past nor turmoil, only *bliss that can be measured, sorrow that can be healed*, like this woman sitting close to him who laughs and laughs and laughs.

With both hands on the nape of his neck, rumpling his hair, she forces Julien to look up again.

"What hair you have, it's as thick as the fleece on a sheep's back and the colour of a *marron glacé*!"

Her bright and merry eyes try to capture Julien's fleeting gaze. She is patient. She will wait as long as is needed until he does something, says something.

Her soft warm hands on his neck, on his brow. Later perhaps, once it has been surrendered to the wonder of memory, this brief moment in the hands of the woman from Les Billettes will seem to him delectable and harrowing, like the gift of a day that passes and never returns.

She has risen, now stands erect in the light, already caught up again in her own unknown life that awaits her out there, somewhere in this city, beyond the gates of the garden and beyond Julien's grasp. He says goodbye to a stranger who eludes him, who is reaching out towards an immediate future, one from which he is excluded.

They were taking their leave of one another as the gates were closing and the slow, tired stream of donkeys and ponies were returning to the stable for the night. He was so afraid of not seeing her again, of losing her face in the nameless crowd. He makes her promise to come to the Ravel concert two days hence, at the Salle Pleyel.

◆ ◆ ◆

It rained all the following day. The trees of Paris, and what little earth there is at the base of trees or inside the iron gates, are fragrant now as Duchesnay once was. Thus did Lydie in a bygone life smell of damp earth, in the fox shed.

Wandering from café to café, breathing in the fresh smell of the rain, Julien waits for the arrival of the day, the hour, for the concert at the Salle Pleyel.

If at times Aline's image forces itself on him, at a café counter or the corner of a street, it is in red shoes and a flowered dress that she appears, impalpable and transformed. When that happens Julien may reread one of her letters, conscientiously, as if reviewing a lesson, while he is surrounded by cigarette smoke and the jingling cash register and pinball machine.

Don't catch cold. Don't drink too much black coffee. And most of all don't forget your sweetheart who hugs you and kisses you and sends you all her love.

Aline

With Aline's letter slipped inside his wallet, between the oversized banknotes, Julien sometimes catches himself murmuring: *How tiresome are the demands of the beloved heart and the beloved body.*

Julien readies himself for the concert, carefully dresses in evening clothes, dons a starched white shirt, a black bow tie as if he was in mourning. His thoughts about his mother have been quiet now for some time.

◆ ◆ ◆

She insisted on paying for her ticket and now she has taken a seat next to him, on the threadbare velvet bench. Their two profiles stand out, somewhat solemn and overlapping slightly, like royal profiles on a postage stamp. He keeps brushing against her with his knee and shoulder. The music absorbs them and exempts them from any movement, any word. Their deepest complicity comes from their twofold living warmth, perceived through their garments that touch each other in the muggy darkness of the concert hall.

Her hand, burning hot, somewhat limp and relaxed among the folds of her skirt, the smooth cold ring on the fourth finger. Julien has brushed against that hand, has felt the hard ring under his fingers. From that moment on, he became less attentive to the concert, as if irritated by a sudden dissonance, shocked by a false note that reverberates and echoes all through the hall.

Several times she has looked at her watch and now, barely seated across the table from him on the terrace of a café, she announces that friends are expecting her, that she promised them long ago . . .

Julien says:

"That ring you're wearing?"

But the ring is no longer on her finger, for she dropped it into her bag as soon as the concert was over. Her hands are perfectly bare now, long and smooth. She shrugs.

"I wore it for the concert, that's all. Afterwards it's too much trouble. I have no need of jewellery, since I'm sober and austere by nature — and divorced into the bargain."

She speaks quickly. Seems anxious to provide whatever information he may request.

"What are your friends like?"

"Young, happy, a little crazy. I have lots of fun with them."

"And with me?"

"With you? It's rather the opposite. Aside from your eccentricities, which intrigue me, I wonder what it is about you I find amusing. Unless your dear bewildered face secretly makes me swoon?"

Everything she says is murmured very softly, in a sweet voice filled with laughter and tender irony.

He has only a little time to be with her. At any moment she may disappear, taken up by her hidden life. And then Julien's loneliness in Paris risks becoming very great. He questions her like a judge who persists in trying to compromise someone who is slipping away. How long has she been divorced? Does she play a musical instrument?

"I play the piano sometimes."

She becomes impatient, leans across the table towards him.

"You spoil everything with your questions. I am the way I am, just as you see me here, across from you, only passing through, with no past or future."

She rises, both hands pressed against the table.

"My name is Camille Jouve. I'm thirty years old. My double life is none of your business. Imagine whatever you want. Doctor Jekyll and Mister Hyde, if you want."

With every word she laughs and mocks him. Her teeth are very white, her mouth red. He wishes she'd stop talking and leave, right now. All he wants to do is finish his coffee in peace and think quietly about what astonishing things are happening to him with this woman. He stands up, too, waving his hand as if to dismiss her. She moves closer to him.

"Will you be at the bar in your hotel around five tomorrow? I'll be waiting for you."

She dives into a taxi which starts up right away then disappears into the stream of cars.

Julien sips the rest of his coffee, which is getting cold. He is glad that her name is Camille Jouve. It's a beautiful name. He repeats it to himself like a litany. He scrutinizes everyone who walks past along the sidewalk in the hope of recognizing Camille Jouve's friends, of calling to them, of intercepting them then and there, of reducing them to nothingness before they can catch up to her somewhere in Paris and dine with her in a restaurant he doesn't know.

◆ ◆ ◆

With shutters closed and curtains drawn Julien detaches himself from the city for the night. He piles his clothes on a chair. The bedside lamp lights the carefully made-up bed. It is a banal hotel room, good for rest or for love. Julien is alone and naked in the room while Paris rumbles and roars beneath his windows. Would it be so hard then to bring Camille Jouve up to his room, to sleep with her, then throw her back into the heart of the city and forget even her name? Julien would have nothing to do then but depart for the New World, where Aline is waiting, round and without mystery and as fresh as fresh cream.

But now he is tormenting himself and life isn't quite so simple. The light has scarcely been extinguished, the darkness scarcely settled in the room, and he is like a traveller stubbornly trying to read a city map in the gloom. Paris is open before him like an atlas. He thinks about the streets he knows and even more about the ones he doesn't know. He imagines deep avenues lined with trees, then smaller streets that hide in the shade, public squares, famous or obscure, neighbourhood cafés or those on the *grands boulevards*, restaurants filled with people. He is trying to discover the one, unique brasserie, sparkling with light and noise, the one out of all others where Camille Jouve has gone, is holding court surrounded by her friends. Barely an instant before giving in to sleep, he sees behind his closed eyelids the moleskin banquette where she sits, the white tablecloth on which her elbows rest, the freshly opened oysters in front of her, while uncertain men lean towards her across the table, their unattractive features almost touching her pretty face with its pale cheeks, her dark hair.

At dawn, only barely awake, Julien is exasperated that there are still so many hours ahead of him before he meets Camille Jouve at the bar on the Quai Voltaire.

He gets up, stretches at the open window, looks at the Seine flowing by and at the still-sleeping Louvre. An unopened letter from Aline lies waiting on the tray with the crumbs from his breakfast.

Heat haze rises from the water. Rare strollers appear and disappear into the morning. On the quay the booksellers' closed boxes look like great green padlocked crates in a railway station.

Julien reads Aline's letter. A scant few lines in a childish hand, as if she's written them along a ruler line.

Oh how I long for you. I want you to know, staying in the old country so long is a strange thing to do. The weather here is fine. I'm counting the weeks, the days, the hours, the minutes you've been gone. I think about you all the time. I am pregnant.
Love,
Aline

* * *

Without taking time to shave or knot his tie, Julien is outside, cast out onto the street. He does not know where to go, wants to find under his feet as soon as possible the noisiest, busiest promenade, crowded with people and cars, wants to be swallowed up by it body and soul. There is too much tumult within him, too many contradictory ideas jostling one another.

Delivery trucks unload their goods, obstruct sidewalks and streets. Passersby hurry through the fog that is lifting now. The day will be muggy and hot. High summer. People are going wherever obligations or desires push or pull them. Julien follows close behind them. Eyes fixed on the shoulders of the person immediately ahead of him, Julien matches his pace, tries to lose himself in the wake of this total stranger so he can stop being a bachelor who is caught in a trap, and who is expecting a child. How can it be? What ruse of Aline's? What carelessness of his own? A child, a child . . . He tells himself again that he has a rendezvous with Camille Jouve and that he's as free as the air. A whole day still to get through, the sun's journey from its beginning to its end at five p.m. in the bar on the Quai Voltaire.

Across the Atlantic, blind life is following the course of its thoughts in the belly of Aline Boudreau, secretly taking root. Now Julien need only match his steps to those of a stranger along boulevard Saint-Michel to savour the beauty of this day that is settling in all around him.

Successive waves of men, of women, break one against the other, mingle inextricably then come apart, touching as they pass. Julien catches here or there a word, a glance, a fleeting smile that lights an unknown face, he delights in this living anthill, says "Bonjour" and "Salut," as if he knows everyone in the world.

He is outside from morning to night, eating and drinking while he stands or walks (sandwiches and bottles), tirelessly crisscrossing the city, having left behind him closed rooms and the heel of the mother who crushed him. He is like a snake that has escaped from under a rock. Presently, noon. Flurries of bells soar into the warm air over Julien's head. A festival of bells at high noon. Again and again he says "Bonjour" and "Bonne journée." He speaks to anyone who will listen,

anyone who will reply. A dialogue has been opened between
the city and Julien. Street vendors, a budding grove. The
world is torn open from top to bottom like a piece of fabric
ripped in two. *Between other men and Julien what has changed
is this: he is going to be the father of one of them.*

At Place Furstenberg he wonders if it would be good to
live inside this perfect square, with its four trees and a lamp-
post. He would bring his round-bellied wife there and their
twofold existence, now made one, would be priceless. On rue
de Buci, flowers tumble freely onto the cobblestones, from
sidewalk to street, in a tide of colours and scents. Julien buys
a nosegay of violets for the woman who awaits him in the bar
on the Quai Voltaire.

For the first time he has the impression he is making his
way through a city that belongs to him, a city that is visible
and palpable and coming from all sides around him. He is
the mature man who measures his power on both sides
of the Atlantic at once. Across the world, in the darkness of
his sweetheart, Aline, a child is slowly growing, while
Lydie's shadow soars above the country, like a kite scarcely
visible, high in the world of dream. On the Old Continent,
in a nearby city with uneven cobblestones he can feel beneath
his feet, a woman in a black dress waits for Julien a few
streets away, at the bar on the Quai Voltaire, and the muted
light of her body is secretly aflame.

◆ ◆ ◆

The bar, faintly lit as if by a lantern, dark silhouettes, muffled
murmurs, ice cubes clinking in glasses.

Julien stands in the doorway, dishevelled, unshaven, his
shirt unbuttoned and no longer fresh, utterly weary.

Elbows resting on the bar, a man and a woman perched

on high stools are deep in conversation. Their faces are visible, reflected in the mirror above the counter among the rows of bottles.

Julien has a rendezvous with this woman. Holding a small bouquet of faded violets, he stands, unmoving, back pressed against the glass door, and stares fixedly at her in the mirror, wanting her to turn her head without his having to call her.

Now she swivels on her stool until she faces Julien. Briefly he glances at her superb legs, crossed high. She stands and comes to him. Her earrings tinkle when she moves her head. Without smiling, all black and erect, she says, "Julien." Now the man at the bar spins around. He looks at the man and woman in the doorway. Jiggles the ice in his glass.

Julien has gripped the women's wrists in both his hands. He says very quietly, all at once, without catching his breath:

"I'm leaving tomorrow. I won't see you again. I'm getting married. I'm going to have a child. We won't see one another again."

She straightens the gilt chain of her purse on her shoulder. She stands and waits at the door, her hand on the knob. Julien takes two steps in the direction of the bar. Tosses the violets onto the counter in front of the man who is shaking the ice cubes in his empty glass.

He returns to Camille Jouve. Steps aside to let her pass. The old staircase carpeted in red velvet with brass rods is right there, in the hallway.

◆ ◆ ◆

Julien lies on the unmade bed. He looks out between his lashes at the woman putting her clothes back on.

She has plucked her dress from the floor where she had tossed it. For a moment she holds it at arm's length above her head. Let her pull the black garment over her head, over her face, without delay, then let her disappear forever. As a dark cloth is dropped over a bird cage at nightfall. The woman is only the stuff of dreams: What is she doing in Julien's bed?

They have done what is necessary to slake desire and to let separation come. She has moaned till she could moan no more against him, concerned for her pleasure alone. He has barely emerged from between her thighs when already he resents her, for she is more beautiful than Aline and should never have been born.

And so much for their brief encounter. Now they have separated as if they'd never met.

She picks up the garments scattered on the floor and shakes them. Half huddled against one wall of the room where this woman is taking forever to dress, Julien thinks of the offence to Aline.

It was just a way to mark the end of bachelorhood, he keeps telling himself while she approaches softly to bid him farewell. At peace and free once more she leans over him. He feels her warm breath on his face. He is feigning sleep even as his whole being rushes towards her to take her in his arms one last time.

For a long moment he persists in lying there in the dark, tries to put his thoughts in order, pleads in vain for sleep, desires with all his might that deep oblivion, that solid mooring in the depths of night. The sleep of a dumb beast. His whole life is jostled every which way in his mind, holds him spellbound.

As the night slips away, Julien lies with eyes wide open on the disorder of this room with its drawn curtains and can think of just one thing: to inquire about the *Homeric*'s next departure. Reserve his ticket as soon as he can. He gets up and performs his toilette. His journey to the Old Country is over.

Camille Jouve continues to exist, beyond Julien's reach. Now she is sitting again at the bar on the Quai Voltaire, crossing her legs, applying lipstick. She hasn't redone her chignon. Her heavy hair falls to her shoulders. She noticed immediately the absence of the man with the ice cubes. Orders herself a scotch, neat.

All that remains now is to leave again, cross the sea the way he came. Travel across the ocean a second time. The promised land shifts now to the other shore. He has only to make the crossing in the opposite direction. The Atlantic again, as far as the eye can see. Julien imagines long days watching the sea till land appears, half liquid and barely emerged from the water. Aline is that dark land on the horizon, trembling with its fruit. Aline is the source and the beginning. Julien has a rendezvous with her. Once again, dreams are before him.

He has not lifted the curtain or looked out the window. His eyes have not followed the woman who is moving away with tiny steps along the sidewalk of the Quai Voltaire. No foreboding tightens his throat at the thought of an unknown man moving in the shadows, through the city's streets — a dark silhouette that stands out from all the rest, as solitary and idle as Camille Jouve, of the same evanescent race, walking towards her while she senses him in the distance, hopes for his company, for a few hours only, until the end of night.

Aurélien, Clara, Mademoiselle, and the English Lieutenant

I

It happened abruptly, in lightning fashion. A sort of savage illumination struck Aurélien Laroche. In that harsh glare nothing of his old beliefs survived. Suddenly everything within him was devastated, like a field of grass delivered to the fire. Present, future, past, eternity — at one stroke all were abolished. Neither Christ nor the Church nor redemption nor the resurrection of the flesh: Aurélien had lost his faith the way a person loses the key to his house and can never go home again.

Aurélien was standing at the edge of the freshly filled-in grave, wearing his black suit for weddings and funerals, hat in his hand. It was July. The sun was beating down on his lowered eyelids. At his feet, flowers dusted with sand marked the place where his wife now rested, in the cemetery, next to the river.

The separation was now complete. All that remained was for Aurélien to trot back home at the leisurely pace of his old horse. At all costs he must avoid having all those people clustered behind him extend their hands and offer their condolences. His youthful face with its dried tears is no longer to be looked upon here until its final state of dead stone.

A house built of poorly squared planks, on the bank of the river. All around it, a sort of cage of thin grass. Obscure outbuildings, half-collapsed. Fields running close by the edge of the forest. From the road could be heard now and then the crying of Aurélien's child. In vain the village women offered to help: Aurélien chose to take care by himself of the small creature who had emerged from between the thighs of her dying mother in a fountain of blood.

Sometimes at night when Clara was asleep in her wooden cradle, a sort of evil shadow that did not belong to the night would circle the house, enter it, and make its way into Aurélien's chest, gripping his heart in a vise. He told himself then that he was locked within injustice, as if in a prison from which he would never be able to escape.

The days of diapers and bottles passed nearly without incident. Lines draped with baby clothes were hung once a week between two stunted trees. The rest of the time, Clara, in her diapers, smelled very strongly of urine and of milk gone sour.

Aurélien took his daughter with him everywhere, rolled up in a faded sweater that had once been blue. He would lay her down in the grass in the shadow of the trees, under cheesecloth because of the mosquitoes, when he had to earth up plants or reap or plough. From time to time Aurélien would pick Clara up and hold her against his chest, to console her for being alone and so tiny, lost at the edge of a field or at the foot of a fir tree. He would decide on occasion to go to the village, do his errands with his daughter on his back, tied into the faded blue sweater, its sleeves knotted under Aurélien's chin.

With the image of his wife buried in the very marrow of his bones, all lament, all desolation forbidden him, Aurélien cared for his daughter and cared for his fields. The village people were kept at a distance in the same way as rebellion and tears.

Shaving before the pocked mirror above the kitchen sink, he would see his own face come to meet him like a taciturn stranger, and he would think about human dignity, which forbade him too much hidden aloofness or secret tumult.

Life flowed by, silent and monotonous, between the father and his child, along the bank of the river. It passed beneath the vast country sky, slack and bare, forever stripped of its angels and its saints. At no time would Aurélien, in the simplicity of his heart, dare to apply the name despair to the dark hole that moved along with him, under his feet, wherever he might be — in his house, on the road, or in the fields.

Clara grew up amid her father's silence and the voices of the countryside. Long before acquiring any human speech, the little girl could chirp, cackle, purr, coo, moo, bark, and yelp. Her imitation of the great horned owl when dusk had fallen was so true that the blood of the field mice froze in their veins.

Sometimes Clara would surrender herself to the trills of birds known to her alone, so limpid and pure that she would abruptly fall silent, choked with happiness.

"What an opera singer my Clara could be," thought Aurélien, having picked up the word "opera" long ago, during a conversation he overheard at the general store between the notary's wife and a passing traveller.

At the age of ten Clara was unable to read or write and her vocabulary was as limited as that of a child of three.

◆ ◆ ◆

Three times already the new village schoolmistress had come to fetch Clara and take her to school. Just out of normal school, her zeal was extreme, and she taught her class as if the salvation or damnation of every one of her pupils depended on her good will.

The schoolmistress had frothy red hair that made a halo around her in the sun, and goldrimmed spectacles that gave off flashes whenever she moved her head. She sat very erect in the cluttered kitchen while some round-eyed white hens pecked beneath the table that was never cleared. The schoolmistress accepted the glass of dandelion wine Aurélien offered her, drained it in one gulp, wiped her lips with an embroidered handkerchief, and began to extol the benefits of school for children. According to her, all the knowledge in the world was to be found collected in texts and exercise books, coloured maps that hung on the wall, and on the enormous blackboard which was gradually inscribed with the rapid signs of knowledge on the march.

It was a whitewashed village school, under a pinnacle of grey shingles, and in it children of good will were promised that they would possess the earth.

"You understand, Monsieur Laroche, your daughter is as beautiful as the sun and moon combined, but the mind inside that curly head lies fallow, fallow . . ."

She repeated "fallow" despairingly, and Clara thought she

could hear beneath the leaves the muffled lament of an animal unknown to her. And then it occurred to Aurélien that the entire earth was lying fallow, resembling in that way his own fields filled with rocks and sand, as well as the devastated sky above his head and his heart, which was equally mute and stony. He asked himself if it was good for his daughter to leave abruptly the deep dark life where things are never expressed or named, to go and lose herself in a garrulous and pretentious world. At the same time, though, Aurélien was filled with pride because the teacher had acknowledged Clara's beauty and had compared her with the sun and moon.

As for Clara, from the schoolmistress's first visit she was dazzled by the light that glinted from the young woman's red hair, from her gold-rimmed glasses, and from the rings she wore on both her right hand and her left — rings that wedded her to all the earth.

And as the teacher spoke, all her unfamiliar and mysterious words were charged with the same gilt and reddish radiance, so superb one could die from it.

Soon Clara had but one thought, to learn to read and write and count, simply so she could spend the day under the influence of that radiant redness.

After several days of grim reflection, Aurélien finally gave in to his daughter's pleas. The next day he bought her patent-leather shoes with straps so she could make her entrance into the school. Very soon it turned out that Clara's feet, accustomed to running about quite bare, could not tolerate the fine shoes Aurélien had bought. She carried them all the way from the house to the village and only put them on once she was within sight of the school, and she entered it very erect, standing firmly in her shiny shoes.

Seated in the first row with the youngest nursery-school pupils, facing Mademoiselle, fiercely flashing, Clara learned to read and write in record time. It seemed to her she had to run with all her might across shifting ice that was constantly threatening to shatter. Even more than the tiny black letters in her reader that she gradually deciphered, Clara loved the ringing sound of the new words in her teacher's mouth, as if she were discovering some new music that enchanted her.

One day, when the little girl had worked particularly well, Mademoiselle took her white hand bedecked with rings and lifted Clara's face up to her own, gazing very deeply into her eyes, and she murmured so softly that only Clara could hear her, as in a dream:

"In the depths of those eyes, *the river is deep and all the king's horses could drink there together.*"

These remarkable words, like a sigh against Clara's cheek, scarcely surprised her, so certain was she that all the wonders in the world would soon be revealed to her. For were not the king's horses and the king himself, wearing his crown, advancing solemnly from the end of the horizon on their way to her, to drink from the pupils of her own dark eyes?

Time seemed suspended between Clara and Mademoiselle. The entire class, from nursery school to fourth grade, became more and more agitated, buzzing like a flight of hornets. Mademoiselle, bending over Clara, did not speak and did not stir. Clara came to fear her teacher's stillness, her feverish pallor which she now saw up close, with the freckles drifting across her linen-white skin.

The little girl lowered her gaze and for a long time she concentrated on the knots in the wide boards at her feet.

While Clara had easily won the admiration of the nursery-school pupils, thanks to some ringing imitations of roosters at sunrise and of barn swallows at sunset, such was not the case with the older students at the back of the classroom. Girls and boys were constantly nudging each other and snickering because Clara's dresses, which were too short for her, resembled faded calico sacks, her unkempt hair a black-bird's nest after a storm. But what soon proved to be the last straw for the class, the older children and the younger ones united in their resentment, was their certainty that Mademoiselle's lessons were now addressed only to Clara. Numbers, letters, words, whole sentences now flew over their heads, floating in the stuffy air of the schoolroom like a wild swarm that had broken free, to settle solely on Clara's mop of tow-coloured hair.

For the teacher it was a question of delivering to the daughter of Aurélien Laroche, as quickly as possible, before it was too late, all the knowledge stored up in her blazing red head.

Clara, for her part, was keenly aware of her teacher's urgency. Her intelligence was wakened at the speed of the day when it emerges from the darkness, then climbs to the horizon, leaps across the pebbles on the river's banks, skips over the dark crest of the trees, gallops full speed across the water's flat surface, intoxicated by its own movement, by its singular dazzle, as it emerges from the night.

Though Clara did not leave her place among the nursery-school children in the first row, very close to Mademoiselle's platform, after two years she reached the point where she could share the lessons and homework of the grade four pupils at the back of the class, where there were mainly girls, since schooling beyond grade three was considered by the parents to be something that might unman their big boys.

Often Mademoiselle kept Clara after class, explaining to her very quickly problems that had to do with faucets and trains, then lingering briefly over the agreement of participles before moving on to fables and tales, sometimes even progressing to poems, while her cheeks were stained with red and her voice became increasingly choked.

One winter night, when darkness had long since fallen and the fire in the schoolroom stove died out completely, and Clara was ready to leave, with her tuque on and her coat buttoned up to her chin, she gathered up her courage and decided to speak to her teacher. All in one breath, with her eyes fixed obstinately on the floor, she said that this could not go on, this haste, this extreme impatience, this lack of time in which they were both trapped, she said that this was no way to live, that she could not breathe, and that it frightened her. Saying this, Clara dropped her head lower and lower, as if some explanation of the mysteries of this world would come to her from the wide grey boards that lay barely touching at her feet. Soon the young girl had lost her voice and she finished her tirade in a nearly inaudible gasp.

"Why are you in such a hurry, Mademoiselle, why? Will you go away soon and leave me all alone in my house by the river, with the cries of animals and the songs of birds?"

Mademoiselle shuddered under her black woollen shawl, a little as if an icy weapon had touched her back between the shoulder-blades.

"I need to tell you everything I know, give you everything I have. It is like a legacy I want to leave you."

"Are you going away then?"

Two small red circles appeared very clearly on Mademoiselle's pale cheeks, like make-up applied with too heavy a hand. Clara thought this sudden redness was caused by her teacher's bewilderment at the thought of a mysterious journey of which she could not speak.

"I don't want you to go away!"

As she cried out, Clara's voice had the tone, familiar and harsh, of the inhabitants of Sainte-Clotilde.

Mademoiselle pulled Clara's woollen tuque further down over her ears and told her that she should leave, that it was very late.

Once she was on the road home, which followed the frozen river, amid the vast solitude of a winter night wherein the only sign of life was a thin thread of water that glistened black in the middle of the current, Clara found herself regretting the fact that Mademoiselle had never taught her how to ward off the ill fortune that was moving through the snow-covered countryside, in the very heart of the shadows, where there were neither moon nor stars.

Mademoiselle lifted her two diaphanous hands into the light; one after the other she pulled off all her rings and let them fall onto the little iron bed edged with flowered cretonne. She said to Clara:

"Pick the rings up. All of them. They're for you. It's all for you. Books, linen, dresses, everything. The others will have nothing."

Clara asked who these others were. Mademoiselle shrugged her shoulders, as if she considered the question to be annoying.

"The others, all the others, the family, every last one of them. They'll have nothing. Only you."

And at the same time she was saddened to be reduced to material gifts, with nothing left to offer from her country schoolmistress's mind. Had she not already given Clara everything — reading and writing, arithmetic and sacred history, even stories and poems that were not on the curriculum but were the very substance of the singular flame that was burning inside her?

It was then that Mademoiselle thought of the recorder as her supreme offering, the little instrument she sometimes played when she was alone, that she carefully concealed under piles of linen in the fir chest of drawers.

Clara was in Mademoiselle's bedroom for the first time, and she was astonished to find it so cold and bare.

"I must teach you how to play the recorder, this minute, this very minute! I forgot to teach you to play it!"

The schoolmistress sat on the floor, her back against the wall. Little by little the circulation was restored to her icy fingers and her harsh breathing softened, became pure and limpid. It was as though the voice of an angel were bursting from the magical instrument, to the amazement of Clara who had never heard anything like it.

All this was taking place in the dead of winter, in the snow-covered countryside around Sainte-Clotilde, in the heart of the schoolmistress's little bedroom adjoining the village school. The schoolmistress who now was crumbling like a dead leaf.

Day by day, Clara was learning to play the instrument. Mademoiselle was growing more and more exhausted and her breath had the taste of fever.

When the little girl knew how to produce a tune, how to modulate and to play trills and runs quite easily, Mademoiselle said that her days as a teacher were now at an end and that she had nothing more to give Clara, save her living woman's vermilion blood, and that soon it would be done. Saying this, she smiled. Clara had hardly enough time to be astonished at so strange an utterance when already her teacher had taken to her bed to die, half-sitting, with her back propped against a pile of pillows.

The death throes lasted all day and all night. Clara watched over Mademoiselle, wiping the sweat from her forehead, the blood from her mouth. Clara thought about the shattered order of the world, about her mother who had died giving her life. Twice begotten, by two different women, Clara secretly weighed the twofold mystery of her mingled legacy.

Mademoiselle's sisters, who arrived the next day, at first resembled her like three peas in a pod, with their russet hair and their gold-rimmed spectacles. Little by little, each of them took on a fierce expression that did not evoke Mademoiselle at all. Little red-headed vultures, for had they not come to observe that nothing was left of their youngest sister's belongings, neither in the drawers of the fir chest, nor in the battered old raffia trunk, nor on the roughly peeled wooden shelf, nor behind the door where big black nails had been planted for clothes to hang on? Clara had taken everything away with her to her father's house on the bank of the river, according to her teacher's wish.

Her name was Blandine Cramail. She was nineteen years old. Sainte-Clotilde was her first post. It was said in the village that the schoolmistress had been carried off by galloping consumption.

Clara did not attend the ceremony in the Sainte-Clotilde church. She stood at her window, unmoving, her face turned towards the church, while the bells tolled the knell. When silence had been restored to the countryside, in the way that ice re-forms and solidifies from one end of the world to the other, Clara improvised funeral music on her recorder, so heartbreaking and pure that Aurélien's walled-up sorrow erupted again as it had in the early days of his widowerhood. Then there was only a single mourning, celebrated by the sound of a recorder: that of the father and of his daughter, on the frozen earth on the bank of a white river, like a field where white foam had been spilled.

II

In the heart of the day, the heart of the night, time passes. On the river, in the fields and the woods, birth and death reign in equal measure, with no beginning and no end, from the minuscule mayflies skating across the river on long thin legs that dissolve at once into the blue air, to the children of men who are astonished at the speed of the light as it makes its way towards the darkness.

Clara's age changed so quickly that she scarcely had time to carve it with her knife, along with the date, on a heavy brown beam above her bed in her attic bedroom, amid the garlands of onions hung on the walls and the shrivelled, sour little apples that sat on the sill of the dormer window.

Twelve years, thirteen, fourteen. Soon, she will be fifteen years old.

Clara no longer reads tales or poems. She no longer reviews in her head the knowledge bequeathed by her teacher. Clara is bored.

For a long time, when the wind blew in the evening, Mademoiselle's dresses would sway gently where they hung on the wall near the poorly sealed dormer window, breathing in the shadows and seemingly alive. And now little by little Mademoiselle's dresses are losing their colour and becoming as thin as onionskin. The day is approaching when the very image of Mademoiselle in Clara's memory will become like a coin that has grown faded and worn until it is no longer legal tender.

Clara did the laundry for women from town who spent the summer in Sainte-Clotilde, and hung it on long cords stretched between two trees; she cared for the animals, hoed the garden, and prepared the meals.

In the evening, taking shelter in her attic, she would sometimes feel in her entire weary body how deeply she resembled the grass and trees, the animals and fields and all that lives and dies, without complaining or breaking any silence.

Some evenings, though, when the newborn moon, red as a sun, spread out in broad streaks across the river, Clara's heart would leap in her chest, would pound against her ribs as if it wanted to break out and roam the world. Under the russet moon the earth's beauty would weigh down on Clara, seeming to demand that her life burst outside her and that she offer up entirely her remarkable and fierce little self.

And then Clara would sometimes play the recorder late at

night, sitting on the grass beside the river. She would go through her entire repertoire, and when she ran out of pieces to play, she would improvise strange, strident music that would rend the air around her.

Aurélien would put his hands to his ears then and beg for mercy. He wanted nothing so much as for ordinary life to resume its course, calm and monotonous, both inside his own house and over all his sandy, rocky land. Above all else, he liked evenings without music, when Clara would prepare food and drink and set it on the table before him, with no useless words or gestures.

As she was then during the childhood that wears out and worsens, Clara would remain the salt of Aurélien's life.

◆ ◆ ◆

For two years now, war was being fought in the old countries on the other side of the Atlantic Ocean. And at this moment, signs of that war could be discerned even in the countryside around Sainte-Clotilde, on the opposite bank of the river, where a military camp was going up at Valcour not far from the house of Aurélien Laroche.

Whenever Clara happened to be travelling around the countryside on her father's old bicycle, she had to give wide berth to the soldiers scattered along the road and to the trucks with their right-hand drive.

They would materialize here and there, in twos or in small groups. They spoke English or French. Called her "darling" or "*chérie*." They would invite her to go to bed with them. But Clara merely greeted them, very softly, without moving her lips. "Hello, hello all you men who are watching for me along the road like cats watching for a mouse, let me by, I'm not for you, not for you handsome gentlemen in your khaki shorts, raised in a military camp amidst all sorts of murderous weapons that could mortally wound any girl in the countryside around Sainte-Clotilde who found herself in your way."

Then Clara would pedal away on her bicycle as if she had an appointment to keep beyond the horizon, on the other side of the mountain stripped bare by firing exercises.

There are so many wild strawberries that summer, they don't know what to do with them. Clara spends long hours crouched in the grass by the fields, close to the fragrant earth that exhales its warm breath onto her face. From morning to night, to say nothing of the noon-hour when the Angelus drops its clear notes onto the mountain brimming with fire, Clara picks the berries that are hidden under the leaves. Every evening, she brings home big buckets filled with carefully hulled fruit. Her red-stained hands seem not to belong to her.

"A dollar a bucket! A quarter a box!"

Clara sells strawberries to ladies from town who are on vacation in Sainte-Clotilde. Hunched over her bicycle, its baggage-carrier laden with boxes, she travels through the countryside riddled with sun, her nape roasted, and her arms and calves. That sweatiness in her hair.

She comes and goes from one house to the next. Her hoarse voice, half-swallowed, barely audible, tirelessly spouts her song: "A dollar a bucket! A quarter a box!"

No cool spot anywhere in the countryside. The dry shade spread along the road in broad deceptive patches hardly less blazing than the shimmering sun. Customers are increasingly rare, the houses farther and farther apart, nestled under the trees.

Here the road is so narrow that the trees' shadows seem to touch above her head. A thin thread of unshaded light still persists on the sand in the middle of the road, where Clara has been pedalling ceaselessly since morning. Something stronger than the wind — though wind is absent from the heat-numbed countryside — urges her along on her clattering bicycle, forces her to go deeper into this unknown country.

It is no small thing to cross through the absolute newness of the air along a deserted road, to breathe great gusts of it, of this air that has never been breathed before, to sense its resistance with each turn of the wheel, to feel its warm breath over every inch of her skin.

It cannot continue like this, this midday with no point of reference, always advancing but arriving nowhere, pushed from behind and urged to cross the line of the horizon.

Fir trees and spruce, as far as the eye can see, choking each other, and here and there a solitary pine, nearly transparent tamaracks, a few birches on puddles of green moss. The vast murmur of July rises from all sides at once. Thousands of wild little voices accompany Clara, deafen her, merge with the giddiness of the sun.

◆　◆　◆

Trees with freshly lopped branches, their wounds white in the harsh light, are a sign that someone has only recently carved this path out of the forest. Clara did not see the mailbox at the edge of the ditch, half buried in the undergrowth, with a foreign name written there in capital letters. Now she is setting her foot on the ground, pulling her heavy bicycle like a horse by its bridle and entering the path where pebbles and tree roots are strewn on the surface of the earth.

Amid the chirping of crickets, the fragrance of resinous trees warmed by the sun, the odour of yellow and russet needles turned over beneath her feet, Clara continues making her way. Her bicycle tires leave sinuous traces on the sand behind her that are soon erased.

All at once, the desolation of the little log camp, blackened and rusty from inclement weather, is there before her, in the centre of a tiny glade that has been barely cleared. Clara realizes at once that the river is nearby and that reassures her, like a familiar presence.

Her vigilant blackbird's gaze looks all around, peers at the rare trampled grass, the fresh stumps, the still unpeeled tree-trunks, the branches covered with dried and curled-up leaves, a cord of wood stacked carefully next to the little camp with its closed windows.

And now she turns on her heels and sees him, sees a man sleeping in a canvas chair. She takes her time to look at him while he cannot yet see her. He is stunned by the heat, with a book open on his lap, his unseeing face offered to the sun. She stares at him shamelessly, the part of her that is still a child urging her to study thoroughly and unblinkingly all the visible and invisible things in this world.

She sees him now as she will never be able to see him again, with the freedom of the first glance, all the while judging him severely. Tall, thin, bony, bare-chested, khaki shorts, this man who is dry like a flower pressed inside a missal resembles those soldiers hungry for girls and alcohol who travel around at the heart of the day, fair weather and foul, along the narrow roads from Valcour to Sainte-Clotilde.

No doubt she should not let her footsteps decide for her and bring her so close to the sleeping man; this has nothing to do with her, or so it appears. Now she examines him as if through a lens. This man's solitude, as he lies here abandoned to sleep, is exposed to the devouring sunlight. His ribs, visible beneath the suntanned skin, rise slowly, the heartbeat of his life laid bare, and Clara is unable to move, caught as she is in a kind of distraction that will never leave her again. From now on, without thought or reflection, she will be reduced to the movement of the earth's blood within her and around her in the countryside.

What the sleeper sees inside the darkness of his night, under his closed eyelids, will never be revealed to Clara during the brief acquaintanceship they will subsequently share. Only barely does she become aware of the invasion of fear on the foreign face that undergoes a change as he dreams in her presence. Presently he trembles so hard that she will have no peace until she makes him emerge from his night. Very softly she calls to him:

"Monsieur! Monsieur! You're dreaming!"

He wakes with a start, shrinks back towards his house until he can feel the poorly squared treetrunks against his thin back. He says *"My God"* in his language and his gaze measures the narrow space that separates him from this little girl, who is staring at him like some strange animal.

She does not move, she is rooted to the spot. Her eyes like lustrous coals. Her faded calico dress, long in the back, short in front, reveals her knees.

"My-God-my-Lord-goddamn," says the Lieutenant in one breath, in a single devastating word.

And he moves towards Clara. His long dry body folds like a breaking tree, leans up against her. The heat of the sun on the Lieutenant's skin envelops her in a deadly and powerful smell. She sees from very close the long hands covered with blisters.

Caught in the act of dreaming and dread, he apologizes with foreign words she does not understand.

"I apologize for the fear on my face and the shame of the fear on my damn body, it was only a nightmare, dear child."

He says *nightmare* again and laughs a great thunderous laugh. He pulls on his shirt and picks up his dark glasses that have fallen in the grass.

From this moment, Clara will no longer see the Lieutenant's pale eyes. Scarcely does she notice at times her own oddly shaped image reflected in his glasses as in a distorting mirror.

He takes a long look at the chalky sky through his dark glasses, one injured hand shielding his eyes. He says "Hush," one finger to his lips. He seems to be waiting for something to shatter and break in the overly calm sky. He says in an overseas French, learned in the region of Tours, that one must never trust the gentleness of the sky and that the fire is hissing and spitting, every night that the good Lord brings us, in the sky over London. Then it turns so bright above the city gleaming with light that you could thread a needle with your eyes closed, as long as you do not tremble, of course. *To tremble or not to tremble, that is the question.*

In the sultry air all around them, like stagnant water which they swallow and breathe at the risk of losing their footing, the Lieutenant's laughter bursts out again and then abruptly cracks.

She continues to stand motionless and mute before him, an entire line of ancestors rushing through her veins and forbidding her any fury or exultation, save for prayer or blasphemy.

"You're not very talkative, my dear!"

The Lieutenant's English voice is deep, as if it were emerging from his belly. Again he peers at the sky overhead.

"There's a storm heading our way," he says.

Clara raises her eyes towards the sky that has started turning white like a blister and shakes her head, No.

"Are you afraid of storms?"

Again she shakes her head, even though she feels as if she is lying, and suddenly she fears the storm more than anything else in the world.

The Lieutenant's fine heavy voice deteriorates, resembles the drone of an insect shut up in a jar.

"How old are you?"

"In two months I'll be fifteen."

He tells her he likes that and laughs, half hidden behind his dark glasses. The only light in his dark face is the dazzle of his white teeth.

The Lieutenant abruptly stops laughing, as if he has been ordered to be silent in the stifling air.

Now she asks for something to drink.

He goes to fetch a glass of water and he waits until she has finished drinking. She clinks the ice, surprised at the mist on the glass, having never seen ice cubes in a glass. She takes pleasure in leaving the warm mark of her fingers on it.

Now the Lieutenant has only one thought in mind: that this little girl who is lingering here should disappear as quickly as possible. For it is the Lieutenant's most fervent wish to be again as he was before her appearance, utterly alone and nonexistent, stretched out in his canvas chair like a dead man, delivered up to the sun here in this place, which under his closed eyelids could almost be fire set loose in the sky over London.

This time the Lieutenant's voice is nothing more than a breath that she reads on his lips rather than hears:

"You should go home now, right away, or you'll get a scolding."

The Lieutenant gestures broadly with both arms. He

points to Clara's buckets and boxes, scattered over the grass.

"I'll buy it all!"

She has gathered up her empty buckets and boxes and mounted her bicycle and now she is pedalling into the dying sun, the shadows all but imperceptible at the feet of the trees.

On the return trip as on the outward journey, she is surrounded by the rumour of July. Along both sides of the road, myriad voices form her retinue. Crickets and locusts drone, here and there the acid song of the cicada rises in the air, and on powerful wingbeats comes the call of an invisible bird.

And now these many familiar voices and the blazing vibration of the air withdraw all at once, like the ebbing tide, while the Lieutenant's foreign voice fills the space, seems to well up from everywhere at once, along the ditches, on the grass of the embankments, and in the distance, behind the edge of the woods, deep inside the moss and underbrush.

His voice, nothing but the Lieutenant's voice, its hoarse foreign sweetness lacking in sense, with no perceptible words, only the enchantment of his voice, accompanies Clara long after she has taken her leave of him.

Not until she has crossed the bridge over the river and passed through the village is the song of the earth around Clara reduced once more to a chirring of insects along the side of the road, into a confused murmur in the countryside.

◆ ◆ ◆

Wielding the axe until his strength was exhausted, he has carved into the countryside. Fifty feet long by fifty feet across. He has appropriated for himself the little abandoned log camp on the bank of the river. He has cleared the view onto the river. During all the time that he will pass among us he will not unpack his valise, which sits on the ground, wide open, between the camp cot and the deal chest of draw-ers. See him now on his knees on the floor, rummaging in the tangle of his clothes, searching for flasks and bandages. His hands are covered with resin, with gum, and with the blisters he has just burst that now are oozing. He wraps his hands like Jesus and waits until it is fully dark before lighting the gas lamp that sits on the table.

Someone who is invisible in the shadows, mingled with the indistinct breath of the shadows, murmurs that this child is really too self-indulgent, and that this must change.

Sitting there into the night, on a kitchen chair in the middle of his one room, any voices or whispers having retreated to the four corners of the shadows, little by little John Christo-pher Simmons is filled with the silent night, filled to the brim, passive as a bucket plunged into black water.

Soon it will be possible for him, here in this silence, to feel the forest that is coming closer to the little camp, slowly encir-cling it; one day it will take back the land that has been cleared all around it, like its own sovereign possession, ravaged by the violence of the axe and of the furious man who held it.

He had not known that he possessed such fury and resent-ment against the trees.

One day the grown-ups rose in a tall forest at the heart of a noble dwelling in the West End. Their horrified faces could be seen hoisted to the summits of enormous tree trunks. Amid the foliage of the ceiling their dark faces were uncovered, bent over a scrawny little boy only to reproach or to show wrath. Nurses and governesses, tutors and chambermaids, cooks, butlers, chauffeurs formed an endless hedge in the Lieutenant's memory, standing there to welcome solemnly the parents of the little boy who were moving forward now, overflowing with fierce energy and equine odours.

All must be felled, must be prevented from growing back, the pines, the firs, the spruce, and the birch, all around the log cabin, to ensure the space he needs for his ruminations, here in this land of exile. So thinks the Lieutenant as he lies on his narrow bed, an army blanket drawn up over his face. While set loose forever in his veins, despite space and time, a British child tries to hide his frightened face beneath the authorities' reproachful gazes.

"That child is afraid of his own shadow, we'll never make a man of him."

Born into fear, brought up under the shame of fear as beneath a she-wolf who might have nourished him, now he lies on a camp cot in a god-forsaken cabin, on Canadian soil, thinking he is safe in the dark, breathing the cabin's musty air, sensing the field mice nibbling under the floor.

"If the lad falls off his horse we shall put him back in the saddle at once, despite his cries and his tears, so he will learn that fear, like hunger and thirst, heat and cold, can be controlled and ordered at will."

Wherever he goes, whatever he does, the Lieutenant is always being put on trial. From beyond the ocean he has crossed, from the very end of the British Isles now left behind forever, come to him voices of majesty and authority telling him over and over that he is a coward.

Already he has twice gone to the window and pulled the cretonne curtain over the pane, as if recreating the blackout, as strictly as possible. It would take only a hole in the curtain, an infinitesimal tear, and the blitz would be visible again, released into the darkness. Horror and folly. This night is flawless, utterly black, calm, warm, and soft. He may as well get used to the goodness of the world and roll himself up in it as if it were a blanket.

The Lieutenant climbs back into his bed only inches off the floor, where he can hear close at hand the mice that squeak and nibble more vigorously than ever, as if their days were numbered.

An ancient and tiny terror. Now the Lieutenant is moving his bed so he won't hear the mice.

English courage has no example in the world but English courage, that's well known; the Lieutenant snickers, his head in his pillow, while the whole family council assembles in his head, to judge him and condemn him.

"Lieutenant, miraculously or inadvertently this lad has been lost to England's honour. Anyone who has seen him in a local shelter during a bombing raid can testify to that. Tears and fits of hysterics. We shall send him away to regain his health, *out of this world of sound and fury*. The Commonwealth is great. Surely we'll be able to find a peaceful part of it where he can pursue his military service in perfect tranquillity."

From his first day on Canadian soil, the Lieutenant knew that nothing was finished, knew that everything was beginning again as if he had not crossed the Atlantic, as if the savage expression that passed over his face was the same as the London smog on the nights of bombardments.

It took just one normal day at the military camp in Valcour. The ravaged hills of the firing range, the smoke escaping from the mortars, the detonations rending the air, the military orders like streams of abuse shouted by officers and NCOs. And life had become intolerable again.

It was he who chose this refuge in the middle of the woods, along the river between Valcour and Sainte-Clotilde. Neither radio nor newspapers, a woman to clean every Thursday, auburn and plump, pallid and strewn with freckles, who gripes and who blithely breaks the few dishes put at the Lieutenant's disposal. Too much noise. The woman makes too much noise. And she's too fat. In a little while he will send her away, as he himself was sent away from England and from the military camp at Valcour. Let each person remain ashamed to be hunted down. For in the secrecy of his soul each has good reason for his shame and for being hunted down. This morning, for instance, that little girl dismissed from the sight of his man's face, her hands red from berry-picking, her eyes open too wide, her entire slim, hard body no doubt already suffering the ravages of the menstrual flow. Too many grown-ups in the world. Too many little girls who cross the frontier and meet up with the cohort of grown-ups who are huge and without pity. Only little girls with smooth bellies, asleep amid their rumpled wings, can lay claim to the sweetness of the world.

He opens the plank door that gives on to the river and the night. Breathes deeply. There is no salt in this air, it is muggy and pervasive, like water that is too soft. It is pointless to live here, in parentheses, separated from everything. Life here, life there, like two sections of the Red Sea that has been parted to allow the Lieutenant's boundless solitude to pass.

The heat persists though it is night, it has stopped moving, is slow and viscous, flows between the trees, through their needles and leaves, it floats upon the river.

Sweltering heat like that in a steam room fills the enclosed space where one must, after all, live until tomorrow.

Even before dawn comes to light up the black sky, the birds have begun cheeping very softly and a muted rain has started to fall, small, wide-spaced drops, clearly perceptible but hard as pearls spilled onto the leaves and the log roof.

The Lieutenant listens to the rain fall, distinguishes each drop, each hard pearl in the noisy air, his hearing increasingly keen and quick, suddenly alert and awake, eager to know what kind of day it will be.

Soon everything grows hazy in the countryside and in the Lieutenant's ears. He has shut the door behind him and now he is alone, in the middle of a violent downpour that is coming from everywhere at once, pouring onto the roof, beating against the windows, streaming in rivulets onto the floor.

Little by little the smell of damp earth penetrates the Lieutenant's house, seeps into his clothes, clings to his skin. The furious summer rain awakens the black heart of the earth, pulls from its entrails its primeval breath, fills the Lieutenant's nostrils, his throat and his skinny chest. In the same way, the little strawberry-picker yesterday was as fragrant as the earth, filled with wild scents beneath her faded calico skirt, every time she moved under the intolerable sun. Nothing else to report. He does not even know her name.

The next day, Thursday, John Christopher Simmons dismissed the woman who cleans his house.

◆　◆　◆

For several days Clara is unable to go back to the Lieutenant's house because of the storms. She uses that time to tidy the house (as if she were leaving on a journey), and starts mending and darning, while violet glimmers rap at the windows to enter the kitchen, and the river studded with lightning rises before her very eyes.

This girl would like to play the flute amid the storm and the desolation, but she is unable to do so. What is inside her resembles nothing that is known and it ravages her like a fever that cannot be expressed in words or in music. At this very moment something is being decided in the rain-drenched countryside, something deaf and blind and terribly opaque, of which she can see neither the beginning nor the end, and which concerns her. If she should happen to lift her head from her work, it is to look out the window at the river rising in the rain, like someone spying from the corner of her eye a pan of milk that is boiling over on the stove.

Long attentive to the disasters inside him and around him, Aurélien peers out at his garden and his flooded fields. Has on his hat, his old jacket. Rain is falling onto his face, running down his neck and inside his sleeves. Endlessly he checks the level of the river. Aurélien has planted a post on the bank and he waits for it to be completely submerged or swept away by the current. He is apprehensive about the moment when he will have to make a decision about the imminent disaster caused by the rising water.

She is the only daughter and he the only father, and she is making ready to betray him in secret.

Accustomed since childhood to this rumbling of the water at her door, day after day, more powerful or less, more lilt-ing or less, at times elusive and disappearing suddenly amid the regular respiration of the earth, then coming back in force very close to her ear and enchanting her again, Clara has come to confuse the beating of her own life with the river's rise and fall. And now she is astonished at her inner confusion and tumult, which are reflected in the eddies in the rising river.

Clara's hands grow languid as she works, and she lets them drop side by side onto her knees like two small animals that have been killed. Naive as the angel ruffling the feathers of his white wings in the sunlight, her heart is filled with dark zones that disturb her. She tries to take her own inventory, in order to see a little more clearly in the growing night. She is thinking very hard, as if she were carefully writing in a schoolgirl's scribbler.

My name is Clara Laroche.
I am nearly fifteen years old.
My father, Aurélien Laroche, a farmer at Sainte-Clotilde, is a widower, my mother having died when I was born.
I know how to read, write and count.
Everything I know I was taught by Mademoiselle, who is dead.
I weigh about one hundred pounds.
I stand five feet and some inches.
I am growing before your very eyes,
I am dark as a crow,
I play the recorder.
I think I've fallen in love with the English Lieutenant.

Seeing her so absorbed and so remote, so near to being lost in thought, Aurélien cannot help asking his daughter the question he has always been careful not to ask, one he could not bear to be asked himself.

"What are you thinking about?"

"Nothing, really, nothing."

Saying that she lowers her eyes, sticks her needle again and again into the coarse fabric of an old skirt; her mouth is shut, her eyes closed, and her heart is brimming with uncontainable joy.

Thinking of his harvest that is rotting where it stands, Aurélien has gone outside to look at the disaster. The door slams behind him.

Clara has not stopped sewing. Each small stitch, even and straight, that she tirelessly sews in the cloth seems to be speaking in her stead, repeating like a monotonous litany: "I'll do it. I'll do it. I'll do it."

After she has cut the thread with her teeth, she lifts her shining face from her work. She looks at the blank wall before her and murmurs, talking to herself, as if she cannot help it, her voice hushed, softly, for herself alone, each syllable standing out from the others, holding back her laughter as the amazing words are whispered into the silence of the empty kitchen: "I'll do it. I'll do it. I'll do it. I will be the wife of the English Lieutenant."

She is astonished that she wants it so badly, as if her life depended on it.

That evening in her attic, she stands for a long moment undecided before Mademoiselle's dresses hanging on the wall, like a woman choosing a dress in a shop who does not know which to select. Clara finally decides on the most beautiful one, both skirt and top a slightly faded red, with bursts of colour deep in the folds. She spreads the dress on a chair, placed on the floor next to the chair the high-heeled patent-leather shoes. For a long time she has been holding a tiny lipstick in a golden case that turned up in a surprise package she'd been given at the general store.

Beneath the downpour tumbling from the sky and against the earth that steams from its own warm breath for long days still, coming and going from the house to the outbuildings and from the outbuildings to the house, Clara is now waiting only for good weather, like a fiancée who has secretly prepared her finery, who goes about her usual business and now, in her head, is counting the hours until her wedding day.

Sometimes at night she gets up to look out her dormer window at the rainwater that can no longer disappear into the earth, that is creating a slack lake around the house.

◆ ◆ ◆

He saw the bright sky move across the countryside. He shaved closely then, sprinkled himself generously with rainwater from head to toe, donned fresh clothes and waited until the fine weather had fully arrived.

There are still too many vague glimmers hanging in the electric air for the Lieutenant to feel truly at peace. It would take only one small match held high above his head for the entire sky to be set ablaze once more and look just like the nights in London, under the bombardments.

The Lieutenant's windows are as narrow as an arrow-loop in a castle wall. He looks out through the dirty panes, riddled with green and violet bubbles embedded in the rough glass. All he can see before him is the lane lost beneath the trees, like a lumberjack's path. Any trace of footsteps, either coming towards him or going away, has been washed away by the rain. He is alone, as though on a desert island.

The Lieutenant's supplies have been dwindling visibly now that the cleaning woman no longer comes.

And now he tests the sodden ground with his foot and sets out like someone who does not know what he is doing, letting his steps decide, leading him where they want to go, where he must go if he is to survive.

Once he has come to the end of the path and is facing the main road covered with puddles and mud, his feet no longer hold him up. He no longer has the courage to advance. The fear of facing up to this unknown village where he has never set foot freezes him where he stands. Besides, he is well aware of the true reason for his visit to the village. Though he will ask in a confident voice for milk, eggs, flour, tea, and potatoes, there is a serious risk that in the dim light of the shops he will arrive at the essential questions about the little girl that are tormenting him. Her name, her address, her house, and her garden. Her parents and her grandparents. Her friends. Her fields and her outbuildings. Her language and her religion. Her innocence, like a green fruit to be picked in the storm-furrowed countryside.

He retraces his steps. He goes back inside his house and heats up his last tin of Campbell's soup. He will wait until there is nothing at all left on his shelf to drink or eat before he turns back to the village. That way he will be able to arrange matters so that his hunger and his thirst for the little girl are null and void, for long days yet to come.

III

There is a rainbow, all its colours laid out clear and precise, while a second arc is forming behind the first, fragile as a glint in the water.

Clara is on her way to marry the English Lieutenant.

Dressed up and made-up, hat, gloves, and purse, perched on her high bicycle, Clara is making her way towards the luminous arches spread before her. She is paying close attention to the puddles that spatter her legs and are liable to ruin her wedding dress. Low branches drip onto her skirt and leave streaks of a deeper red than the rest of the dress.

Amid the imperceptible vibration of the day and the prism colours streaming before her, Clara pleads with a god she does not know, trembles before his hidden face, prays very softly that the Lieutenant will not take her as a cat takes his mate, sinking his fangs into her neck to keep her there beneath him while he tears her open.

The Lieutenant sees the red of Clara's dress coming in the distance, moving very quickly beneath the trees along the path.

When she is very close to him, all decked out and smeared with paint, her bicycle tossed into the grass, he does not recognize her at first. For a long moment he does nothing but look at her in amazement. He says:

"My God!"

And he rediscovers the fierce and joyous laughter of circus afternoons in his childhood.

"I was not expecting such a lovely clown!"

Clara does not stir under the laughter that tumbles onto her and insults her. Her high heels seem to put down roots in the floor. She has come here to be married to the Lieutenant and nothing and no one can prevent that from happening. Not laughter. Not tears. She is waiting for him to come back to his senses and stop laughing.

Now he becomes excessively grave, as if he were about to risk his soldier's life in a battle already lost. He takes the time to note meticulously everything about the little girl that bothers him. The dress, too long and out of date, streaked with grease, the high-heeled shoes, the little hat with its veil, the lipstick, and above all the ridiculous little gilt-clasped purse that she clutches as if her life depended on it. He doesn't know where to begin to rid her of all that, so that naked childhood will appear before him.

He wipes her cheeks and lips with a damp towel. He cannot bear Clara's eyes, which are open far too wide in her freshly washed face. He tells her to close them. He walks away from her in the room. He says some words in hushed tones, making them stand out clearly from one another, like pebbles he would fling into the water.

"Good girl, funny girl, good childish stuff, gorgeous gift from God to my poor soul."

The Lieutenant's words, incomprehensible, do not reach Clara, they seem to die along the way, having to cross the entire room in a foreign language before they reach her.

She has taken off her hat, her gloves, and her uncomfortable shoes. She is waiting for him to approach her. She has closed her eyes. She does what he has asked her to do.

In two strides he is beside her. He says again and again, "*Good girl, good girl,*" and strokes her frizzy hair as if he were trying to soothe a small animal which is at his mercy. The scent of Clara's hair is on the Lieutenant's hands. He sniffs his hands after they have left Clara's head. He is wild about its smell. Again he takes her tousled head in his hands. All the perfume of the little girl in the red dress rises to his face in warm exhalations, like the acrid odour that escapes from gamebags filled with wounded birds after a day of hunting, when the men return home staggering from a strange, cruel intoxication.

He sniffs her neck, under her arms, the folds of her dress, the hollow of her thighs. He drinks the tears from her blazing cheeks. He beseeches her to close her eyes and not to cry.

Amid a sound of old silk that rustles and tears under the Lieutenant's fingers, Clara is quickly undressed, having had nothing on her body but her bridal dress.

She does not open her eyes. She does not say a word. She lets him do what he wants to do. She learns from him what she was supposed to learn from him, for all eternity. Clara utters only one little cry, the cry of a dying child, when he enters her.

In the semi-darkness of the closed house they get their breath back, both of them, like castaways flung up onto the sand, with the ocean's backwash still beating inside them. For the Lieutenant, the sadness has already begun. Clara seeks him and calls him with her closed mouth. With the sensitive hands of a blind woman she tastes the sweetness of the Lieutenant's skin. He barely flinches under Clara's fingers, as if a light breath were brushing, in a dream, his sleeping body, his disarmed sex.

The kitchen table between them. The red-and-white checked oilcloth. The last package of crumbling biscuits. The boiling water poured over the last tea-leaves. The Lieutenant's provisions are exhausted.

They sip very pale tea from the chipped cups that came with the house. She has donned her rumpled dress again. Across from her there is a man dressed as a soldier who is drinking tea and crushing a biscuit in his saucer. A vague smile is frozen on his lips, is intended for no one, seems to drift in the stuffy air of the room with its drawn curtains, its locked door.

Already there is misunderstanding between them because of their different notions about the time that has been given them to be together, time that is ending and soon will be taken away.

She would like very much to stay with him in his cabin until the sun comes back and the roosters of Sainte-Clotilde and Valcour answer one another in the countryside, all together, upright on the first rays of dawn as on a high-wire, trying to outdo each other as they celebrate with a single raucous, strident fanfare the marriage of Clara and the English Lieutenant.

And she laughs because her notion is extravagant and fills her with joy. The Lieutenant will not know Clara's dream, any more than she will know his.

He waits for her to finish drinking her tea. He is filled with impatience and fear. His solitude is already there in the room, wary, only awaiting Clara's departure so it can take back the Lieutenant and close in around him.

He looks on his wrist for the time. He lifts the curtain at the window, sees that the daylight is fading, fears more than anything in the world being surprised with Clara here in his house.

"It's late, very late. You must go home now. You'll come back another time . . ."

He repeats "another time" and muffles his words so well that, later on, Clara will never be sure that she really heard them.

She picks up her hat, her purse, and her gloves, puts the high-heeled shoes on again. She stands facing him, expecting no improbable mercy from the Lieutenant. Perhaps she has already long been aware, in the darkness of her veins, of separation, of the brevity of love, its slight passage upon the world, like the swift shadow of a cloud across the fields.

Heels together, his tall body folded in two, he bows over Clara, kisses her hand, ceremonious and preoccupied. He says *sotto voce*, as if afraid of waking someone who is sleeping in the room:

"*Farewell, my love.*"

◆　◆　◆

Aurélien is outside studying his garden that has been devastated by the storms. He is utterly unable to comprehend what is happening to him. He resembles a drunken man after a brawl, uncertain of what has gone on but struggling now to remain erect and ringing from head to foot from the blows he has received.

Perhaps he should not have tempted the devil and called

out to his daughter after waiting for her such a long time, at the supper hour.

"You're home late!"

It was then that he saw appear suddenly on the mute face of his daughter, by way of response, something at once blazing and consumed that has been intolerable to her.

She nevertheless prepares everything as usual, despite her tardiness, cooking the potatoes and heating up the salt pork, before taking her place at the table. But suddenly, there across from Aurélien, is a strange woman who is his opposite, in place of the little girl he is accustomed to having in the house.

Late into the falling evening, Aurélien's gaze wanders here and there over everything that is broken, smashed, crushed, rotted all around him, from the fields to the garden, from the garden to the fields, without managing to settle down anywhere, as if he were searching vainly for the soul of the disaster that has gone astray in the countryside. But now Aurélien's gaze is suddenly fixed on a row of collapsed suns along the length of the henhouse. Amid the withered stems, flowers, and leaves, at the very heart of each great sunflower, the little burned face of his daughter endlessly appears and shows itself, for the damnation of Aurélien.

◆ ◆ ◆

This man is preparing to go away. He looks without seeing at the river fringed with foam that carries along broken branches, bits of wood, all kinds of nameless debris from its flooded banks.

The Lieutenant has packed his bags. It is the slack hour of the night. Long before dawn arrives and long after the day has ended. The dreary moment when nothing more will arrive. Save tedium. The middle of the darkness. The moment in sleep nearest to death. He must follow his own deepest law and flee before it is too late. So many hasty departures already in his life. So many little girls adored and then abandoned, amid the blood of the first embrace, while the fear of standing trial grows, before judges in wigs of white string.

The Lieutenant sets out, his pack on his back, carrying his suitcase. His heavy military shoes make a sucking sound on the waterlogged earth. Like a thief, he enters the opacity of night. At daybreak he will be thirty years old. His solitude on this deserted road fills him once more to the brim. Father, mother, masters, and governesses seem to be sleeping in the deepest part of his memory, carefully hiding their irritated faces in dark rooms cluttered with Victorian furniture. John Christopher Simmons might think he has had no childhood, no original curse, while a sentence from Rilke obsesses him and comes to him incessantly, assuring him that *while he was still a child they struck his face and called him cowardly.*

He would be content to mark his birthday by hitchhiking. But no car appears on the road. Too early or too late. He cannot see two steps ahead of him. Just enough ground to set his feet down, cautiously, between puddles. It is as foggy here as at the bottom of the sea. Who knows though what city, what unknown village might loom up at any moment at a turn in this endless road? The tall wet grass at the edge of the ditches, when his steps leave the path, grazes him as he passes, and the mingled perfumes stir all around him. The rain has started falling again, in slow, fine drops.

Very far away, in a landscape the Lieutenant has left behind on the bank of a wild river, in the heart of a frame house shut for the night, an adolescent is turning over as she slumbers. She finally fell asleep at dawn, exhausted as a child who has run all day into the wind and for whom tears are secretly lying in wait. Clara sleeps while the light spattering of rain on leaves and roof penetrates her night and gently lulls her, even slips into the strangest of her dreams.

The English Lieutenant strides away into the streaming countryside. Ahead of him, on the horizon, a vague glimmer beneath a mass of grey clouds. It resembles the day.

AM I DISTURBING YOU?

I

Delphine died in my bed last night, shortly before dawn. And I, Édouard Morel — a man without grace, and rather unsociable, too — have been forced to keep watch over her for a good while now, as if she'd been a woman dear to my heart. Now that the doctor has been advised, I just have to wait for them to carry her away.

She is here, stretched out on my unmade bed, the sheet pulled up to her chin, as I arranged it after I closed her eyes. I'd never noticed before how blue her eyes could be.

And now she is playing dead, conscientiously, unreservedly, as if she were at home, alone in the world, and with a kind of supreme wilfulness absorbing her entirely. I'm looking at her as I've never looked at her before. I exhaust myself looking at her. You'd think I was waiting for a sign from her, an explanation, the confession of a secret, whereas I know perfectly well that, right here before my eyes, she embarked upon an endless task, a ferocious and sacred one, and that no one will be able to distract her from it until she has turned to dust.

I swear, I'd stake my life on it, that this girl is nothing to me and she had no more reason to end her days here in my bed than anywhere else. She did it deliberately. I'm sure she did it deliberately. Considering how long she's been following me everywhere, clinging to my skin, gnawing at my bones.

"Am I disturbing you?"

The silence of death isn't altogether impenetrable then, for Delphine's voice persists in the muggy atmosphere of the closed room, tirelessly repeating her eternal, pointless question.

I've called the doctor, who is taking his time, and I've pulled the sheet over Delphine's face.

I've thrown open the shutters and I'm leaning out the window as far as I can. I seem to be looking for some kind of help in the grey dawn rising over the one tree in my building's tiny paved courtyard.

"Am I disturbing you?"

Scarcely a few hours ago. Her doleful, stubborn voice close to my ear. No doubt she'd kept a copy of my key, and she came in without making a sound. Her flat little Chinese shoes brushing the rough sisal of my rug. Suddenly she is there in the room where I'm asleep. She bends over me in the darkness as if she wants to force her way into my sleep, to interfere with my most secret dreams. Her long hair tickling my cheek, her breath racing on my neck.

She climbed the four flights of stairs without breaking the silence of the sleeping house. No witness to her light passage. Behind their closed doors all the tenants are asleep, ignoring one another in the dark as they do in the daylight. Right away she starts to undress, her movements strangely slow, as if each article of clothing were wrenching away her soul.

Though I tell myself there's nothing all that unusual about some unimportant woman undressing at my place uninvited, just to annoy me, my attention is extreme, almost overcharged.

The faded jeans, the worn T-shirt, the frayed briefs fell around her untidily, onto the rug. When she was fully naked, standing in the middle of the room with everything that adorns, dresses, and covers tossed away from her, I knew that Delphine's pure nakedness, her devastating poverty, were intolerable to me.

She steps over her scattered garments with their sweetish smell, curls up under my blankets, sighs contentedly, and says it's as warm as if she were under the belly of a warm beast. She closes her eyes and seems to sleep right away. She talks as if in a dream:

"Sore feet. Sore legs. No money. Totally exhausted. Grandma's inheritance all gone. Too much walking. Days of it. Nights. Afraid to stop. Afraid of being killed where I stand. Taken by force. I'm insulted on the sidewalks as I walk along without stopping. Evil men stare at me as I pass, touch me with their dirty hands. Sore back. Sick to my stomach. As if I were pregnant again. Nothing to be done now. Nothing to say. Nothing to explain. Nothing to laugh at. Nothing to cry over. Nothing to eat, either. Only myself, all alone. Myself, less than nothing. Myself, and I've been walking for days. For nights. Thirst. For a good ten minutes I follow close behind a man who is eating grapes and spitting their skins onto the sidewalk. I eat the skins of the grapes spat out by the man who's walking down the street ahead of me. My stomach aches. Everything aches. The poor little thing who aches all over, as my grandmother used to say."

Delphine's usual chatter, inexhaustible. Herself, always

herself, reflected in a mirror that is itself reflected in another mirror, and so on from mirror to mirror till her head spins, while Delphine's voice dwindles away. Pointless to prick up my ears. The bits of phrases that I hear suffice and I can't stand them.

An odd little laugh at the very back of her throat quavers like a sleigh-bell.

"I ripped off some shampoo at the supermarket."

I approach the bed, wanting to make Delphine feel ashamed about the grapes on the sidewalk and the stolen shampoo.

She moves her head and her hair falls onto her cheeks and her nose, long black threads. She talks and gets winded, lifts locks of hair with every breath, every word she utters. Doesn't even try to toss it off her face. Says she's just washed it, in the fountain in Place Saint-Sulpice.

"My hair's the only thing I love."

She tries to laugh again. Shows her teeth. Props herself up on the pillows. Raises her arms above her head. Her small breasts are flattened, disappear altogether. Her ribs become visible. I can't help thinking of the skeleton of a little ship in distress, washed up on my bed.

Delphine is stubborn; she resumes her monologue, seems to be trying to thumb her nose at some invisible person who's hidden in the bedroom, who would force her to get it all out very quickly — everything she's never said or even imagined saying to anyone.

I talk to her about her country, which she should never have left.

She replies:

"I have no country. My country is any city that has sidewalks where I can walk. Railway stations. Trains. Hotels. Airports. When I can follow someone everywhere. Shadow him. Wait till he turns around. To see me and be seen by me. In the hope that he'll take me home and adopt me. The way my grandmother came to my parents' house to get me the first time I nearly died. The last time, it was on account of Patrick Chemin and my child who is dead and gone now."

She goes on talking, chewing away at her words, while I'm no longer sure I can hear anything she says. In any case, I refuse Delphine, body and soul, and I haven't finished protesting her presence in my bed.

Now she is pronouncing my name slowly, distinctly, as if she were taking pains to decipher something strange that was written on the wall in front of her.

"Édouard, dear Édouard, let me sleep here. Only sleep. One more time. Only once."

She says again, echoing her own voice:

"Sleep. Sleep."

I lean over the untidy bed. I move her hair off her face, which is changing. Delphine's last sigh runs over my fingers, between the long locks of her black hair.

◆　◆　◆

Doctor Jacquet moves slowly, like someone who has been snatched from sleep. There's no end to his examination of Delphine's body stretched out on my bed. He grumbles as if this examination annoys him more than anything else in the world. Seems not to believe what he sees. He turns to me.

"Are you a relative?"

"No, just a friend."

My face, turned blue by my overnight beard, seems to hold his attention as much as Delphine's overly white arms, where he's straining to look for needle marks. Is he trying to catch someone out, someone dead or alive, over this incongruous death?

"Did she shoot up?"

"Not as far as I know."

"Was she suicidal?"

"Not to my knowledge."

"In short, you don't know very much about this person."

"That's right, not very much."

I think, *I do know a couple of things about her*, but I'm not really sure what I mean by that and I remain silent.

Dr. Jacquet's broad, clean-shaven face betrays deadly boredom. Sitting at my work table, he pushes away my papers, then writes his report. He mentions permission to postpone burial and says a post-mortem is essential.

"I warn you. If you're interrogated, you'll have to be more precise about this person."

"Her name is Delphine and I've known her for a few months."

I repeat "a few months." I meditate on the word *month*, the word *day*, the word *year*, and on time in general. I try to find the secret relationship that may well exist between measurable time and the scandal of Delphine's death.

All at once, abruptly, I remember that Delphine has just turned twenty-three. I've been thirty for two months now.

◆　◆　◆

Two men in white smocks came to get Delphine. They took her to the place where dead girls are opened and emptied, and their hearts are weighed in rubber-gloved hands.

Nothing else to report. Leaning on the windowsill, I wait for the day to arrive altogether before I turn around to face the untidy room at my back.

The deserted courtyard is gradually waking. Cheeping of birds. Clatter of shutters thrown open. Broad shafts of soft September light. Through bursts of ringing bells I hear the streaming of the fountain at the church of Saint-Sulpice.

The sun is high now. It penetrates everywhere in the room, sheds violent light on last night's disorder, which is frozen in its tumult like the hands on a watch that has stopped.

Gather up Delphine's things, scattered all over the room. Make a tidy package of them. Change my soiled sheets. Pull the plaid blanket tight, without a crease. Sweep. Dust. Erase all fingerprints but my own. Chase away the shadow of Delphine's fingers on any object they have touched. Let in lots of air between kitchen and bedroom. Alone once more. Pick up the thread of some copy I started last night. Line up words underneath realistic colour photos. Push mass-produced furniture for a mail-order catalogue. I'm used to it, though my aversion is intact.

"Mini-price. Maxi-quality. Guaranteed value. Super-sturdy. Multi-purpose. Melamine-surfaced particle board."

The term *melamine-surfaced* delights me, as if at one stroke I've achieved the most grotesque perfection of my soul.

Glued to my table. Move on from the convertible banquette to the stylized Louis XIV living room suite. Wait for the day to end. Act as if Delphine's bird-claws had never settled on me.

II

Who was the first, Stéphane or me, to notice Delphine beside the fountain, in the glow of the pink chestnut trees that line the square? Afterwards, that would prove to be a lively topic of conversation between Stéphane and me.

There was a girl who hadn't moved for quite a while, who was sitting on the rim of the fountain with the water streaming at her back. There was something surprising about her stillness. From her entire little person there emanated a kind of obstinacy at being there in the mist from the fountain, an unwillingness to exist anywhere else — elbows on her knees, folded in on herself, slightly shocked at finding herself in the world.

She sees two young men coming towards her, one stocky and dark, the other lanky and fair, and she acts as if she sees no one. Is it Stéphane? Is it me? One of us asks:

"Can we do anything for you?"

She doesn't reply right away, as if it were difficult for the question to make its way into her stony stillness. Her eyes looking up at us, open too wide, as blank as a statue's.

I repeat — this time I'm sure it's me:

"Can we do anything for you?"

We hear her voice, reluctant and remote, murmuring as if from the bottom of a well:

"If you want."

Stéphane and I take hold of her under the arms and pull her up. She doesn't resist and says:

"Thanks. But you really didn't have to."

And she worries about her baggage.

Once she was on her feet, her dress pink, as if the colour of the chestnut trees were rubbing off on her, we saw that she was pregnant.

She smooths her rumpled dress and her big belly with hands like a child's, slender and white. She speaks with excessive, nearly unbearable softness.

"The Fat Lady mustn't know I'm in Paris."

Just then the bells of Saint-Sulpice unfurl onto the square like an equinoctial tide, loud and joyous.

She smiles and tells us it's the angelus.

◆ ◆ ◆

After she's settled on a café terrace in the square, she goes on looking at the fountain she's just left.

I point out that her coffee's getting cold, that she should drink it.

She takes a few sips, makes a face, pushes the cup away, says it's too strong and makes her feel sick to her stomach.

155

Stéphane offers her some tea, and she drinks it with a lot of milk.

She acts as if she's not with us and gazes attentively at the women who walk by. She stares at them. Knits her brow. Disparages them to her heart's content. None of them finds favour in her eyes. There's not one woman parading in the square who isn't caught in the act of resembling the Fat Lady.

"Too fat. Really thick. Too big. Wouldn't get through the door. Arms like boas. Legs like tree trunks. Above all, too old. Oh my, old, old, old enough to die. She ought to make room for the young."

She leans on the table, puts her head on her arms and cries. I wish I weren't there, across from Delphine, when she's crying. Stéphane offers her some cake.

She eats and she cries.

With her mouth full, she tells us that the Fat Lady must be somewhere in the city and that she absolutely has to be found, without her knowing it, and stopped from doing any harm. As for Patrick, he won't be here till tomorrow.

I ask who Patrick is.

She stands up and points to her big belly.

"Patrick, Patrick Chemin, sales rep, fishing tackle, he did this to me."

She slowly strokes her belly.

She sits again and gulps down the rest of her tea.

Then Stéphane steps in:

"And the Fat Lady, who's she?"

"Patrick's wife."

Exhausted by these confidences, reproaching herself for divulging them, she is absorbed for a moment in her desolation; then in a flash she fixes both of us, from across the table, with a look that seems not to belong to her, a look as sharp and cutting as a blade.

"What's most disgusting in this whole business is Patrick."

She falls silent at once, having reached the limit of what you can say and show in a glance without dying of shame.

She turns towards the fountain again, as if some reassurance could come to her from the streaming water. All around us, the murmur of the city has grown so loud that we can no longer hear the murmuring water.

And now a little voice, high-pitched, soft, sounding almost worldly, emerges from the scraping of chairs being pulled or pushed, the clink of glasses, the orders shouted or whispered, from the mingled conversations, the clatter of cars and buses.

She says:

"I'm Delphine."

She points to each of us in turn. Touches Stéphane and me on the chest, the shoulder.

"And you? And you?"

Our first names, which we offer immediately, seem to surprise her, to put her into a strangely joyous state more worrisome than her tears.

She repeats after us:

"Édouard. Stéphane. That's great. That's funny. Fantastic."

During her brief time among us, the list of names that sounded so joyously in Delphine's ear would hardly be longer than that, going from Patrick to the Fat Lady — if that Lady had a first name.

◆ ◆ ◆

Aside from the fireplace and the logs piled next to it, the table littered with papers, the two straw-bottomed chairs, and, in the place of honour, the double bed — usually only half occupied — there's nothing here.

I read and I work, I sleep and I eat, I drink, I wash and shave. Twenty metres square. Whitewashed. Lime wash with a tinge of blue, like a country dairy. There's no one here but me and my passing shadows reflected on the bare walls as the days go by. I myself cast a shadow on the white all around, as if I were a thick tree, a kind of dense spruce, from root to head. Myself to infinity. Just me repeated on the walls, the ceiling, on the creaking hardwood floor. My own memories flutter like moths in the room. Always the same, devoid of interest. My everyday movements here, near Place Saint-Sulpice, fourth floor, overlooking the courtyard. A studio apartment twenty metres square. Enough room to live and die without making a sound. No strict, pure angel, his crumpled wings grey, rust, and brown like those of a partridge, stands behind my chair and blames me. I am free, if I want, to be nothing and no one.

Above all, let her not come here to mix her traces with my own. Let there be no memory of her within these walls.

She was there next to the fountain, like a little heap fallen from the pink trees, half girl, half plant, like a swollen bunch of grapes. Her round belly. Her wrinkled dress. And I'll probably never know whether this creature is opposed to me or not.

Her image is too fresh. Without past or patina. Only from yesterday. Thin. Without depth. Leaving no trace on me, like distemper drowned in water on a smooth wall. Not deserving to live inside me, like the signs of my own passage. Pathetic Delphine, swallowed up at once by me, sole master of my dark memory.

Too many glimmers, too many spots of sunlight still persist in my eyes. No doubt they come from spending too long, yesterday, looking at the chestnut trees in the square.

◆ ◆ ◆

Pale, thin, and long — like me, a specialist in little dead-end jobs — Stéphane experienced incredible ecstasies while listening to Bach and Mozart. His face then resembled those of the saints captured in mystical mid-prayer by painters of bygone days.

Very quickly his face came to bear the same expression when he looked at Delphine, who didn't look away; she was not at all uneasy under Stéphane's gaze, being fully taken up with herself, untangling the inextricable.

Around noon the next day, she turned up at his place on Rue des Anglais. Hadn't he given her his address and phone number?

He thinks:

Good God, I haven't made the bed, there are crumbs everywhere, my records on the floor . . .

She says:

"Patrick's plane has been rerouted to Marseilles because of the fog."

He thinks:

My God, what a mess, she turns up at my place out of the blue, on Sunday of all days, and I've slept in as I always do on Sunday, dirty shirt on the chair, socks on the floor, on the glazed tiles, my room a disaster, what will she think of me?

She says:

"I came to ask what I have to do to get to Marseilles."

He rubs his eyes. Explains that Marseilles is far away and that once the passengers are off the plane they will most likely be put on a train to Paris.

She wants to know what train, what station, and she's afraid the Fat Lady knows much more about it than she does,

159

that she'll be the only one able to greet Patrick Chemin when he arrives in Paris.

He thinks:

Not here, I don't want her here, not today, I'm not ready for that, it's too small here, too dark, my room under the rooftop, the neighbours' dormer window right across from mine, my neighbours and I look at each other every chance we get, gimlet-eyed, like fighting cocks, and here she is in the middle of my room, so visible with her pink dress and her big belly, in a little while they'll see her too, those malevolent neighbours, they'll think she's an ordinary person paying an ordinary visit, but she's a marvel, my extraordinary guest.

She says again that Patrick Chemin's plane is lost in the fog. She's on the verge of tears.

Craning her neck, she looks out the window, the sky barely visible high above the narrow courtyard, a well of black light rather than a courtyard. She thinks she can hear the murmur of the sky above the rooftops.

"His plane. That's his plane. I'm sure it's his plane. I can hear it roaring and circling in the sky. I can hear it using up its fuel by going around so much, like a bumblebee, in that thick milkiness in the sky. This morning everybody was looking up at that sound. Even the Fat Lady was afraid it would burn up all its fuel, and fall and crash at our feet. The Fat Lady was frozen there like a statue. Like everyone else, for once. You could see that her big fingers were no longer moving on the yellow book she was reading. In the end, we were told the plane would land in Marseilles. So I came to find out what I have to do to get there."

He phones. But all the lines that have anything to do with Patrick Chemin's plane have been busy since morning.

She says again, "Marseilles." Swallows. Gathers momentum, and disjointed words tumble off her tongue — "Patrick

Chemin," "airplane," "fog," "Fat Lady." The rest is as mud-
dled as the tears on her cheeks, which she wipes away with
her sleeve.

But now Stéphane must lend an ear to what is new in
Delphine's confused remarks.

She talks about her grandmother, who died and left her
an inheritance. She says she'll spend that inheritance, penny
by penny, to travel, to follow Patrick Chemin to the ends of
the earth if she has to.

She pronounces "grandmother" slowly, cautiously, as if it
were a precious, fragile word, and her face lights up. Again
she emphasizes the syllables in "grandmother," and she is
absolutely happy.

"Do you want to see my inheritance, Stéphane dear?"

She pulls up her dress. He can see her Petit Bateau under-
pants. She undoes the little brown leather pouch that she's
fastened around her waist with a belt against her bare skin.
Shows him the coins and bills. Scatters them around her in
the room. Then she runs to pick them up, like a hen picking
at grain scattered in a barnyard.

◆ ◆ ◆

Not knowing what to do with Delphine, who had started
crying again, Stéphane brought her to my place, holding her
hand all the way along the boulevard.

Later he would tell me all about Delphine's intrusion into
his place, about the route they'd taken through the city.

He'd assure me that she'd neither seen nor heard anything
around her. The new leaves at the tops of the trees, the scaly
trunks of the plane trees, the song of the invisible bird, the
round grilles at the foot of the trees, the captive roots beneath
them, the light mist everywhere, the great murmur of midday,
the busy passersby — life, all of life, had rained onto her and

she hadn't been aware of it; she had shed it as a duck's back sheds water.

Once they reached Rue Bonaparte, outside my building, she cast away any trace of absence or daydream. All at once she dropped Stéphane's hand, surprised she'd held it for so long. Suddenly clear and precise, with no hesitation, she declared:

"Poor Stéphane, your hands are wet."

Very quickly she was standing in my doorway, saying, "Bonjour." And then Delphine walked into my place for the first time.

◆ ◆ ◆

She's out of breath and she looks bigger to me than she did yesterday. She sits on my bed. Piles the pillows behind her back. All her attention is devoted to recovering her breath and settling in comfortably. Delphine is at my place but it's as if she weren't here, she's facing me as if I didn't exist.

Then, abruptly, she springs to her feet and comes to stand next to me.

"I have to know. What station? What train? What time? Hurry, Édouard dear, please. Or I'll die right here, right now, on the ground at your feet."

Immediately I abandon my scattered papers, my catalogues and dictionaries. I pick up the phone. After listening to bursts of soft music for a long time, I finally get the information Delphine is waiting for.

She repeats after me, ten times at least, as if she were singing:

"Four p.m., Gare de Lyon, four p.m., Gare de Lyon, Gare de Lyon, four p.m., four p.m. . . ."

Stéphane and I decided to show Delphine around the city while we were waiting for the train from Marseilles. The three of us walking. The mocking expression of some passersby. Which of the two of us is the father of that child who is practically visible through its mother's pink dress?

She already likes the *bateaux-mouches* and the banks of the Seine. She shuns monuments and museums like a child who's afraid of grown-ups. Despite the hazy day, like a December morning, we take her to the banks of the river. Her round belly thrust forcefully ahead of her seems not to belong to her, she is still so slender and frail, separated from her burden by steadfast childhood.

She's careful not to stumble on the paving stones. Then she sits on the ground, her back against the stone wall, despite our protests. The dampness doesn't bother her, or the cold stones.

Delphine looks at the Seine stretching out before her.

A white mist rises from the water. We can see the boats through the mist. At times half visible in the white mist. The lights of the *bateaux-mouches* slice through the fog in long luminous beams, and we hear them glide along the water. As if it were night.

She says:

"At my grandmother's house there's a river running nearby. Sometimes it runs through white mist, other times it's very bright because of the sun shining on it. I like it when my grandmother is rocking on the verandah. When she died, the rocking chair kept going back and forth in the wind all by itself, and I couldn't stand that rocking without my grand-mother's slight weight. That rocking on the verandah drove me crazy and I ran down the road, carrying my inheritance against my belly, till I was out of breath, and then I met Patrick Chemin, who drove me to the nearest town."

Stéphane stands, I stand facing her, both of us shot through with mist, looking at her and listening to her, shivering as if it were winter though it's April already, while she sits on the ground, her back against the stone wall, her eyes vague, as if she's seeing her grandmother through the mist.

She says, suddenly very close, very alive, like someone stirring after a waking dream:

"Patrick and the Fat Lady haven't been married to each other for very long. It can't last. I'm pregnant. Patrick's real wife is me. He'll have to realize that."

On the bank in front of us is a man getting ready to fish. We watch him get ready. He sits on the paving stones, arranges his glittering metal line, rummages in a green plastic bucket.

Delphine assures us that the angler is poorly equipped as regards line and hook, and that he'll never catch anything.

"And besides, the Seine is rotten, everybody knows that."

She laughs, showing all her little white teeth. She points at us, at Stéphane and me.

"Little Frenchies, little Frenchies, your Seine is rotten!"

Stéphane clears his throat.

"And what about your river? What's your river like?"

"Wide and deep, with rapids. The Thibaud boy drowned in it, between the island and the mainland. The water was as black as hell."

The fisherman is standing in oversized trousers that hang loosely on his scrawny legs. He casts his shiny line onto water that recedes gently into the mist.

It's not possible that this girl has a grandmother like everyone else. A father, perhaps a mother? In vain I search her peculiar face for some sign of belonging, some slight trace of a resemblance. I look at her stretched out on the ground, propped up by the wall. Her pure stranger's mask positioned over the fine bones of her face. She has a touch of an accent.

Pronounces her *a*'s like *o*'s and her *o*'s like *a*'s. Perhaps she's never lived in a real country, just in some hinterland known only to her, beyond sea and land, at the slender line between life and death.

"Let's get out of here. There's too much fog. We're getting all tangled in this cotton batting."

Delphine gets up and shakes out her dress, which is short in front, long in the back. Stéphane holds out his hand to her. He asks:

"Where do you come from?"

She points to the white sky above our heads, to a passing gull. Says, "Up there." Laughs.

"I took a plane to come here. My grandmother's inheritance was eaten up in one shot when I bought the plane ticket. One way. I'll be there when he arrives. The first one to greet him. Before the Fat Lady. Didn't see the Atlantic Ocean. Too many clouds. White. Thick. Just like meringue. Very white. Verging on blue. Dazzling. Flew too high. Didn't see the ocean. Cotton batting everywhere. There's no ocean. My mouth is full of cotton batting. I suffocate. Too high in the sky. The birds are dead. Too high to build nests. I'm coming, dear Patrick. Four p.m., Gare de Lyon. I'll be there. Before the Fat Lady."

The fisherman's line goes taut. A little fish is wriggling at the end of the line. The fisherman quivers with joy from head to toe.

Delphine declares that it's high time we went to the Gare de Lyon. She takes us by the arm, Stéphane and me. She is between us, clinging to us for all eternity, or so it seems.

Which of the two of us will draw the child from between her thighs and give it to her, as childlike and virginal as she is herself?

◆ ◆ ◆

I write: "Checkerboard table. Solid exotic wood from South America, top stained and finished with nitrocellulose varnish."

Glance out the open window. And that's it for my peace of mind. Just long enough to gaze at a tree in the courtyard. I envy that tree, envy its fullness as a tree, utterly wrapped up in its branches and its leaves, shivering in the light wind. Whereas I am reduced to the most infinitesimal part of myself, typing nonsense for a mail-order catalogue.

A hundred times in a row I write "nitrocellulose." To calm myself. The clicking of my typewriter bears me up and carries me away. Is this any way to live?

Again I glance out the window above my typewriter. The tree in the courtyard is standing there, tranquil. I take a breath. The tree and myself, both perfectly calm.

Suddenly I spy her coming along the paving stones, between flower-beds that aren't yet in bloom. Have heard nothing from her for several days now.

She sits on my bed, winded.

"Too many stairs, Édouard dear. It's too much. Too much."

The same pink dress, more and more shabby. She apologizes, her voice barely audible, assures me none of her clothes fit now except for this pink dress her grandmother gave her a long time ago.

She comes very close to me, says into my ear:

"Stéphane promised me he'd put this dress in the washing machine when he goes to his mother's, and iron it himself."

She appears very pleased with herself and with Stéphane, whereas I become furious with her and Stéphane both.

Delphine pursues her thinking:

"Patrick and the Fat Lady: their marriage won't last long, I don't think. He promised to phone me."

She settles in among the cushions. Begins to recount,

speaking to no one in particular, her eyes focused on the open window as if, through the grey day, she sees images that stand out powerfully before her.

"You dumped me at the Gare de Lyon, you and Stéphane, like a package to be delivered. The huge station, the crowds going every which way, people, people everywhere, breathing in my face, bumping my belly as they pass me, my child cries, I hear him crying inside me, I'm afraid for my crying child, afraid for myself lost in a station, Patrick arrives with his suitcases full of flies and fish hooks, just one change of clothes, his razor and aftershave in a toilet-case, right away she wraps him in her great big arms, hides him from me with her broad shoulders, any more and she'll have him on her lap, her fat thighs, her enormous knees, and there will be nothing for me to do but die with my child, who is crying and crying."

Delphine comes so close to me that I can see a little green vein on her temple. She speaks into my ear again:

"All the money is hers, the Fat Lady's — the Paris apartment, the house on Ile de Ré. Everything. Everything. All he has is suitcases filled with sparkling flies and deadly fish hooks, his brown velvet eyes, and his soft, hesitant voice, that knocks me off my feet."

I pick up the sheets of paper scattered over my table. I make piles of them and clip them together. Make a pretence of being very busy. Soon nothing is perceptible in the room but Delphine's voice, uniform, unwavering, too clear. She goes on talking, like someone recalling how she's spent the day before she falls asleep.

"The apartment all sparkling white like a bathtub, the matte white marble fireplace, the fire in the fireplace like the red tip of a lit cigarette against all the white everywhere else in the apartment, the white rug curly as a sheep, a kind of white city all around the living room, with corridors like streets and doors shut like the doors of houses. So magnificent you could die. Patrick inside it like a prince, resting after making his rounds all over the world with his flies and fish hooks. He's earned his apartment on the Trocadéro. And she's there talking to him and calling him 'darling.' If she only knew why I'm so big . . . And she's invited me for dinner, with lighted candles on the blue tablecloth, a beautiful deep blue against all the white. So gorgeous you could die. The gleaming silverware heavy, very heavy, and glasses that sing under your fingertip, three for each person, a big one and two smaller ones, for drinking different wines, and even water if you want. She's the one who invited me. She had no choice but to be there with him to welcome me. Very polite. Asked me about the baby in my belly. Pretended to know about the backaches, the nausea and all that. Finally asked with seeming kindness: 'When are you due?' All the old questions that old women ask young ones who are swollen like balloons and filled with future. You could see she was polite and well brought up. He must have had to teach her. She'd certainly seen me at the station, waiting for Patrick. She was waiting for him too. The two of us waiting for Patrick. And he pulled in on the train like a prince who travels with suitcases filled with fish hooks and flies. When I turned up for dinner they kissed me, both of them, the way you kiss a well-behaved child. When we were all alone in the living room, with her in the kitchen making coffee, he came up to me, looking like a bereaved man who does what he must to look bereaved, but who deep down is waiting for this difficult moment of sorrow and boredom to be over. He spoke very softly. His brow was knit behind the round lenses of his glasses. He said: 'Be nice, be patient, it will all work out. Give me time . . .' Then he added very quickly, as she was coming in with the coffee: 'I'll call you as soon as I can . . .'"

Delphine sits across from me. Rests her elbows on the table. In a voice that is suddenly close and familiar, she repeats her same little litany, which she's no doubt been repeating time and again throughout her pregnancy:

"It can't go on. Patrick and the Fat Lady married to each other. Patrick's real wife is me. They'll have to face up to it."

Very quickly she goes back to her daydreams, right under my nose, as if I weren't there.

"The apartment — all white and vast, like a white city, a private apartment so luxurious you could die . . ."

Delphine is startled again. Her sharp clear voice. She is looking at me. Two pale sparks come into her eyes, cross the table, and flash in my face.

"And now, Édouard dear, I'm staying in a small hotel, a very old one on a very old little street, Rue Gît-le-Coeur it's called. A tiny little heart that lies there. At night I can hear that old little heart as it beats within the walls. It keeps me awake."

Stéphane has arrived, all out of breath. He claims that Delphine's ears are too sensitive for her to sleep all alone in a residence so old, so given over to the strange sounds of an ancient time and of the pitch-black night.

After not finding Delphine in her hotel, after running over to my place so he's out of breath, Stéphane seems relieved, as if he was afraid he would never see Delphine again anywhere in the world.

◆ ◆ ◆

Delphine had very clear ideas about what had to be seen in the city. The fountains, the bridges, and the banks of the Seine attracted her particularly. Whether it was the traffic circle on the Champs-Élysées, the Pont d'Arcole, or the fountain in Place Saint-Michel, we had to wait for Delphine to emerge from her fascination and come back to us.

The great lake and fountains of the Place du Trocadéro. The night, humid and mild. In-line skates. Skateboards. Boys, girls, perched on passing flashes of light. A rumbling hum. The city two steps away. The gushing water. The long liquid flames, white and shuddering. The spray that touches Delphine's hands as she draws near. Again, her stonelike stillness. Her perfect solitude once more.

Nine p.m. at the Place du Trocadéro. A girl and two boys at a table on the terrace of a café they can't afford.

Here she is accepting the cake Stéphane offers her. Didn't see Stéphane order the cake. Didn't see the waiter take the order. Sudden laughter on Delphine's face, where warmth and vivacity have returned. She's laughing because she likes cake, and because she feels she has to laugh to say so. She speaks with her mouth full.

"You can see Patrick's embarrassed to go out with me because of my condition. He bought me a big loose coat that goes down to my heels. He wrapped me up in it. Asked me to wear it all the time when we're together, even when the weather is warm. I don't wear it if he's not there. But when he takes me out, like yesterday when we went to the movies, I keep it on all the time. Even at the restaurant after the movie. I'm suffocating from the heat. But I do what he wants. While I wait for us to get married. He's always asking me to be patient."

Stéphane says:

"The bastard! The bastard!"

Delphine doesn't hear a word Stéphane says. She goes on with her story.

"Once, at the hotel after the restaurant, he didn't want to make love. For fear of squashing the baby. Wouldn't even kiss me. But we could talk with no one else around. I made a scene. He started quivering like a little puppy. To calm me down, he promised he'd tell his wife everything. And he will. He'll tell her and he'll marry me. He has to, after all. I'm pregnant."

She rests her elbows on the table, lets her tea get cold. Loses sight of us, of Stéphane and me, like small figures becoming smaller and smaller as you move off in a boat and little by little the shoreline disappears.

Again her ventriloquist's voice, remote and subdued:

"I think he's very bored in his wife's lovely apartment. A kept man, that's what Patrick Chemin is. His white leather easy chair. I'm sure he's sitting in his white leather easy chair. Looking preoccupied, he sips the coffee the Fat Lady serves him. He'll have plenty of time tomorrow to complain about the coffee keeping him awake."

Stéphane says again:

"The bastard! The bastard!"

I too intervene. I take Delphine's wrist, I squeeze it in my fingers very hard, I shake her arm all the way to the shoulder to make her face me, alive, to make her look at me and talk to me. Her transparent skin. Her green veins visible on her too-white skin, all down the length of her arm.

"Get out, for Christ's sake! Get out girl, before it's too late. You can't stay in limbo like this. Forget about Patrick Chemin and go home."

She looks at me, alarmed. Rubs her wrist as if we'd hand-cuffed her.

She says:

"You're nasty, Édouard dear. Patrick is a good man. He's the first one I saw on the road, in his old Ford that was falling to pieces, jolting and clattering over the bumps. He picked me up right away, when I'd been racing down the road since morning, the swaying of my grandmother's rocking chair in my ears, my grandmother dead beside her chair, a sudden death, fallen from a rocking chair that went on rocking as if nothing had happened, an evil chair that did it on purpose, the wind that joins in and carries the swaying and breathing of death down the road and far away, that breathing and swaying on the back of my neck as I run, the scent of fields for as far as the eye can see on either side of the road, mixed with the breathing of the wind and of death, the scent of daisies, buttercups, vetch, yarrow that you start to smell in the fields on either side of the road, and even the grass along the ditches, salted with dust, is perfumed by the wind and the breathing of death, and me, I've been running down the road since morning, scented by the fields and by death on the back of my neck, and Patrick drives up in his old car, his suitcases full of flies and fish hooks, and he takes me in, it's the first car I've come across since morning, since the breathing of death on the back of my neck, and I run away, I run till I'm out of breath, the swaying of the rocking chair in my ears, death on the back of my neck, and he is the first one — Patrick Chemin, fishing tackle sales rep — he's the one I have to marry, he's the first, it's an obligation I have."

Stéphane leans towards her as she strays from the point, no doubt hoping to bring her back to us by means of cakes and tea. He calls out:

"Waiter!"

I think, and my chest swells at the thought: she followed the first person who came along, like a baby goose. A phenomenon of her pregnancy, most likely. With Patrick now, and it's for life. Pointless to insist. It could just as well have been me or Stéphane. But it was Patrick. The first person who came along. To replace the grandmother. A question of time and place. Of country. Chance in all its necessity.

Can it be that I'm no longer a man? I just have to do what

a man does with a woman. Take her as a man takes a woman. Remove her from her repetitive childhood without delay. Right here, maybe, though it's a busy place, with cars, and blind, deaf people jostling one another while they wait for the 63 bus. Ophelia, Iphigenia, Antigone, and some other diaphanous creatures, doomed to an early death. I'd open her belly, in keeping with male custom, that humped belly of hers, and I'd draw out the little occupant cowering in there. I'd save her from the affliction of being an unwed mother — and crazy on top of it. But I'm not up to that, I don't even deserve to lick her ear in my dreams. And what's the good of losing myself in my savage ruminations? I'm bored to death here between Delphine and Stéphane. I wish I were somewhere else, someplace I'd be alone again.

Still, I miss nothing of what Stéphane and Delphine say or do as they huddle with me around a little table covered with cake crumbs and dirty cups.

Stéphane has just laid his big pale hand with its knotted knuckles over Delphine's little hand, which has wandered onto the table.

"Don't touch me, Stéphane. Your hands are damp, and that gives me goose pimples."

This remark slipped out, but she neither moves nor takes her hand away. No sign on her face of either speech or anger. Delphine sits there motionless, exposed to all and sundry, without modesty or hope.

Stéphane hides his big offended hand in his pocket. He hastens to offer a chocolate eclair to Delphine, who is smiling vaguely.

I go home alone, walking along the quays. The Seine gleams in the night, brighter than it is by daylight. The echo of my footsteps follows me like a noisy shadow, rapid and rhythmical.

◆ ◆ ◆

For three weeks we didn't see Delphine or hear of her. As if she were no longer in Paris. She didn't show up at my place or at Stéphane's. She didn't slip in between the tables with her big belly to join us at a café or restaurant. No one spotted her sitting on the stone with the Saint-Sulpice fountain at her back.

Stéphane even wondered if Delphine might be giving birth all by herself in some private clinic, like a cat who goes into hiding to have her kittens.

And then one fine day she rang the bell and walked right into my place, not waiting for me to open the door. She plunked herself down on the rug, in the middle of the room. She lifted her faded pink dress and undid the leather belt she wore against the skin of her waist. She opened her pouch and flung a shower of coins and bills around her. Then her nimble little bird-claws picked everything up, as if thieves were pursuing them. She made piles of coins and bills on the rug. She gazed at what was left of the inheritance from her grandmother, she counted it, and she was desolate.

"I'm ruined. Ruined. All those trains. All those trains. Nice, Toulouse, Poitiers, Brussels, La Rochelle. The money slips away, along with the trains and hotels. And Patrick, who pretends not to recognize me in the stations and hotels. Who goes marching across hotel lobbies. His long legs like scissors cutting, kicking through the air. Who pretends not to see me, walking fast so he'll lose me in the crowd of travellers. Who's always surprised by my appearance, like a wild animal chased by a sudden storm. Carrying his big suitcases, full of fish hooks and flies, at arm's length. While I have all my belongings on my back, and my inheritance tied around my waist. I was like a lost soul in drafty train stations filled with people weighed down like movers. Despite their haste and their burdens, the air of insult written on their faces, I'm sure all those people who were leaving were judging me on the way by, condemning me as a slut because of my belly and my dress that's too short in front and hangs down in the back."

She is loudly indignant; she curls up and lies on the rug, protecting her belly with her hands. Says she hasn't slept for days and her legs are very cold. I carry her to the bed and cover her with the duvet. A moment later and Delphine goes on talking, as if she's telling herself a story before she goes to sleep.

The story is all about spending long hours in the waiting rooms of strange railway stations, about how hard it is for a pregnant woman to stand up for so long, about her fear of falling and being trampled by travellers.

Delphine suddenly throws off the duvet. She sits on the edge of the bed.

"Good thing I swiped Patrick's diary from his coat pocket last time we were together in Paris, in a sleazy hotel hidden away on the second floor of a fancy restaurant on the quays. I learned it by heart, the way you learn your lesson before you leave for school. I just had to go wherever Patrick was going with his heavy suitcases. To surprise him. To see and be seen by him. Without really wanting to. Or deciding to. Only a diary in my head that I had to follow to the letter to fulfil my need to be with him. A sort of obligation, stronger than everything else. A tremendous stubbornness. I followed him from station to station, from train to train, from town to town, from hotel to hotel. Always, I was there waiting, and he thought he was going crazy. And I thought I was going crazy. Always, he was surrounded by people he knew. They mustn't see us together. Pretend not to know each other in stations and hotels. Me with my loose coat down to my heels. Him with his suitcases, his doe eyes constantly on the lookout in case someone saw him with me. Around three a.m., when no one was there to catch him, an adulterer, in the hallway, he'd come to me, all excited, in his stocking feet on the hall carpet. He worried about the baby and he said that one day he'd have to marry me. All the time he was talking, he kept looking at the time on his wrist. Before he left I'd always create a little scene, and he would too, quietly, not letting himself be too angry for fear someone would hear him in the silence of the night hanging heavily over the hotel."

Alone within herself, no longer facing me as I listen, Delphine recounts her own life, never tiring of it. I let my pen fall to the floor. The blue ink makes a tiny dark stain on the blue carpet. As if it were merely the shadow of the fallen pen.

Delphine is shivering on the bed. I heat water for tea. I ask if she's seen a doctor since she's been in Paris. Delphine's teeth chatter against the bowl of tea. She looks at me, outraged. Says I mustn't mention doctors to her, ever, or she'll throw herself in the Seine.

◆　◆　◆

High summer over the city. The light on all sides is white, dry, blinding. The shade gnawed away in all its nooks and crannies. The stone radiates, dry as crumbling chalk. White dust. Sweltering heat. Pollution. Sheltered from sweat and tears, Delphine resembles a little fish that's been salted dry. Her baby curls up inside her and is silent.

She casts no shadow in the strong sunlight that devours her. Only the fleeting shadow of her big belly against a wall when she goes into town, pushing her belly before her like a steep rock. Under these conditions — extreme weight in her centre and a ravenous beast deep in her entrails — she raises frail, green-veined arms to the sky. Yells. Demands justice.

Absolute justice that would depend only on her own law, Delphine's law, an ideal law, despite the common sense and notions of justice held by married women and timorous men. With the railway timetable carefully memorized, and Patrick Chemin's schedule at her fingertips, she tracks him down and runs into him in out-of-town hotels located near the train station, just long enough for them to exchange the resentment they both feel, to whisper it in strange bedrooms, stopping themselves from bursting out, the way people hold back their cries when making love, because of the neighbours.

"I forbid you to follow me around like my shadow. If anyone sees us together I'll be ruined. You're in my way. I can't stand you. I'll see you in Paris, as usual."

"I have to be where you are. To shame you. So you can see me as I am, in a terrible state. So you can learn me by heart and never forget me."

Could anyone but her do that better than she does, and plead her case? Could anyone proclaim louder than her the wrong that was done to her when she was numb with horror after her grandmother's death, and death has been hard on her heels long enough that the cold breath on her neck has stopped, and the cold wind at her back, and the funereal scent of late-summer flowers, usually unscented, that had begun to smell strong like graveyard flowers, and he was inside the heat of the world, he took her inside his own heat, which was the radiant, penetrating heat of the world. The road was deserted, like a bare hand separated from its arm and shoulder, all alone in the naked air. He arrived in the bareness of the road where she'd been running since morning, her elbows close to her body, the wind on her neck like an icy knife. His clattering car, his fishing tackle in the black suitcases on the back seat. He had her get in the car beside him, choking, nearly dead from having run so far. He gave her a big white handkerchief. Told her to wipe her eyes and blow her nose. She does everything he tells her to do. He takes charge of her. He consoles her. He repeats, "Such a terrible affliction," and he cries too. She says she has nobody now. She clings to him like a lost cat. It is autumn everywhere along the flat road where he picked her up, suffocating. They drive over the mountain, where the maple trees blaze here and there against the blackish green of the spruce and the gold of the birches. A glimmer, like light seen through stained glass, enters the clamorous little car when he offers her candy. For the first time she sees his doe eyes with their long black lashes against his pale cheek. She starts to cry again, repeats that she's alone in the world. He squeezes her fingers hard enough to make her cry. A little more and he'll claim that he's all alone too. Which would be true in a way, though he has recently married. It doesn't make sense to say he's all alone, even if he secretly feels he is. With his wife or without her, moreover. An irreparable solitude, no doubt. This man has never in his life consoled someone else, always being the most unhappy. He is elated and comforted to be able to do so with Delphine. To deliver her from tears and from the suffocation of tears. He desires this for the first time — the power of the stronger in the face of the weaker. He melts with gratitude. Feels infinite pity. He drapes his jacket over Delphine's shoulders. Now that she has stopped crying, she's freezing from head to toe as if it were winter.

They pull into town around six p.m., in the little dark green car that bounces and rattles.

All that happened in Delphine's country, well before Patrick's return to France, where that woman was waiting for him — she who remained, in his most deeply hidden thoughts, his wife and sovereign for all eternity.

◆　◆　◆

Stéphane insisted on going with Delphine to the Gare Montparnasse. She departed for Nantes without seeing Stéphane, as she was busy having her ticket punched and trying to locate her railway car on the platform.

He comes to my place as soon as he can get away from the record store where he works. He's waiting for Delphine. Though he appears to be as drained of all passion as a little dead fish on a plate. His blank eyes gaze at me, unseeing.

Delphine has come back sooner than expected. She assures me that she'll never see Patrick Chemin again as long as she lives, that she'd rather die.

She pats her belly and seems close to giving birth. She creases her eyes in her little freckled face, makes an effort to see the shadows breathing in my paper-littered studio. She even declares that she can discern very clearly, directly ahead of her, the troubled face of Patrick Chemin. This man hasn't been doing at all well since Delphine cursed him in Nantes.

"He's very pale and he's sweating bullets. His wife wipes his forehead with a Kleenex. She fixes him a soothing drink. Her movements are those of a giant who is doing her best to care for a normal-sized human being. Though his legs are too long. The tiny torso of a sick child. Narrow shoulders. No one sees him more clearly than I do, with his flaws and his good points. His incomparable eyes. He has the brown velvet eyes of a doe. His long, long lashes cast a shadow on his cheek. I've never looked at anyone the way I look at him. I carved his name on my heart with a sharp little knife, all the letters of his name in capitals. All the features of his face in large characters. His legs like scissor blades. The stupid look on his face when I told him he'd have to choose between his wife and me. The fat old lady or me — young and full to bursting with life. I have double everything:

kidneys, liver, heart, arms, legs, sex. I'm a double-yolked egg. Carefully hidden behind my navel there's a living beast that swells and grows from hour to hour, that eats me and drinks me, that presses on my bladder with all its weight, sucking its thumb and making itself comfortable as if it were at home."

She looks us in the eye, Stéphane and me. Her laughter tumbles from her like a shower of hail.

"Would you like to know, my little papas, exactly what Patrick Chemin said to make me curse him in Nantes? 'I'll never marry you. I'm tied to another woman in spite of myself, by a powerful force that comes from her alone, that binds us to each other until death . . .' I told him that real life was on my side, and that, if he didn't marry me, he'd soon be dead and buried, rotten from remorse and sin."

From laughter Delphine moves on to tears. Then laughs again. She is shaken by laughter interrupted by sobs.

"The worst part was when he asked me to forgive him and he wanted to put his ear against my belly and listen to my child's heart, like a doctor. I couldn't bear having him so close to the frantic beating of my life, so I scratched him on the cheek. Then I jumped to my feet in the hotel room. I buttoned my long coat up to the neck and I left, all alone, in the middle of the night. The wait till morning in the empty railway station at Nantes was the longest of all the times I've waited in stations and on platforms. But I'll never again go anywhere to see him and touch him, to be seen and touched by him. Lovers who see each other and touch each other in the madness of being in love. I think I'm going to give birth right away, at your place, Édouard dear. I've been looking so long for a quiet, comfortable nest . . ."

Threat and counter-threat. At once I talked to Delphine

about a doctor, a hospital. In one leap she was at the door. Raced down the stairs. We could hear her shouting from one floor to the next:

"I'll give birth the way I want, when I want, where I want. It's nobody's business but mine."

Leaning on the windowsill, I see her hurry across the courtyard and disappear under the porch, with Stéphane following and shouting at her.

He caught up with her at the corner of Rue de Rennes, as she was turning onto Rue Cassette, just as school was letting out. They talked together, surrounded by the crowd of children, breathless from running.

"Do you want to marry me?"

He was panting so hard that the words broke off in his throat. She kissed his cheek to thank him. For a moment his hurried breath and hers were mingled.

"No, Stéphane, no, I can't."

He was wrong to insist, because Delphine's anger came rushing back. She ran away again, shouting insults at Patrick and at Stéphane, who fed her anger because he was within her reach just then. She cried:

"No, Stéphane, no, Patrick Chemin is the one I want. And anyway your hands are damp, poor Stéphane, I don't want you to touch me!"

Stéphane let her dash away, bumping into the tables and chairs lined up on the sidewalk outside the corner café. Very quickly he lost sight of her.

We heard nothing more about Delphine for several days. Her baggage stayed on the floor of her hotel room, and her bed wasn't slept in.

Stéphane told me all about it, and I pointed out to him that the girl was crazy.

◆ ◆ ◆

What can be done for Delphine who has disappeared? Her pregnancy. Her madness. Her threadbare cotton dress. The inheritance from her grandmother, which is dwindling visibly. The man who made her pregnant. His refusal to marry her. Stéphane and I have decided to adopt Delphine and her child. We've bought a layette, baby clothes, and maternity clothes in a shop that caters to pregnant woman. We've started looking for her in the city.

No doubt it's pointless to shake the city in every direction, like a rug, in the hope of finding Delphine. Streets, squares, alleys, cafés, railway stations — ah yes, especially the stations. She cannot be found.

Stéphane says her name to anyone who will listen.

"Her name is Delphine. Have you seen her? She's a pregnant girl who . . ."

Lost from the outset, like a puppy found in a garbage can — wandering since the dawn of this world in some vague country we can only imagine — Delphine well and truly cannot be found. The two of us, Stéphane and I, can trace her appalling little life no farther back than a grandmother and a rocking chair that moves back and forth on a wooden verandah. Delphine says her grandmother no longer has milk or periods. That reassures her. The old woman cannot release some noisy baby from her dry womb, from under her pulled-up skirts. She won't insult her granddaughter by replacing her with another brat. An only child forever, she breathes and settles herself in her grandmother's lap, against the big, dry, warm breasts. Even though she is ten years old. Childhood rediscovered seems eternal. But now things are falling apart and the whisper of death can be heard. That bitter whisper cannot be the wind, though the rocking chair continues to move back and forth after the grandmother has fallen dead to the ground. Such swaying back and forth in her ears, and the road before her so she can run away until she's out of breath. And now, on this side of the Atlantic, it's beginning again. Once again Delphine is running away, with death at her heels, or so she thinks.

◆ ◆ ◆

The Fat Lady is here before me. Now I can see her up close. The texture of her skin, the curl of her hair, the breadth of her hips, the blaze of her anger, the passage of words on her red lips, her carnivorous teeth. I can hear her breathe.

Having emerged from Delphine's story as if by magic, the Fat Lady is at my place. She is sitting on my bed and crossing her legs. But how can this be?

She dragged a sheepish Patrick Chemin to Rue Gît-le-Coeur in the hope of finding Delphine and taking the child from her. With Delphine gone, the hotel-keeper insists that someone get rid of her baggage.

At that very point in the conversation with the hotel-keeper, about the baggage, Stéphane turned up, and the three of them met and recognized one another, making Delphine's world virtually complete. All that remained was for me to join them and to join in their commitment to find Delphine.

All Patrick does is plead that we go to the railway stations and look for Delphine there.

Her fury paces the narrow room. Her long strides. Her endless legs. My back is to the wall. Shut away with her inside her rage and her insults. I, with my restricted life, my limited desires, I am suffocating in here with her, between the table and the bed.

She strides back and forth. She has the ceiling at her head, the walls at her fingertips, she need only reach out her arms. Now she is circling me, glaring, dancing. Her short linen jacket spins around with every step. Her odour is on me. She speaks into my face.

"Patrick has told me everything about that little girl. He was trembling from head to toe. He looked like a stuffed toy being shaken."

Shall I take advantage of her anger, rub myself against it like a match, and blaze in turn from a strong and violent life?

But look at her now, outrageously mild and asking for something to eat and drink.

I offer her bread and cheese. I set a half-full bottle on the table.

I watch her eat and drink, standing across from her, arms hanging by my sides but somehow awkward, as if I were holding a hat in my right hand and a bouquet of flowers in my left, the better to salute her rapacity — or perhaps this fury of hers, that is soothed as she eats and drinks.

"I'm very greedy, and my greed will be the death of me. I like *choucroute*, bacon omelets, good ripe Camembert, and my dear little husband — oh God, how dear he is, my dear, dear, dear husband who has cheated on me . . ."

Her deafening laughter makes the windows rattle.

Not a drop left in the bottle, not a crumb left on the plate.

She gets up from the table, stretches and yawns, her mouth wide open as if she wants to swallow everything around her — invisible pollen suspended in the motionless air, every living particle eddying within my walls, and me, standing there before her like an edible insect.

Something infinite in her arms and thighs. The giantess moves like a panther in a cage.

"I have to adopt that child. He's half mine as it is, since Patrick is the father. I'm ravenous, and everything I lust after is already mine."

She has started to smoke. She blows smoke-rings big enough for me to step through, like a circus act, wearing all my clothes and with my big boots on my feet.

This creature is beautiful and terrifying. Her name is Marianne Chemin.

◆　◆　◆

The waiting room, Gare Saint-Lazare, seven p.m.

Marianne is the first to recognize her, having looked for her more zealously than anyone else. The crowd walks by, going in every direction, dazing her and jostling her. Now she has neither grace nor beauty. Her dress is a rag on her skin. Her head is as empty as a black hole. You can see beads of sweat on her forehead.

From very far away, Marianne has seen the pink stain of Delphine's dress as she stands pinned against the wall. She moves towards her, picks her out, holds her. With her head thrown back and her hands on her belly, Delphine is without defences or vivacity. She is ripe like a fruit that is past its prime, one that holds within it another fruit that is practically overripe and ready to fall to the ground.

Once they're in the taxi on their way to the Hôtel-Dieu hospital, amid countless cars driving along in the sunlight, the two women are so close to one another on the back seat that Marianne can feel Delphine's contractions through her own sterile body, resonating in her like waves against a seawall. And if Delphine turns around, she can feel Marianne's gaze fixed on her like the black eye of a squirrel preparing to break a nut to get at its kernel. *I want that child and I'll have it*, thinks Marianne.

Delphine is moaning continuously now. She has arrived at the peak of her lie and of her little drama.

The over-abundant life she thought she possessed has been taken from her. Her imposture has been found out and she is dumbfounded.

Her cries through the walls of the Hôtel-Dieu.

Marianne, Patrick, Stéphane, and I confined to the waiting room. Cries everywhere, all around us. What goes on here is like the earth forced open so new blood will come.

Patrick never looks up from the tiles at his feet. We can see the top of his head, his thinning hair. You'd think that his misfortune was hidden down there, between two tiles, that if he bent down he'd be able to rip it out like a weed.

Briefly he raises his head, and I observe the eyes that Delphine praised so highly. Excessively gentle, with an otherworldly velvet smoothness, Patrick Chemin's eyes express what he will never say to Delphine. Tender compassion is lost between his eyelashes. At the peak of disaster. Doesn't know whom to ask for forgiveness. Delphine or Marianne? Wants above all to be rocked and consoled.

The midwife approaches us. Tells us that the girl was full of air, like a wineskin. She laughs reluctantly, too surprised to poke fun openly.

"False pregnancy! Did you ever hear the like, I ask you? A unique case in the annals of the Hôtel-Dieu."

More exhausted than if it had all been real, a cry caught in her throat, Delphine finally dozed off long after she was placed in a hospital bed, an injection in the crook of her arm.

As she walks past the nursery, Marianne carefully studies the newborns behind the glass, as if she were looking through the impassable waters of birth. Her long hand, with its gleaming wedding band, raps against the glass wall.

◆ ◆ ◆

She is silent on her hospital bed. Utterly mute. Still as a stone. Flat as a sole. A dead fish. Nothing is happening any more, in her belly or in her heart. She has been burst open. Stripped of her heaviness. Now she is reduced to her empty form. Narrow and thin. The imaginary fruit has been tossed into the naked air, mingled with the nudity of the air, sucked in by the naked air, reduced to dust and powder, spread, impalpable, through the great void above the rooftops, disappearing on the horizon like the ashes of the dead, vanished over the sea.

A beautiful summer. Paid holidays. Vacations planned since last year. The sea. The mountains. The countryside. Children. Parents. Grandparents. Evanescent loves appearing on the horizon. They all go away. Nearly everyone. Pretend they know nothing of Delphine's extravagant dream that has been swallowed up by the chalky air of a summer day.

They have not seen her thinness, the sheet that her flat little bones barely lift as she lies tidily on the hospital bed. They have taken advantage of her absolute silence and her refusal to see anyone at all to leave on vacation as usual.

Marianne has taken Patrick to Ile de Ré, to the big house that has been hers since her parents' death. Ashamed as though he himself had given birth to a chimera, Patrick has sworn that never again will he be taken in.

I brought flowers to her in the hospital. She closed her eyes so as not to see them. Pinched her nose so as not to smell them. Her hand came away with difficulty from her chest, where it had been fixed like the dead hand of a martyred woman, palm open over her heart, in old paintings. She gestured for the flowers and their odour to be taken away, and went back to sleep, the sleep of the dead.

Stéphane no longer listens to music — or if he does try to listen to some kind of music he used to like before he knew Delphine, his pale face looks drawn, as if he were hearing discordant notes ringing in his ears.

After the hospital discharged her, we checked out the classified ads in *Le Figaro*.

"'Villa Anthelme. 17th arrondissement. Métro Wagram. Room and board.'"

Stéphane and I went there, accompanying a sleepwalker who mustn't be wakened for fear she might throw herself under the first car that came along.

The narrow sofa was covered with a rough fabric in a dark blue that was nearly black. The double window open to the stifling summer didn't stop the musty smell from tickling our noses.

Delphine has been leaning out the window into the sticky heat, looking at the long inner courtyard with its paving stones pried partially loose, and she declares that this is fine, that no one will dare cross the bumpy courtyard to come and disturb her for fear of spraining an ankle.

She turns down the blue blanket. Sees that the sheets are clean. Gets into bed fully dressed. Turning to face the wall, she asks us to let her sleep. While Stéphane and I are still there looking at her, Delphine sinks into sleep, tired from the move by taxi and from life in general.

Stéphane says that he loves Delphine more than his mother, that it's terrible, and that Delphine doesn't love him at all.

The telegram arrived almost immediately after Stéphane's declaration: "Mother sick. Asks son to come. A neighbour."

Stéphane took the train for Meudon the next morning. He wouldn't come back to Paris till after Delphine's death.

◆　◆　◆

I believe I can picture Stéphane comfortably ensconced in a seat on the train, heading for Meudon, travelling full speed through the countryside, not so much as moving his little finger, inert and taken in charge by one of the powers of this world. I know, however, that his musician's soul distinctly hears Delphine's little voice, lilting and insidious, amid the deafening clatter of the wheels along the rails.

As for Stéphane's mother, whether she's sick or not, I have no precise idea of her, having barely seen her, a dark widow, one night in her house at Meudon. With Stéphane on his way to her, it's a little as if he were sinking gradually into the opacity of the earth.

The air is like oil. A heat wave in all its splendour. My solitude restored. Quick errands between two paragraphs. Stairways rushed down, then right up again, on the double. Baguette. Coffee. Ham sandwich with butter. Cheap red wine. Cheese. Summer berries. I barely exist and I write paragraphs. I abandon Stéphane's loves and plunge into maxi-furnishings for mini-salaries. All's well that ends well.

The world is in order. I work. Delphine sleeps at the Villa Anthelme. Stéphane is sinking into the maternal shadows before our eyes. Fear the mystery of the other like my own forbidden memory.

I'm at home, revelling in the stuffy air, when Delphine comes bursting in, shining from head to foot as if she's just out of the water. Her maternity dress, brightly coloured and unwrinkled, hangs loosely over her tiny body. Her high cheekbones seem freshly polished.

"See how nicely I'm dressed, Édouard dear? Everything's new. The dress, the shoes, all of it, all of it. I just had to choose from the trousseau you and Stéphane bought me! Down the toilet with my pink dress and the lump that was inside it. I'll never see Patrick Chemin again. Take a good look at me — alone, thin, and flawless! A genuine marvel!"

She spins around. Her oversized dress is like a swollen lampshade around her. Her crepe-soled shoes squeak on the carpet. Her long hair flies over her face and down her back.

"I came to tell you about the Villa Anthelme. Would you like to hear what goes on there?"

She is here, at my place, in a room littered with papers and catalogues, all vibrant with laughter and with the secrets of the Villa Anthelme.

"At first I thought no one was there. Except the maid, who seemed to be the real mistress of the house. It suited me that there was no one in the house except for the maid and me. Silence everywhere, as dense as water. She brings my food on a tray. I don't eat. I pretend to be always asleep. The silence from me is added to the silence of the house. Outside, it's summer. I rage and I cry in my bed against the wall. The maid calls me Little Misery. There's a tiny washbasin with an S-shaped pipe. I wash my hair in it. I plug in my hair dryer. Immediately, there's a rustle of slippers everywhere, coming awake in the house. Going up and down the stairs. Brushing against my door. Feet scuffling everywhere. Buzzing like a swarm of flies in the dark.

"'Somebody's blown the fuses!'

"The answer echoes back:

"'Who blew the fuses?'

"I huddle in my bed. The shattered silence of the house is intolerable. The silence ought to be glued back together so I can hide deep inside it again. I don't want anyone to see me. I pull the sheet over my face. There's a knock at my door. I put my hands over my ears. The maid bursts into my room. She unplugs the hair dryer. Says it's forbidden. She's very angry. My eyes are wide open at the maid's anger. I see her thick lips quivering with anger. Now there are old people all over the landing, craning their necks to look through the open door into my room. The old people have emerged from their holes like rats. I hide in my bed as best I can. I'm so afraid that all at once I get my voice back. I scream:

"'Shut the door!'

"Once the door has been shut and the maid has gone, I cry my eyes out, I can't stop, till evening. It's a change from the silence that's been stifling me for days. Around eight o'clock the maid comes to see me with bread and ham on a plate. She says:

"'You're carrying on too much, Little Misery. Now stop it. Your pillow's soaking wet.'

"She wipes my face with the hem of her white-flowered red dress.

"Her name is Farida. She's the real mistress of the Villa Anthelme. The old people just have to behave themselves. She scolds them one by one, each in turn, and she runs everything like a real queen."

Delphine is talking faster and faster. She can't get the words out quickly enough. The tempo of her speech has been restored to her a hundredfold. After a very long silence she really gets going.

"If you only knew, Édouard dear, the things that go on at the Villa Anthelme."

She delights at the rest of her account in advance, as if it were an avalanche of words preparing to tumble down.

The heat seeps in through the closed shutters. Delphine looks out between the slats at the courtyard baking in the sun. She comes back to me.

"I wanted to take a bath before I came to see you. Soap myself from head to toe. I washed my hair yesterday, but already it's like spun glass. So much accumulated sweat, grime, and tears. I want to erase every sign of my past life. Forget Patrick Chemin. Get a new skin. Into the sea at noon. Start from square one. Never be fat again, or sad. Here I am before you for the first time. Take a good look at me. See how clean and new I am. My imaginary child is in the garbage. As for the bath, Farida told me I could. She assured me that the youngest of the old people bathes on the days his girl-friend comes to visit. The bathroom is big and high like a chapel, and the tub sits on a platform like an altar. Four doors flatten the four corners. No key. The tub as deep as an abyss. The still, hot water Farida has run. The verdigris copper taps. I'm in water up to my chin. My hair in a chignon on top of my head. The delight of all that water. I breathe under water. I blow bubbles. In a little while, a strange rustling comes into the gentle foaming of the bubbles, from the other side of the doors. The old people are spying on me through the keyholes. I hear them breathing and stamping at the four compass points. I get out of the water as fast as the wind, and wrap myself in the huge towel Farida has laid out. The one and only big, white, soft terrycloth towel in the Villa Anthelme. The other towels are the size of a gauze pad, they're scratchy and they don't dry you properly. Farida brings me something to eat and drink. She tucks me in even when I pout against the wall. She scolds me and wipes away my tears. Her big breasts. Her swollen mouth. If she looks away for just a minute, I go back to the street and follow the first person who comes along, dogging his footsteps till he turns to me and takes charge of me."

I point out to Delphine that it would be best if she stayed at the Villa Anthelme as long as she can before she goes back to her country.

"I don't have a country. Get that into your head, Édouard dear. No country at all. Where I come from was my grandmother, only my grandmother, and she's dead."

◆　◆　◆

The beautiful summer is stagnating in the courtyard and above the city, is ripening gently, secretly preparing its decline and its end. I'm reading *Murder on the Orient Express*. I lose my way in the obscure plot. I think I hear a steam engine whistling in the night, while in full daylight, at home on Rue Bonaparte, the muffled sound from the porte-cochère rings out and slowly fades.

It's her. It can't be anyone else. I listen for her footsteps on the stairs. I drop my book. I hear a child's voice calling to me through the door:

"Are you there, Édouard dear? I need to talk to you right now!"

Her hair, plaited into two long braids that pull at her temples, makes her look more offended than usual.

"I'm not hanging around the Villa Anthelme any longer. I'd rather go back to the street."

She stretches out on my bed, slaps her braids against her shoulders like whips. Straightens up and says in a strained voice, urged by I know not what wild wind that presses on her and leaves her breathless:

"I have to tell you. Since yesterday, Farida has refused to bring my meals to my room. She flung me into the dining room with the old people. I have to face the old people at the table in the dining room of the Villa Anthelme. My arrival creates a sensation. They all look up. Their gazes all focus on me. They stop chewing when I sit down. They drop their forks and knives to look at me. The silence they cast over me is like black ice. A field of black ice to catch me in, to put me into the same state as them, like poor frozen beasts."

Nervously Delphine undoes her braids. Her hair, set free, corkscrews around her. She brings her hands together, groans in a barely perceptible voice:

"Farida doesn't look after me. She leaves me all by myself. I'd got used to her warmth, the warmth of a living creature. The others give me goose pimples. Their cold hands. The way they roll their eyes — the eyes of a malevolent dead fish. And Farida, who goes from table to table dishing out the meat, rice, or vegetables, the cheese or stewed fruit. She refuses to change Madame Lebeau's plate between the meat and the fruit. With her hands on her hips she declares, so all the people in the dining room, who are listening in silence, can hear:

"'You old owl. Are you the one that washes the dishes?'

"I saw that Farida was as fierce with the poor creatures as an animal tamer swinging his stick inside a cage."

She talks. I listen. The long hours of midsummer, drop by drop. Suddenly she falls silent. Gathers her impressions. Doesn't know how to approach them. Steeps herself in silence again. Silently regains the power of speech. Broods on the insult to Madame Lebeau. Swallows at length. Briskly flips her hair over her shoulders. Decides to say something but doesn't know quite how to go about it. Thinks very hard about Madame Lebeau and how she was insulted by the maid.

"She left the table without picking up her napkin, which had fallen to the floor. She walked right across the dining room, head high, feet awkward in her house slippers. Everyone watching. Everyone listening. It's so rare that anything happens at the Villa Anthelme. We hear Madame Lebeau shuffling up the stairs, step by step, breathless and plaintive. Her door on the second floor slams in the vast silence. We go back to eating, but more slowly, moving food from one cheek to the other, like a child who doesn't want to swallow. For three days, not a sign of Madame Lebeau. Nowhere. Not in the dining room. Not on the stairs. Not in the hallway that leads to the bathroom. By the third day I wondered if she was dead in her room. I knocked on her door. Several times. With a pause between knocks. Eventually she came to the door. Brusque, like some crank. I asked how she was. I observed that she was very much alone. She jumped out of her room. A little grey viper about to bite. She came into my room. My door stayed wide open. Her amazing speed. Her quick little movements that could stagger you, body and soul. She repeated 'alone,' 'alone,' as if she were tearing the word between her teeth, spitting it on the ground, then picking it up to bite it again.

"'Everyone's alone. I'm alone. You're alone. Or maybe you're hiding someone? Under your bed? In your closet?'

"She looks under the bed. She looks in the closet. Shaking like a leaf.

"'You can see there's nobody anywhere.'

"She whispers, like an echo, 'nobody,' and 'anywhere,' breathing very fast, looking deathly tired.

"Then she totters out and double-locks herself inside her own room."

Delphine ends her speech with a great sigh, brings Madame Lebeau's solitude back to herself, is engulfed in it for a moment.

"Once in my life I was more alone than Madame Lebeau, the very worst of all the times in the world, and that was after my grandmother died. And now that Farida has kicked me out, it's starting again."

She is talking in her stranger's voice again, very low, her soul and her heart so far away that I feel I'm hearing her in a dream.

Caught in the act of listening and heeding, I refuse to follow this little girl along the uncertain roads of loss and desolation. For want of anything better to do, I offer her food and drink. I set the table and heat up a pizza.

She eats and drinks warily. Barely sips her wine. Spits the anchovies onto the edge of her plate, the olive pits into the ashtray. She gazes fixedly at me across the table and prepares what she is going to say. Lays down her knife and fork.

"Please, Édouard dear, let me sleep here, only sleep. I've left the Villa Anthelme."

She wants me to be kind and compassionate, while I rage and refuse.

◆ ◆ ◆

I make her lie down in the bed right against the wall. I, the true master of the bed, stretch out at the other edge. I leave the light on. I look at her. She's pale and thin. She looks at me. I am heavy and dark, with curly hair. When I pull off my shirt, she turns away. I switch off the light. Undress in the dark. Stretch out again. A lock of her hair brushes my shoulder. I lift it off at once. I establish a clear boundary in the very middle of the bed, a kind of no man's land where it's best not to venture. It's not that this girl excites me, but I'm afraid of I know not what sombre power emanating from her small person as she is given over in the darkness to the old demons that torment her.

She is lying there perfectly flat under the sheet, moving neither her head nor her body. Her profile indistinct in the dark. Barely audible words break away from her, move across my cheek like warm mist.

"At the Villa Anthelme there's someone who's hidden, someone more highly placed than Farida, who gives orders to the whole house in secret. Someone authoritarian and sacred stands behind a closed double door with dark mouldings, on the ground floor just next to the front door. She's the one who is really in charge of the Villa Anthelme. When I was walking down the hall this morning, I heard her voice, an old woman's voice, bellow and break. No doubt angry at having played dead for so many days and nights now, she was crying out to make up for the time she'd lost. Farida received her anger, flung by the bucketful. I saw Farida go in like a little girl waiting to be punished. I saw her come out again, all limp in her floral-patterned dress, like a big red and white flower withering and drooping on its stem. Farida saw me — saw that I knew everything, that I'd been standing there in the lobby for several minutes. She couldn't bear no longer being the queen in my eyes. She turned on me. Her eyes were bulging out of her head like shiny marbles, black and white. She cried out in turn:

"'Get out of here, Little Misery! I don't want to see your face any more! Get the hell out!'

"She helped me pack my bags. Her hands were trembling. She threw me out on the street. And she hailed a taxi, waving both arms over her head as if she were calling for help."

What do I do with this girl lying beside me in my bed, like an old wife telling me about her day? I think I'll dream all alone at her side, like a very old husband. She says good night, and she drapes her hair across her face, to hide.

◆　◆　◆

She pretends to be drinking her café au lait, face buried in her bowl up to the eyes. Confesses that she's not crazy about coffee.

I make her some tea.

Between us, no conversation is possible. She's too sleepy, it seems, to launch into one of her customary long monologues. And I'm too much on my guard again to want to listen to her. I'm annoyed at her for having slept in my bed. I retreat into silence in front of her and wait for her to go away.

A sleepwalker who butters slices of bread and dips them in her tea. Her slow movements nearly coming to a standstill above the plate and bowl. A little more and her knife and her little spoon will fall to the tablecloth, and sleep will make her head droop to her chest. She murmurs that she's very tired.

I tell her that if she wants to stay in Paris, she'll have to look for work. She admits, her lips barely moving, that she's never worked and doesn't know how to do anything.

She closes her eyes, turns very pale, speaks softly — listening to a voice, it seems, that repeats as an echo in the absolute void of the room.

"My grandmother used to say that I was a poor little thing who hurt all over, and that I needed to rest."

Her blind face comes very close to me above the table. She speaks with her mouth shut. I guess at, rather than hear, what she is saying.

"They stole my child at the Hôtel-Dieu. They told me he was dead. They said I was stark raving mad. How do you expect me to work like everybody else?"

And all at once she brightens up, grave and in full possession of what she sees before her.

"My grandmother spends all Sunday afternoon rocking on the front verandah. On Sunday the rockers of her big, shiny, red straw-bottomed chair go back and forth on the floor of the verandah for hours. I like their smooth sound, it joins the murmur from the fields all around. I can hear that gentle rubbing of wood against wood in my head day and night, in Paris, Nantes, Aix, on Rue Gît-le-Coeur, at the Saint-Sulpice fountain, at the Villa Anthelme. When she died, my grandmother fell out of her rocking chair on the verandah. Not one moan. Not one sigh. Not a single cry for help. She fell like someone who has finished rocking and lets herself drop to the ground. A sound both muffled and light. The wind was blowing so hard that day, the empty chair kept rocking by itself in the wind while my grandmother was lying there dead on the ground. The doctor. The priest. The notary. I did what had to be done. At the house. At the church. At the graveyard. In the notary's office. I went to all the places you have to go to in cases of death, burial, and inheritance. The wind was still blowing. The rocking chair kept moving back and forth by itself in the wind. I couldn't stand that relentless creaking and I set out down the main highway, leaving the house I'd inherited to squatters, and the chair rocking on the verandah. Safe in a small leather pouch that I fastened to my belt was the other part of my inheritance, in coins and bills. Just enough to survive on until someone took care of me again. I walked along the road for hours, over the horizon, I think, and I thought I would die."

Both her face and her body change before my eyes. Here she is in front of me, filled with terror and tears, running away from her grandmother's death on the road. Too much, it's too much. I'm disgusted and I turn my head away. All this girl wants is my tears in return for hers. I will not grant her that complicity. Dry as an old tree against a stone wall, I inform Delphine that she'll have to find another shelter for the coming night. I give her the address of a small hotel in Montparnasse that someone told me about.

◆　◆　◆

Édouard dear, do you want to know what's going on in the Rue J. C.? It's a street full of girls swaying on their high heels. Red-heads, blondes — they lost their original colour long ago — they blaze in the sun or the rain, among the gaudy neon signs. Starting at four in the afternoon. The tallest one has the red mane of a mad mare hanging all the way down her back. Her gleaming black boots come up to her thighs and they are inlaid with bits of mirrors. We meet on the sidewalk. She's constantly parading back and forth. I'm looking for my hotel. She despises me, she hates me from the first hard, furtive glance. Édouard dear, why did you drop me there in the middle of all those hookers? The hotels are named for flowers: Les Hortensias, Les Glycines, Le Volubilis. Only the Saint-Gildas displays its name, the name of a Breton saint, in phosphorescent letters. That's where you sent me to sleep. I was wide awake all night. The big clock on the wall in my room sounds the quarter-hour and the half-hour with a muffled thud. Beneath my window the red mare paces the sidewalk and hates me along the way, through the closed shutters. I'd rather sleep at your place, Édouard dear. It's more peaceful. Just sleep. I'm so tired. Ever since I've had my grandmother's death chasing me, and Patrick Chemin, who is rotten. So long, big brother. Till tonight.

Delphine

I found this letter when I came back from a long stroll along the quays. The Seine was flowing slow and grey in the mist, and the edge of the water disappeared into the hazy sky. A wan light rose from the river, as it does when there's snow on the ground and the earth is brighter than the air. It was the beginning of September. The thought of Delphine followed my every step, like a stray cat that twines itself around your legs, that you refuse to look at for fear you'll have to take it in.

I barely have time to read her letter, which she's slipped under the door, when there she is, with her bundle on her back. She says she's tired. She stretches out on my bed and stays there, fully dressed, listening to her weariness. She spies on her motionless body, searching for the deep-seated reasons for her distress.

"'Where does it hurt, sweetheart?' my grandmother would ask."

She repeats that she's tired. I tell her she'll have to get a job like everyone else. She laughs. Gets up abruptly. Swears she doesn't hurt anywhere. I notice how small and white her teeth are.

Delphine is telling her story again, as if she can't stop, regardless of what it may cost her.

"Excused from dishes, housework, cooking, from mending, from hens and rabbits, by my grandmother, who does everything in my place, I rest. At night I no longer hear the cries of hungry infants piercing my skull. I sleep to my heart's content, day and night. Between naps, I read. A huge fatigue turns up between books, between naps. A black hole to swallow me up. The poets keep me company, and I'm damned along with them, in the books and in my room in the country where I read. I read and I dream about hell and about the scarlet sky at the end of hell, like a bright border of flames. Always, my grandmother comforts me and says sweet things to me, things so comforting and sweet after my huge storms of incomprehensible pain. I hear her empty chair rocking on the empty verandah. I escape from that

intolerable rocking by hurrying down the deserted road. My
footsteps resound on the asphalt. Tap, tap, tap. A real runaway
horse. But smaller. Not so strong. A little clicking of hoofs on
the asphalt. A very small runaway horse. Driven onto the
road. A very small, panicky clicking along the asphalt. And
I'm nearly out of breath, close to dying. The first car stops.
The first person appears. His head out the window. His head
bent towards me. His gaze, like no other. Let him look at
me just once more and I'll be his entirely. Let him recognize me straightaway as his inexpressible soul, let him take
me with him right away, to a life that is comforting and
sweet. Out of this world. Let him settle me in a safe place
filled with incomparable love. An impenetrable place where
I'll be safe from terror. There are black suitcases piled on the
back seat of his car. He gazes at me with his doe eyes. His
long lashes. He is Patrick Chemin. He comes from another
land, across the ocean. He sells flies and fish hooks. I have to
be picked up right away or I'll drop dead on the hill. Too many
kilometres in my body. Haven't eaten. Or drunk. Too much
walking down the road. My grandmother's chair keeps swaying in the wind behind me. I go limp and I fold, like cloth.
My breathing pounds outside of me. Let me get my breath
back. The wet grass where I fall full-length chills me and
swallows me up at the same time. I've passed out in the wet
grass. He carries me to his car, which smells of beer and
smoke. Puts a compress on my forehead. Takes me to town."

She is alone before me, as I am alone before her. She
extracts her life from between her ribs, a little at a time. I
respond with the brutality of the deaf, who hear nothing and
who measure neither voice nor speech.

"You always talk about your grandmother. What about
your parents? Didn't you ever have parents?"

"A father, a mother, brothers, sisters, masses of them,

masses. Everything you need to make a family. To populate the entire world. The only visible problem is the lack of room for sleeping. Three to a bed. Dresser drawers set on the floor. To sleep in. An air mattress in the tub. Diapers drying everywhere. On radiators. On lines strung up in the kitchen. Shot through with cries. I am shot through with cries. I didn't have a childhood. The first-born. Made to pick them up one by one as they come into the world. When my grandmother arrived, I'd been lying on a bed for three days as if I were dead. With my parents' approval she decided to adopt me. As soon as I was at my grandmother's, at her house in the country, along the very edge of the paved road, I settled into a peace like no other. At home, I was replaced right away. Scarcely two days after my departure, my fourteenth little sister was born, chubby and round. I've never heard her cries rip through the air above the rooftops. My grandmother was my nest. I'd never known anything like it. And I kept cheeping to go back to my nest and rest. I didn't return to the house in town, and no one in the family came to the country to see me at my grandmother's. Not my father, not my mother, not Malvina, who's going on six. Not Petit Louis or anything or anyone. All alone with my grandmother. For all eternity."

Her voice monotonous, inexhaustible, lower and lower, muffled. Her story with no beginning or end. I'm becoming exasperated. And my own story down deep inside me is asking to be heard in turn. What a fine dialogue of the deaf Delphine and I would have. I cut short the preposterous idea of such a conversation. I take refuge in the kitchen till she falls silent and my soul does too.

Sleep overcame her as she lay in my bed with her long hair tangled and her clothes a mess.

I lie down beside her. Switch off the light. Listen to her slightly husky breathing in the dark.

The warmth of her sleeping body next to mine. It's so dark in the room that I can't see her face. I feel the desire to do with her what a man does with a woman in his bed. I kiss her lightly on the cheek. I touch her breasts under the T-shirt. She jumps up. Speaks very softly and with difficulty, as if each word were being wrenched from her.

"I'm living through a disaster, Édouard dear. Leave me alone. I followed Patrick Chemin like a dog. For days. Sometimes without seeing his face. Just an attraction, an odour that told me where he'd been. The first time, it was in a town of all levels and castes, the one where I was born. His eye, the eye of a sacred cow, had already ravaged me on the road, before he brought me with him to the hotel in town. I liked his little poor man's suitcases too. I bled a lot onto the hotel's sheets. Patrick Chemin washed them in the washbasin in the room. The water was all red. He kept saying: "Good God! What have I done?" I gave birth to a dead child and my love died at the same time as my child. Patrick Chemin is a pig. And you too, Édouard dear. Men are all alike. No more of that, ever. Now let me go."

The sound of a key turning in the lock. Middle of the night. Delphine has flung my door wide open on the landing. Goes slowly down the stairs. Her fatigue on her back like a stone.

◆ ◆ ◆

What get in my way most are her suitcases; she left them on my rug and I have to walk around them to go from the bed to the table. As for the rest, I'll have to get used to those recurring images of her that make me shrink like an oyster reacting to drops of lemon juice.

Delphine anorexic amid the cheeping mob of her sisters and brothers, who are hungry for her. Delphine at the house of her grandmother, who is showing her how to tear a chicken leg to pieces with her teeth. The grandmother an ogress, Delphine an ogress in turn. The overwhelming love of the one and of the other. For the one and for the other. Grandmother and granddaughter.

Having not yet attained the point of absolute disappearance, the little ogress I found by the side of a fountain continues to eat into my time, to gnaw at my solitude. I can't bear not knowing where she is in the city. It's ten days now that she's been gone. But what can she be doing, with no money, no baggage, in a city crowded by all those people returning from their August vacations?

I look everywhere for her, with no hope, as if for a needle in a stack of hay.

Is it possible I'll find her mingling with the crowd on the *grands boulevards*, trailing behind the first man who comes along in the hope that he will turn around and assist her? I can't help thinking that even if her destitution became extreme, she wouldn't hold out her hand. She would never ask for charity. But she'd be so alone and lost that people would give her alms without her asking. No doubt she'd just have to be there on the sidewalk, waiting for the world to end, her eyes blank, her face pale and insulted, facing a stranger who would turn away, hounded by her for hours now, and she'd attract the most perverse compassion.

I've been walking since morning.

The city is spilled out abundantly around me. A smashed anthill. But shining in the lacklustre crowd, like lighted rallying points here and there, are anonymous joys, furtive rages.

No trace of Delphine.

All I can do is go home. Back to my stairs, my four walls, my catalogues.

Stéphane's mother is recovering slowly. Stéphane won't be back in Paris before next week. Marianne and Patrick are on Ile de Ré till September 15.

I damn myself all alone.

And now she has chosen this propitious time of my own damnation to perfect it in a way, to turn up at my place once again, and end her days in my bed.

A burst aneurysm, the autopsy report will declare.

III

Everything seems to be in order around me. The body removed. The bed made. The room aired out. All I have to do is resume my idiotic work, with complete peace of mind. It would take someone clever to get me out of here now. But here is her little voice, half worn away by the ravages of death, drawing me out of the opacity in which I've enclosed myself:

"Let me sleep here. Only sleep."

She, always she, Delphine. Not sleeping. Acting in secret. Consuming her life and her death amid hidden violence.

Let the frozen ocean spread out between us as far as the eye can see. The pole and its ice. Never walk across the empty space. Between her and me. Between myself and me, I should say. Myself, in the flesh. Childhood abolished, the wish for non-return. Adulthood as a desiccated fruit. Very little air around me. Just enough to breathe between the pages of a mail-order catalogue. Delphine is unwelcome. All compassion unwarranted. Such frost inside me. Such cold, unimaginable for a creature from a temperate country like the one where I happened to be born. Exquisite light of the country around Tours. The banks of the Loire sandy and mild. A father, a mother, planted there, inadvertently no doubt, in the midst of rich, level soil. And the second son, born to them too late, like a bitter root doomed to freeze.

Who talks about breaking the ice? Harsh, forbidden memory (unless it is little Delphine, acid and stubborn). With what highly sharpened axe? What effort on the part of the entire being who seizes the axe with both hands? If by chance I were able to break the frozen sea within me, I would have Delphine at my fingertips, alive and shuddering, and perhaps, as well, a little boy who was killed, who was caught in the ice in the depths of my night. Above all, I must not become emotionally involved. The risk of waking the still water is too great. I prefer to let the dead bury the dead, twenty thousand leagues beneath the sea. The real terror is that the shadow of God's pity should be well and truly lost in the depths of the accumulated gloom.

The greatest disturbance in the world — when the waters were divided from the firmament, with a crashing of foam and molten lava — would likely have had no more effect on me than Delphine, death at her back, climbing into my bed.

"Am I disturbing you?"

To silence Delphine. To exhaust with one stroke the words of the living woman, the silence of the dead woman. To prevent her from coming to me under the ice, like a little smelt. Let her be absolutely dead. Killed by me. Once and for all. Beyond any pity for her and for me.

Am I not free to rid myself of Delphine as something

that's in my way? To sort out her images one at a time before I dump them overboard? Now I am settling her one last time on the edge of the Saint-Sulpice fountain. I leave her for a moment on a country road in a strange land. I push her into Patrick Chemin's arms. I cause Delphine's child to live or die at will under her pink dress. I hear the cries of the imaginary child before he returns to the limbo he should never have left. Delphine's gaze, so blue, slips through my fingers.

Nothing. Nothing more is happening under the transparent ice. Because I assure you that there is nothing alive here, only the pitiful episodes in Delphine's life and death, filing untidily towards the exit. A school of little fish good only for frying. Pointless to lean over the overflowing water. If minuscule eddies persist, their bubbles barely visible, it is only the end of imaginary abysses as they close up over strange, broken memories. Nothing. There is nothing more to see here. Only the echo of some lost words persists, pounds against my temple.

Sounds (nothing but sounds) loom up, syllables assemble and take pleasure in strange couplings. A little more and the words will come into view, sharp and clear; soon they will form complete sentences, and the meaning of the world, long since disappeared, cast back into the darkness, will become as clear as spring water dipped from the depths of the sea when its black crust is broken into pieces. A harsh memory split from top to bottom. I hear Madame Benoît testifying before the court of God:

"I swear it. That child's eyes are filled with tears."

Madame Benoît repeats the same thing again and again beneath the black ice. A very small fissure suffices, a mere thinning of the frozen surface, for the sound to come through. There is talk of a little boy with frozen tears as I find myself again at the age of five or ten.

This woman comes to visit my parents every Sunday, at the hour when they drink a pastis, and afterwards she drives away in her little violet Méhari, going down the roads of the country around Tours to gather up every sign of sorrow or grief for miles around.

And I, I, Édouard Morel — a forgetful man if ever there was one — am I to be placed forcibly in intimate contact with a whining child? Tender enough to die. Am I to be obliged to recognize myself in that child, the second-born of Rose and Guillaume Morel, cabinetmaker by trade? It's no small thing to place my feet in my own footsteps and say: There it is, it's me. Here is the house and the peaceful garden. The hydrangeas, blue on one side of the hedge and pink on the other because of the different soil my father transplanted there by the wheelbarrow load.

Neighbouring gardens, matching hydrangeas, identical houses arranged along a single line, tiny reference points for the great trains that travel across Saint-Pierre-des-Corps day and night. I am haunted by the trains of Saint-Pierre-des-Corps, their broad, fierce music that rends the air like long knives, their absolute energy, hurled from end to end of the living earth, which is furrowed as a field is furrowed by the plough. Under such a din I will see, no longer just hear, what is going on beneath the frozen memory, as if there were no past or present, not even a possible future, once it has been given over to forgotten words and gestures, while lost odours come along in fresh bunches. And I shall never again be free to exist on the surface of myself, like someone standing on a narrow balcony outside his house, with all the doors behind him closed like prison gates.

And if my mother's warmth were to waken, the gentle warmth of her tender, sweet, warm breast where I rest my cheek in dreams, my entire life would be returned to me at a stroke.

But now a series of small and unimportant facts swirls before my eyes like a swarm of gnats.

The odour of pale wood-shavings, eaten away by emanations of glue and varnish, envelops me from head to toe. My father bends over me. Examines me attentively.

"This child certainly doesn't look like the Other. Too dark. Too small."

My mother repeats, echoing him:

"Dear God, how dark he is! Dear God, how small he is! What a shame!"

Between her breasts, the medal worn smooth by the gentle rubbing of my mother's flesh. The Other, the First-born, lately dead, rests there in his unchanging innocence for an eternity of adoration and grief.

His blue eyes. His blond hair. First in his class. First at home. His unchanging qualities of an absolute First. The dead little child I replace. The Other. The daunting example. I may as well resign myself to not existing.

The sea has frozen over all that. God's pity sleeps at the very bottom, in a cold shadow.

I shave at the sink in my kitchen on Rue Bonaparte. A drop of blood stands out on my cheek. No one can know about the poor quality of my blood. First of all, it's perfectly normal blood. Rh positive. Like most inhabitants of the planet. Who can possibly know that one day when I was a child my vermilion blood was changed? Not all at once, but through a series of small bloodlettings. Not that it became blue or green or violet or any other surprising colour; it simply changed into other blood, natural-looking, unobjectionable, irreproachable at first sight, but in reality its very essence is corrupt. My own mediocrity slips through test tubes like some elusive virus. No bitter drama or thundering tragedy when this strange transfusion began. Trivialities at the origin of the world. Infantile behaviour. All traces gone, no sign of the frozen tears of my childhood. And if Delphine disturbs me, it is certainly because of those very tears, buried beneath the sea.

Death from natural causes, Dr. Jacquet will say. She will be repatriated to Canada. Don't worry about the baggage. The embassy will take care of everything.

A Suit of Light

I

ROSE-ALBA ALMEVIDA

It's me that you see through the wide-open window of my lodge. On the street side. Me, leaning out the window for a breath of air. My head, my hair, my beloved face, my round shoulders, my heavy bosom, my pink satin dressing gown — all the most beautiful things that I possess, I show off through the window. I display the top part of myself, fully clothed, for the people walking by. Starting at noon, when I get up, and if the day is fine. As for the bottom part, it's still me, body and soul in satin, my well-rounded rump, my short legs, and my narrow feet. O the little mules that dangle from the tips of my toes, swaying like two flying birds. All of it carefully sheltered, hidden in the shadow of the kitchen behind me. I seem to be looking outside but, in reality, I am caring for my own person, in secret. I think about myself all the time. And about money. The money I need to become more and more myself, without blemish from top to bottom, bottom to top, all of me exposed to the bright sun of fame. My only son, Miguel, is with me, in the same unbearable dazzle of light. A real little torero in his suit of light. Whether he's naked or dressed my son shines and I, his mother, shine along with him. Olé! Olé! I hear the cries of the frenzied crowd. It's my son they acclaim. I inhale the blazing dust of the bullring. The furious gallop of the dying beast goes past my face. The smell of blood and death pursues me all the way to the foreign city where I am a concierge, at 102 rue Cochin in the fifth arrondissement of Paris, France.

MADAME GUILLOU

Her name is Rose-Alba Almevida and she is taking the air at her window. Now, lightly, she moves her elbows on the window ledge. Tiny grains of dry black dust cling to her skin. She spits on her fingers and carefully cleans her elbows. She looks abstractedly onto the street. She sees her son who is drawing on the sidewalk with coloured chalk. This reassures her and allows her to return immediately to the very depths of herself, to the place where everything is dream and splendour. She's well aware that everything is happening in her head, but nothing in the world can stop her from daydreaming as she pleases, until a gnawing hatred for the life given to her sweeps over her like an equinoctial tide.

ROSE-ALBA ALMEVIDA

Rosa, Rosie, Rosita, Spanish rose, fiery and pungent, Rose-Alba Almevida, impulsive and supreme: I rhyme off the forms of your name, a superb litany. Let not a hair on your head move, nor your breath under your satin robe, let nothing reveal the soul you hide.

I plunge into silent furious longings for four-star hotels, for expensive cars with liveried chauffeurs, for luminous makeup, for unctuous creams, for indelible mascara, for vintage wines, for furs, especially for furs, red or silver fox, spotted panther, soft sable, so that I will be forever changed into a wild beast, fierce and splendid, made for love and consecration. These dreams come when I am mad on the inside and appear distracted on the outside.

MADAME GUILLOU

Miguel Almevida. Seven years old. Huge eyes. White transparent skin that, when his clothing allows, reveals a tangle of blue veins. White shirt. Patent-leather shoes. Thin as a matchstick. Too delicate no doubt for the affronts of life.

MIGUEL ALMEVIDA

The sidewalk, grey as boredom. My coloured chalks go back and forth across the grey of boredom. Red, green, blue, yellow, white, violet. I place colour on the stagnant boredom of the sidewalk. The chalk screeches in my fingers, it crumbles and is crushed. I lay down straight lines. I draw the plans for my future house. Sick and tired of the crowded little lodge, of the toilet in the yard, of the faucet on the landing. French people, third-rate like all of them, go back and forth along my sidewalk. Shamelessly, their hurried steps erase my lines and colours. My mother would say that I ought to bite their toes very hard to punish them. That would teach them to respect other people's work. It's what she thinks when she has to scrub the staircase buried under layers of wax and dirty, muddy footprints that come from who knows where and sabotage her work step by step.

I have to pass the chalk over every half-obliterated line, brighten every colour that's been blurred, and then my drawing will be clear and precise and visible from one end of the street to the other. Here is my house, I dream it up as I go. A good twenty rooms, lined up along a corridor that's broad and deep as an avenue at the Place de l'Étoile. Small salon, medium salon, grand salon, small kitchen, medium kitchen, big kitchen, small dining room, medium dining room, big dining room, huge W.C., a second huge W.C., a third huge W.C., an immense bathroom, a very immense bathroom, an endless games room, and a very deep, wide, high, magnificent bedroom. Me, standing in the very middle of that wide, high, deep, magnificent bedroom. I am waiting for my husband and I proclaim it very loudly. Arms crossed, standing in the middle of the matrimonial chamber, I wait for him to arrive. My mother, who looks like an ancient mummy, sticks her head out of her wrappings and very angrily orders me to repeat that remark.

"I'm waiting for my husband!"

She yells so loudly the whole street can surely hear her: "You're sick in the head!" And she pulls the window shut.

My father is back and there are things going on between my mother and him behind the closed window, its drawn curtain. It's always that way as soon as the window or the door closes on them. I've been driven away, excluded, kicked out, and the two of them are inside whispering, arguing, laughing very loudly, and then moaning as if they were sick, my mother in particular, as if she's about to give birth. The silence that follows is like the end of the world. I feel like crying right there, all by myself, all dirty, covered from head to toe with the different colours of chalk, standing on the sidewalk, my feet planted in the middle of an imaginary bedroom. I must wash myself. To erase the sidewalk dust from my clothes and the traces of chalk from all over me. O my beautiful patent-leather shoes, what a disaster! They resemble my mother, they are ruined like her behind her window, and the water that she'll have to fetch in a bucket from the landing, her manner casual, her head high, and her dressing gown all wrinkled. In the middle of the day. A beautiful Sunday when my father looks dashing and has nothing to do. I know very well what they talk about before they collapse into moaning and the great deathly silence that follows. "Money! Money!" demands my mother. My father grunts and claims that she spends faster than he earns. Insults on both sides. Sometimes a few loud slaps on my mother's lovely behind. The cascade of her laughter.

I wait. I pace the sidewalk. I cool my heels. I wear out my wonderful shoes. I wait for the window to open again. One day I'll go away for good.

Three p.m. The window clatters open. The outside air rushes inside again. I follow the air into the house and I say, "I'm hungry." My father shuts the window. I have to sit at the table, my hands daubed with dust and chalk. There's not a drop of water in the house.

My mother doesn't yell at me to wash my hands. She's miles away, farther than ever, and all languid as a result. She has put on a blue dress and bracelets that clink on both arms. My father is puffing away on a Gauloise. His pride in smoking so powerfully and so deeply is equalled only by his dazzling smile between two puffs.

I eat surrounded by his smoke, I drink surrounded by his smoke, I breathe the smoke from after love. My dirty hands are in the shadow of the smoke. The silence around me is so great I can hear the smoke breathing its little mouse breath onto my face. I want to cry.

All at once the half-cold meal, the absence of conversation around the table, their stunned looks, and my own urge to cry — all were finished. Through the window barely open again, people could see that my father wasn't wearing a shirt. All the smoke went outside, swept away the personal stories of us, the Almevidas, evaporated in blue curls, this Sunday, September 25th.

My father's shirt is draped over the back of a chair, white as the Immaculate Conception in the churches, starched as the priest's surplice on Corpus Christi. A ray of sunlight has slipped under the chair. My father's pointed shiny shoes become illuminated beacons.

PEDRO ALMEVIDA

In the time it takes Rosa to get ready, to put on all her frills and makeup, I'll have walked around the block two or three times. My son's hand in mine, my shiny shoes in front of me. The whiteness of my shirt matches that of my son's. Washed and changed at my insistence, now he is trotting along at my side. He insisted on wearing a mauve T-shirt with a green Mickey Mouse, but I was adamant and wouldn't yield. A man has to do what's right. Whiteness and polish on Sunday: that's as it should be. And memories of the corrida pop into my mind and armfuls of jasmine follow after.

If only I knew why my son's hand slips so quickly from my rough construction-worker's grip. The hand is too coarse and virile no doubt for a child who still wavers between girl and boy, whose mother dotes on him five days out of seven. In this foreign city the honour of Spain is assured by me, Pedro Almevida. My son Miguel shares that honour with me, he is bound to me, hand in hand, white shirt against white shirt, pointed shiny shoes — a double pair — walking at a good clip down boulevard Saint-Germain between four and five p.m. on this fine Sunday in September. Anticipation and impatience growing as I watch for the gorgeous embodiment of the fiesta herself, loosed upon the grey city, to appear at the corner of the street.

MIGUEL ALMEVIDA

Here she is! Here she is! She's wearing a miniskirt. You can see her big knees and, higher up, her fat thighs. The skirt stops there. A kind of little shirt cut from the same gold as her dress. I don't believe my father can love. He's too amazed to say a word. As for me, I get used to the idea of a tiny dress made of gold, an abbreviated sun that makes way for my mother's knees and thighs, gleaming and shining in their own way the length of the street.

My father says tonelessly: "We're going back to the house."

We followed my father home. But it was obvious that my mother thought the walk was too short when she'd taken so much trouble to get all dolled up. Her suppressed anger as great as my father's. Both pretended to walk along the side-walk normally, their heads in the air as if they were trying to grab and harness the wrath of the storm clouds overhead, should the need arise.

They've quarrelled. Traded insults. Fought. Roaring like bulls in the ring. Rolling on the floor from one end of the tiny kitchen to the other. Breathing their dying breath. On the verge of a blackout or a fatal cramp.

After they had barely recovered, they took me out of the broom closet where they'd put me. They took stock of the battle's final toll. For my mother, a ruined dress, twisted bracelets, bruised arms and legs, a black eye. For my father, claw marks and tooth marks all over, and a broken rib. My mother weeps for her dress and her eye. My father promises to buy her another dress and a slice of steak for her eye. It's easy to see that he suffers a thousand deaths with every breath. My mother covers his chest with kisses, to glue the rib back together, she says. It's obvious that she is sincere and remorseful.

ROSE-ALBA ALMEVIDA

I'll buy the dress myself from a chic boutique on rue de Sèvres. The most beautiful and most expensive. The longest, too. He'll have nothing to object to as far as the length is concerned. As for the rest, he'll be dazzled. Except for the price, maybe. I'll think of something. That will teach him. I'll be as elegant as Diana was with Dodi Fayed, cruising on a yacht. My husband's head is sure to turn in the presence of such grace and beauty. To make love with him right then — as usual, when it strikes his fancy — I'll take off my new dress and carefully hang it up, safe from the tumults of love.

MIGUEL ALMEVIDA

Home from school earlier than usual and, silent as the air we breathe, saw everything without her seeing me. My mother took the vacation money. She closed the blue box and put it back with the dust bunnies under her bed. She left to pursue her own schemes and I stayed all alone in the deserted house with mine.

I dress and apply makeup carefully, as my mother always does before she steps outside. I take the dress that was ruined in the brawl and tossed in a heap behind a chair and slip it over my head as if it were a golden chasuble. Tubes and jars, brushes of all kinds, stiletto heels, and black tights make me look like some strange and slovenly girl. I have just enough time to rejoice at my weird image in the pitted mirror that hangs on the bedroom door when suddenly my mother is back, carrying a big box marked "Marie-Christine."

You can only be crazy about my mother's new dress. No queen, no movie star has anything like it. Velvet and sequins. No night riddled with stars is as black and glittering. Donkeyskin had better behave. My mother turns and spins at the mirror. I wait for her to see me in all my finery and marvel at me as I marvel at her. The two of us ecstatic at ourselves and at our doubles. Accomplices and sweethearts.

At last! She's seen me!

"Christ almighty! Am I dreaming? What if your father saw you!"

With no consideration for the golden dress or the black tights I put on my head to suggest a woman's long braids, she smacked my rear, and my high-heeled shoes fell off. She didn't hit too hard and I didn't cry. What's most important is that I still have hope in my heart that one day my mother will accept me as I am, outrageously made up, with purple nails, and long hair hanging down.

By sheer coincidence, my father decides that very night that I have to take karate lessons at the local school. One thing is certain, both my mother and I have secrets that must be kept from my father at all costs.

ROSE-ALBA ALMEVIDA

I hemstitch. All day long I hemstitch. The lady on the first floor complains about the heat. I hemstitch. The gentleman on the sixth floor is shivering. I hemstitch. Heat and shivers. They have their problems. I have mine. I won't touch the heat. I have hemstitching to do. I have no time to attend to the heating. The lady on the first floor is menopausal, the gentleman on the sixth is a nudist. What do they expect from me? I have hemstitching to do for Madame Guillou on the fourth floor. Piles of sheets and pillowcases, thread pulled tight and knotted. Madame Guillou, who's very old-fashioned, is preparing a traditional wedding for her daughter. She'll have her trousseau, that overripe girl who is finally being married off. I hemstitch from morning till night. I stop dead and stow it all under the bed when my husband comes home in the evening. It's important that he not catch me sewing. I fear his questions. If he knew why I need money so badly he'd kill me. The blue box for our vacations under the bed — empty. He couldn't bear that and I would be dead in no time. Be brave, poor little me, this is just a difficult moment to get through. Day after day till the whole trousseau is ready. Afterwards I'll rest and I'll dye my hair Venetian blonde. My mind is made up.

MIGUEL ALMEVIDA

My mother is sewing furiously. I wonder what she's going to do with all those sheets. Maybe she'll open a four-star hotel. I'd love to roll around in sheets like those. It would be a change from the rags they make us wear for karate, for the exalted brutality of a deadly virile game. I fall to the floor so often I'm covered with bruises.

Yesterday my father took me to my karate lesson by force, dragging me by the arm the whole way.

There's been a leak in the cellar. My mother still pulls thread. People have been knocking at the door to her lodge for a good half-hour. My mother still does her hemstitching.

"Madame Almevida! Madame Almevida! The place is full of water! The cellar is flooded!"

"I'm coming! I'm coming!" my mother shouts, and she snaps a thread with her teeth before calling the plumber.

My God, this house is exhausting! People going in and out all the time. I don't know where I can go to live the life of a well-behaved child: learning my lessons, doing my homework, examining the bruises all over my body, and cursing my father in peace.

ROSE-ALBA ALMEVIDA

I pleaded, wept, threatened, simpered, and fondled endlessly. To go dancing at a club. To wear my dress from Marie-Christine for the first time. My husband grumbled, yelled, mentioned once again how hard it is to earn money and how easy it is to spend. But when he saw me in my black velvet dress riddled with glittering stars, standing erect in the middle of the kitchen, at the very heart of this rat's nest where the three of us live with no toilet or running water, he said, "Yes." He could only say "Yes" because he didn't suspect the price of the dress or its consequences for our vacation in Spain.

In exchange for all that hemstitching so skilfully pulled and knotted and already dearly paid for, Madame Guillou will look after Miguel until morning. I have the whole night ahead of me for dancing with my husband.

I love dancing, my whole body thrashing about rhythmically, my husband facing me, agitated and glorious. The two of us in the same wild and joyous whirl. Now and then an urge comes over me to try and dance close with someone else, to see if it would have the same effect as with Pedro Almevida, my husband.

As the night draws to an end, as the glimmers of light become ever softer and the cigarette smoke thicker, the slow number rocks the barely standing but warmly locked dancers like a population of the drowned swayed by a rising tide.

I'm drunk, more than from any drink, ready to bed any man who would hold me tightly against him while swords of fire pierced my body through and through. I close my eyes and I melt. My husband gives a hollow laugh and whispers in my ear to wait till we're home to pass out completely. I open one eye a bit and, over Pedro Almevida's shoulder, spy a broad grin without a face, nothing but the smile of an unknown man addressing me quite openly. My husband drags me outside as I cling to his arm and try to erase from my mind the unknown and beautiful strong white teeth that secretly devour me.

MIGUEL ALMEVIDA

It may be a rat hole but it's mine. I'm attached to it. I've been here since my mother left the clinic with a little bundle, me, in her arms. Three days after my birth. That was ages ago. And now they're chasing me out of my home so they can go to a club and live it up like teenagers. It's not the first time, either. Yet whenever they do it I'm scandalized in the same way. My own parents. To ship me off to Madame Guillou's on the pretext of inaugurating my mother's new dress. Under the coloured spotlights and strobe lights. At their age it's absolutely uncalled for.

Madame Guillou's black horsehair sofa dominates her living room. It's like an enormous sea creature glistening with water.

Madame Guillou puts a hemstitched sheet on the sofa and gives me a red-and-white striped blanket that smells of mothballs. Horsehair is spiteful. It's hard and prickly. Slippery. I fall, I land on the floor. Twice. Hard enough to make new bruises. It's like everything else: I have to get used to it.

Morning. Foamy chocolate and hot croissants delight me more than I can say. I'm still overcome with happiness, the chocolate and croissants barely downed, in a state of deep contentment, when I realize that Madame Guillou's wrinkled face is really very kind. I kiss her flabby cheek.

Before leaving I spend a long time gazing at an adorable doll in a pretty dress that's sitting on a shelf. Behind my back Madame Guillou looks at me looking at the doll, her attention equal to mine, intense and indiscreet.

"That doll belonged to my daughter when she was a child. My daughter never liked dolls."

As I make my way home, slowly, dragging my feet down each step, I have all the time in the world to think that if life were arranged better, it wouldn't be wrong for Madame Guillou's daughter not to like dolls or for me to love them.

PEDRO ALMEVIDA

I am the father, the husband, the *paterfamilias*. I have a thick black moustache that's carefully waxed and tapered at both ends, a carnivore's teeth, and a quick temper. Construction worker. Créteil, Nanterre, Villetanneuse, sometimes in the provinces too. My wife, Rose-Alba Almevida, is a concierge on rue Cochin in the fifth arrondissement. When I've made my fortune I'll go back to my native land. Ten or fifteen years of exile, if I have to. I'll exhaust my legal status as a foreigner in this foreign city. And go back home. I'll have a spacious house made of whitewashed adobe. Inside, every modern convenience. A small field beside it, planted with vines, as straight as a die. The ideal would be to spend nothing here. Except for what's necessary. Put everything aside. And go back to Spain. But now Rose-Alba Almevida, my wife, my spendthrift, my glory and my torment, lets my money slip away, fleet as mercury. It's true that I attain seventh heaven with her, both day and night. That's worth a little present now and then. As if I could afford it.

Miguel, Miguel, my son, look me in the eye once, only once, look me in the eye and I'll give you the earth.

I bought him a soccer ball in exchange for the doll I broke. He wouldn't take the ball and he hasn't stopped crying.

Maybe I was wrong to have wanted a boy so badly when Rosita was pregnant. It didn't bring me much luck. Before the ultrasound, I even told her quite seriously as she looked at me with outrage: "If it's a girl I'll throw her to the pigs."

Her grave and quivering voice: "If you ever do such a thing, Pedro my husband, I'll kill you."

ROSE-ALBA ALMEVIDA

"Madame Almevida! Madame Almevida! The garbage stinks in the courtyard! It's been three days now! Get rid of it, woman, and fast!"

Rosa, Rosie, Rosita, little feet, fleshy lips, round shoulders, the most beautiful woman to dance with, people are calling to you from the depths of hell, they want to see you on a dung heap, on a pile of rotting things, with your cool hands, your perfumed breath, your light heart. Use your dainty fingers to sew fine fabrics. Clandestine work, clandestine machinery, in aid of the vultures of the Sentier. Money!

Money! I need money! I'm being robbed! Exploited like a blind negress. Money. Fast, before my husband checks the cash in the blue box under the bed. It could happen though that I'll hang myself first, like a charm at the head of the bed, swaying and sticking out its tongue.

"Madame Almevida!"

They say "Madame" to my face. But under their breath they call me "Marquise." I know they do. I know everything. Oh, if I could I'd empty their garbage onto their heads, but that's not in my contract, and I must fulfill its every clause to the letter. Under threat of being fired. So I'll dump the trash into those big containers, with orange or green lids, that you see on city sidewalks in the morning. But I'll put them out around midnight so I can sleep peacefully during the fine hours of dawn, as I like to do, with the grey shadows holding the chirping of birds as they answer one another from tree to tree.

After Operation Trash I'll take my son to bathe at the Bains des Patriarches, at Censier-Daubenton, where the towels are so big, the water so hot, and the tubs so deep.

My husband is in Saint-Nazaire nailing boards and putting up house frames. I'll be sleeping alone. I'll take the boy into my bed. The two of us in the sweetness that follows a bath. Poor little angel, he cried so hard when his father broke the doll Madame Guillou had given him.

MIGUEL ALMEVIDA

He did it on purpose. He picked her up by the feet and threw her onto the kitchen floor. My poor doll broken into a hundred pieces. Shattered. An old-fashioned doll, very brittle and gorgeous. He was all red, like the flag you wave before a bull to excite him. He's a bull himself, my father, breathing hard in his rage. He said again and again, as if he were cracked in the head: "No you don't, little boy! No you don't! Never!" And went out, slamming the door.

I cried so hard I could have drowned in my tears. A lake at my feet with pieces of doll floating in it, like crumbs on a plate for the birds. And now I've taken his place in the big bed, next to my mother. Too much happiness. Too much. Both of us, my mother and I, smelling good, warm and smooth in the same way after our bath at the Patriarches, close to one another now in the clean sheets. Twins in a single white shell. Yet I'm crying as if I were all alone in my folding bed on the floor of the kitchen, between the table and the buffet.

I finally fall asleep with my mother's feet against mine, "To warm me with your little furnaces," she said.

He came home sooner than expected and carried me, fast asleep, out of the big bed, like a sack of potatoes transported cautiously.

It wasn't till the next morning, as I was getting ready to leave for school, that I started gathering up my things.

Once I was there I told my plan to my friend Karine, who always listens to me and sometimes lends me her Barbie doll. "I'm leaving. My mind's made up. I'm not staying in the house with that stranger."

Karine asked me what stranger I was talking about. I told her it was my father.

ROSE-ALBA ALMEVIDA

That child is going to drive me crazy. My most expensive blush! My finest tweezers! My thickest eyebrow pencil! He took it all away with him in the red suitcase. He did it, he did it, my son Miguel who ran away this morning. It's now five p.m. And I, his mother, am going stark raving mad. My knees are quivering. My hands are freezing. Me, crazy, all by myself in the house. My husband in Saint-Nazaire. My son miles away. What bad luck! I'm suffering like a martyr in the olden days, in the convents of Spain. The police! Should I call the police? To hunt for my son like a criminal. My hair is too black, not yet dyed Venetian blond, I'll pull it out, one hair at a time, as a sign of despair.

For a good fifteen minutes now someone has been pounding on the door of the lodge. Madame Guillou is calling to me as if she were mad.

I'm coming, I'm coming, Guillou, Guillou, you asked for it. I'm foaming with rage and if I open the door to you, you'll see what it means to be a Spanish woman in *la furia* of living.

MIGUEL ALMEVIDA

I roamed the streets. All day long. Dragging the red suitcase. Changing arms. Setting it down on the sidewalk here and there, to rest. I was hungry. I was thirsty. I was afraid. I was cold. I cried a little. Night comes early in November. I felt the dampness of the night on my back. The city was at its worst. Malevolent and foul. The breath of the city on my neck. Hooligans breathing very close to me, their rotten eyes staring at me as I walked by. I decided to take refuge with Madame Guillou. Right away she took my hand and delivered me back to my mother. I didn't put up a fight, I was limp and contrite. Crying my eyes out. My mother held me in her arms, tightly enough to break my bones. I wailed in a voice so piercing that Madame Guillou stood there petrified, stabbed by my howls as if by a hundred Andalusian daggers plunged into her widow's heart.

Another night without my father. An entire night in my mother's bed. Myself all icy up against her, she blazing hot and musky after all the emotions I'd subjected her to while I was a runaway.

At dawn, my mother, who usually doesn't get up till noon, started shaking me the way she shakes her bedside rug from the kitchen window once a month, in a cloud of dust, fine grey incense swirling all the way up to the sixth floor. I thought I'd die from that shaking.

She said again: "No, no, I won't tell your father, I promised, but you do it again and I'll make mincemeat out of you."

I left for school without breakfast, my whole body trembling.

PEDRO ALMEVIDA

I am the husband, the father, the master of the house. I put food on the table for my family. With my pay in my pocket, I go home. Here I am in the train. Ten days in Saint-Nazaire, hammering and nailing in the November wind and rain. I could take my wife right on the doorstep, the minute I arrive, I want her so badly. But first I want to make myself handsome, blazingly handsome, from head to toe. I'll put up with the filthy toilets at the train station for the time that it takes to shave and shower. I'll put on a clean shirt and the shiny shoes that go with it. I'll show up at the door of my house like a knight home from battle.

With every trace of sweat and toil erased, I go home. I close my eyes and already my arms are filled with her, my beauty, Rosa, Rosie, Rosita Almevida, my wife.

ROSE-ALBA ALMEVIDA

I'll have a surprise for him. I'll dye my hair. After a ten-day absence he'll have a surprise. Myself, transformed. Into a Venetian blonde. Claudia Schiffer, but better. More flesh on the bones. A golden splendour emerging from the shadows like a blinding sun too long held captive.

The hairdresser studies me, looks me up and down. For him I don't exist. I'm just a head. No body or soul, just a head at the tip of a lance for him to take and transform to his liking.

He talks as if he were dreaming out loud. He appears to see what he's saying, clearly before him. It's obvious that I inspire him. "I'll dye your hair. I'll cut your hair. I'll transform you drastically. Let me do it, you're too dark, you have the beginnings of a moustache. I'll release you from the darkness. Leave, leave your decapitated head in my hands. I'll make it into a resplendent idol."

What he says, he does. I am delivered into his hands like a dead animal that's turned over and over, washed and embalmed. Once the operation is over, there appears in the mirror before me a golden sparkling creature who claims to be me. I behave myself and dare not contradict her. Absorbed in my infinite contemplation.

"That's 600 francs," says the hairdresser.

I haggle with him. By way of payment I offer him the long hair he's cut off. He studies the heavy sheaf of black hair that has fallen to the floor. Gathers it up, holds it in his hands, hefts it, sniffs it. He maintains that it's Asian hair, straight and coarse, and that it's worthless next to a fine and silky Scandinavian mane. I offer to leave a deposit and come back tomorrow with the rest. The hairdresser smiles, shakes his head, says again softly, tenderly almost, like a cooing pigeon: "Cash, cash, cash, my lovely."

I offer him my gold wedding ring and take back the mass of my hair and cram it into my shopping bag. He accepts my ring after he's felt its weight and clinked it on the counter.

I go home, a tiny white line like an old scar on the fourth finger of my left hand.

MIGUEL ALMEVIDA

What I saw, what I heard between my father and my mother was so frightening, I'll never be able to speak it without dying a second time. The first time, I was hiding under the kitchen table, my jacket over my face, my fists over my ears. Waiting for catastrophe. There won't be a second time, I swear. I couldn't bear it. Yet images, words swirl around me still while I sleep.

"Get out, you aren't my wife any more. I don't recognize you."

A small blond head rises and bristles. "I'm someone else, blond and desirable, a genuine star. Take me and you'll see how beautiful I am."

"What have you done with the long black hair that I loved?"

"Here, take it. It's yours."

She opens her shopping bag and pitches a black mop at his head; he flings it to the floor and stomps on it.

My heart is beating hard enough to crack my ribs. I implore the angels of the night. To come and pull a crimson curtain over the high drama of family scenes. So I can curl up between the sheets.

A little tune, light and persistent, slowly moves away with the dream that's nearly over.

"The ring, the ring you gave me, Pedro my husband, I've lost it, I lost it on my way to the market."

Their voices, unrecognizable, singsongy, die somewhere inside me.

PEDRO ALMEVIDA

She's lying. I'm sure that she's lying. I'll rub her nose in her lie. Oh, she'll admit the truth in the end. There is female deception beneath it. Sly dishonour to a man. It's not clean.

It's diabolical like the Trinity, the Incarnation, and everything else we don't understand. One day it will be crystal clear. Everyone crowded into the Valley of Jehoshaphat. The Last Judgment. The mysteries revealed. It's then that I'll know for certain what my wife did with the gold ring given to her by me and blessed by a priest in a church in Seville on May 28th, 1977.

I take her to the market at the hour when they hose down the square. She and I bend over, looking down at the ground. Among the puddles, the gleaming asphalt, lettuce cores, gutted oranges, apple peels, overripe pears, all rotten things, swept away by the gushing water. Gold ring, little wedding ring, are you here? We might as well be trying to find a needle in a haystack. Rose-Alba Almevida cries and says that it's pointless to look. She asks me to forgive her. For nothing, she says. To do as I want, she maintains. I'll kill her one day.

She is wearing tight black satin trousers and a bright orange shirt with puffed sleeves. With her makeup on, something like shiny little beads drop onto her cheeks from her eyelids. A marvel. I won't tell her that her legs are too short. I feel like being kind to her again.

She takes me to Madame Guillou's. Madame Guillou's bathroom. Tile on the walls and floor. Gleaming, blue and white. I'm here to fix the leaking radiator. Rose-Alba Almevida, my wife and my torment, feasts her eyes on the splendour of Madame Guillou's bathroom. I touch her arm to wrench her from her daze. Tears fill her eyes and her lips quiver like a child trying not to cry. When she's back in the lodge she says again and again: "It isn't fair. It isn't fair."

And she goes to the landing to get water from the faucet there.

I promise her that one day we'll have saved enough for her

to have her own bathroom, white and blue. It will be in Spain, surrounded by vines.

She says that what she wants is a fur coat.

MIGUEL ALMEVIDA

The life that we have to put up with, day after day, ever since the construction site in Saint-Nazaire was shut down for good two weeks ago. My father is at home from morning to night, from night to morning. He smokes cigarettes one after another. When I go outside I can smell the smoke on me as if I were my father himself. I'm like someone walking around with a hundred lit cigarettes in his mouth. I reek of them. I'm only ten years old but it upsets me. I have to step over banks of smoke as soon as I'm inside my house. He is there watching me through the blue puffs of smoke. This is not the time to contradict him. It's as if he's watching a bull being released into the ring. I tiptoe past him. Above all he mustn't know that I skip rope at recess like a girl even though he's forbidden it.

At night I have a dream while he sleeps next to my mother, like a newborn gorged with cigarettes.

A skipping rope hangs down from the ceiling where it meets the wall. It unfurls downwards by itself, very slowly, like a snake descending. I know they're going to beat me with that rope, that's why it's coming towards me. I lie on the ground. I prepare myself for the beating. I beg my father: "Please, not too hard, I'm so tired."

Is it only in my dream that I cry out? The two of them come to my bedside, barefoot and in their nightclothes. They advise me to be good and to sleep the way the angels sleep, without a sound.

The end of a dark childhood on rue Cochin.

II

JEAN-EPHREM DE LA TOUR

Tall stature, small heart, black skin, white smile, green and blue feathers on top of my shaved head, I am Jean-Ephrem de la Tour. Dancer at the Paradis Perdu. Lights pointed all over my skin, from top to bottom, night after night. I'm turning into an American star. Silver wings fastened to my shoulders. I flame and I die in a single breath. I rule over a population of dancers and acrobats. While jugglers and snake charmers in the backstage shadows secretly indulge in base jealousies and the audience rises to its feet, giving me a thunderous ovation.

I meet him around five in the evening on my way to the post office. He, lost child, little heap of dejection, collapsed on a step of a staircase on rue Saint-Victor. I bend over him. "Hey, little beast! Better straighten up or you'll be hunchbacked.

Unfold yourself, little beast, before it's too late."

Frozen with dread, he looks at me unblinkingly. Fear, unalloyed, in his wide-open eyes. I relish it. Will never forget this first fear in his eyes. Bound to him, the frightened child, by the terror that is visible all over his little person curled on a staircase on rue Saint-Victor around five p.m. Such is his destiny, no doubt, to be frightened by me. Such is my own, no doubt, to put the finishing touch on a dread already old, as if it were the original terror, within him. I tell him again to straighten up, not to stay there sitting on the ground. He obeys me as though he can't do otherwise. Fear trembles between his very long lashes. I give him a smile that shows all my inordinately white, strong teeth. I bow to him. I wish him a good day. I wish him a good evening. Ask him not to be afraid of me. Tell him that I'm good when I want to be and that I love him madly, just like that, at first sight, the way we love the sun when we rise in the morning. He says it's not possible and that his mother is expecting him for dinner. He wants to leave. I take his hand. I put his two soft blazing hands in my own hard one. I talk to him about the Paradis Perdu. I tell him about the dancers and acrobats, the music and chatter, the feathers and sequins, the barely pubescent boys and girls transformed under the footlights, carried away till dawn by their passion for life. He listens to me closely and dread works all its tricks in him and on him, skin-deep, like a fever that's subsiding. Seduction has its way and he asks me where to find the Paradis Perdu. I put a pass in his hand. Tell him I'll be expecting him tonight, backstage, and that he'll be able to see the whole show.

"See you later, little beast. Make sure that you're there."

He goes off so quickly, so agile and light, like a squirrel, that I wonder if he will still exist after this first meeting between us on rue Saint-Victor.

His name is Miguel Almevida. He whispered it in my ear before he disappeared like a vision of him that I might have had before dying.

I don't know yet that he has just turned fifteen.

MIGUEL ALMEVIDA

I've waited so long for this night filled with risk, without knowing I was waiting for it, timidly, amid the erosion of childhood, day after day, despondent, often crying. And now the feast for which I was destined, for all eternity, throbs softly like a quivering heart behind the walls of the Paradis Perdu. Slipped through the darkness of the streets for the first time, alone and dressed in my finery in the night. Far away is my father, who's unemployed most of the time, hidden by his smoke like a cuttlefish by its ink. Far away, too, is my seamstress mother with her deafening sewing machine. The thieves of the Sentier who exploit workers will have gotten off lightly. One day my mother will be queen and I'll be the king at her side.

Tonight I make my entrance into the world. The world is opening before me. A little longer and I'll know the secrets of the earth. Dear God, how innocent I am and how my knees are trembling. This is the little hidden gate I must pass through to experience the living splendour of the universe.

He is there behind the door, waiting for me as promised. Half-naked, black, smooth, the eyes enlarged with kohl, the mouth blood-red, the teeth awe-inspiring, green and blue egret feathers on his head, silver wings on his shoulder blades, he is the angel of darkness, born for his own ruination and for mine. His shadow on the wall is that of a giant, bristling with strange frills and flounces.

He tells me to go away and I go. He tells me come here and I come. Upon my obedience my happiness depends. When the curtain goes up on the show, I shall be ready to see everything, to hear everything. The very wellspring of the earth will be revealed to me then, in bursts of music.

He asks for something to drink and I fetch it, wandering the unfamiliar corridors and stairways where half-dressed boys and girls go back and forth, not yet ready for the show, in the process of being transformed into angels or devils.

He says again, Little Beast, do this, do that.

I murmur so quietly he has to bend over to hear me: "My name is Miguel Almevida and I'm not a beast."

He laughs so hard that his wings clash together on his back. He claims that it's a compliment, that for him the word "beast" is sacred and that only gods are entitled to be called it. In a deep voice, almost too deep, he adds: "Little Beast is fine, it's beautiful, it resembles you. Call me Beautiful Beast in return. And everything will be equal between us, the animal and the sacred. Except that I'm the one who is master."

He laughs again. His wings stir. He grabs my hand, places it against his naked chest. "Can you feel my heart beating, Little Beast? Stroke my heart, the way you'd stroke the breast of a black horse to reassure it before a race. In a few minutes I'll be on the track, pawing the ground and scared to death. Call me Beautiful Beast and wish me luck. Say break a leg, break a leg, break a leg, in my ear. Tonight the corrida will be terrible, I can sense it. They might cut off my ears and my tail as they do in your country. You'll no doubt be given the honours of the ears and tail. They'll bring them to you on a silver platter. Little Beast, idiotic and sweet, you'll know this very night what a real feast is. All of life, all of death, on a silver platter like the bloody head of John the Baptist."

He talks like a book that I've never read. He chokes with

laughter. He straightens his wings. I stand there frozen, my hand on the naked chest that becomes misty little by little from a slight sweatiness like dew.

This man possesses the knowledge of good and evil, that's certain.

Three muffled knocks ring out in the dark. Everyone on stage. The feathers, the plumes, the fake jewels, the sequins suddenly appear, jostle me along the way, warm bodies brush against me, the mingled odours of girls and boys prickle my nose, go to my head. The black sun of nocturnal feasts will rise once again above the stage of the Paradis Perdu.

Between the dressing rooms and the stage I listen to the unleashed music, to the dancers' rhythmic feet. Noisy inhalations, laboured breathing dart across my face like quick drafts of air.

After this I'll never be the same, dressed in childhood as in a piece of clothing that's too tight.

The tallest and the handsomest of them all is Jean-Ephrem de la Tour. His long legs, his long arms, his misty chest, the whole of his body that rushes forward and soars, undulates and sways, contorts itself and comes undone, then immediately re-forms itself again, intact and pure, to the sound of some discordant music.

He wraps himself in a big towel and sweats so much it's as if he'd fallen into the Seine. Half-naked boys and girls bring him food and drink. He signals me to leave. "Get lost, Little Beast! I'm tired."

I go home, alone in the night as it draws to a close.

ROSE-ALBA ALMEVIDA

I no longer have a son. I disown him. I mourn him. I hate him. I could tear his eyes out. He came in at dawn, haggard, with circles under his eyes, exhausted as a hooker at daybreak. My husband says that's just fine, his son is now a man and it reassures him to know it. "Involved with a woman at fifteen," he repeats proudly. He laughs. While I cry. Probably Karine, the pale little freckle-faced nitwit who came here from the cold countries. What a disaster! Pedro my husband tells me to be quiet and let his son rest till late tomorrow morning. I obey and I fall asleep in the warmth of my tears.

PEDRO ALMEVIDA

I have just one son who has never been mine. Hardly out of childhood and now he sleeps like a new man after love. Everything is finished between us without ever having begun. I am not the father. He is not the son. He's asleep now. In his dreams he is arming himself against me. He must grow and I must be diminished. So it is written.

I set my mind at rest. For a moment I remind myself of my inalienable rights as head of the household. I dictate my last wishes: a tough virile son finally out of school, which only numbs the mind, dropped into the world of work with nerves of steel and arms of iron. Let his strength have no equal but mine until I die. Amen.

Two men in a house is too many. Who will be the first to drive the other out?

MIGUEL ALMEVIDA

Night poured down over the city by the bucketful, laden with stars or with storms, night keeping watch around the street-lamps, encircling them, night, supreme, spilled out all around, outside, inside, even in the concierge's lodge on rue Cochin at the family dinner hour.

Patience, my soul. Another mouthful or two, another word or two exchanged around the table and the lights of the Paradis Perdu will be turned on like a beacon in the city and I will be free to run towards its strange forms of bliss. I drop my napkin onto the table. In anticipation my heart fills with spells and dread. I slam the door. I'm outside.

"That child is intolerable," says my mother.

"The girl who's got hold of him is a devil, that's certain," says my father.

"Sure, sure, sure. I have to know," says my mother. She gets up from the table, dons her red hunting jacket, her bright earrings, she goes onto the street, follows me from a distance all the way to the Paradis Perdu, buys her ticket, and sits in the front row, between two elderly gentlemen who ogle her greedily.

I don't notice my mother there in the dark until my gaze, shifting from the wings to the audience, settles on her by chance.

She came backstage after the show. They asked if she was there for an audition. A bunch of girls and boys, their makeup half-removed. They measured her, weighed her. Laughed at her. Cried, "Oh!" Cried, "Ah!" While studying the numbers on the ruler and the scale. They told her she was outside the norm, buxom and squat, she repeats "buxom" and "squat," mulling over the unfamiliar words as if they were insults. She weeps with rage.

Jean-Ephrem de la Tour approaches her, wrapped in his big towel. With one movement of his long upraised arm he waves away the mockers surrounding my mother. The towel is half-off him and she can see his black streaming chest. She looks and doesn't blink. He takes my mother's face very gently in his two hands, their orange palms, in the way one might hold a newly opened peony about to shed its petals.

"What a lovely face you have there, Madame!"

I cry out: "But she's my mother!"

He doubles up with laughter. The towel at his feet. He is immersed in his sweat and his laughter, almost naked before her. To her, he represents everything about the Paradis Perdu, its wonders and its infernal rhythms, the entire world of magic she's always dreamed about. My mother's desire to lose herself in the whirlwind is as strong as my own.

He asks for the towel which has fallen to the floor. He shivers and trembles. Says that he's going to catch his death of cold.

My mother's eyes are glued to me as I pick up the towel and drape it over the shoulders of Jean-Ephrem de la Tour in a way that lets my mother know I belong to this man, body and soul.

As I wrap him in the towel and rub him down vigorously, we exist so powerfully together, he and I, that it makes my mother want to fight me. Her dearest wish would be to be in my place, close to Jean-Ephrem de la Tour.

She declares that she's never seen anything as wonderful as the show at the Paradis Perdu. Then she says nothing for a long time, consumed by bitter silence.

Jean-Ephrem de la Tour steps into the shower. He exclaims: "Screw off, Little Beast, and take your mother too, I need to get some rest."

Rose-Alba Almevida leads me away, drags me by the hand as if punishing a child. On rue Cochin not even a small lamp is lit, the lodge is dark, more of a rat hole than ever. My father is no longer there.

PEDRO ALMEVIDA

Out of my home, thrown onto the street, I'm outside my house like a snail without its shell. At the corner café I drink white wine. I search in vain for what's true and what's not. Try to untangle reality from dream. Sourness in me as if I'd eaten sour cabbage. I struggle to sort out my ideas. I kick the bar. Head down. I examine the fake marble. I see in it vague lines like the ones in my head. Determined to shake off all my concerns like dead leaves in autumn, I drink white wine. With shirtsleeves rolled up, bare elbows on the fake cold marble, I consider the twists and turns in my mind and in the shimmering marble. Then all at once, mingling with the glints on the counter and the whirlwinds in my head, she appears and she struts before me as if she were innocent. She takes her black hair that she's had cut off, that I used to love, and flings it in my face. My loved one, my sly one, says "sure, sure, sure," just like that, three times, then runs onto the street and doesn't come back. Setting off on the trail of the ungrateful son we made together one night in Spain at the hour when gardens collapse under their heavy scents.

Suddenly gusts of jasmine and orange blossom sweep into the smoke-filled room where I drain my glass. I'm astonished, for a long time, especially since I'm apparently the only one of the drinkers seated here to detect the sweet perfumes quickly transformed into the most acid vinegar, then all at once I fall asleep with my head on my arms, like a dead beast.

MIGUEL ALMEVIDA

Faster, always faster, I must live without wasting one minute, I've got just enough time, too many minutes wasted in the day, waiting for evening and the enchanted night that speeds along so quickly it's already over by the time I get my breath back. At eight p.m. I start getting ready and I take a long look at my face in the little mirror hanging on the bedroom wall. Behind me, my mother grows impatient and demands her share of the mirror. She doesn't like my face with makeup on and wants to obliterate it, replacing it with her own beautiful countenance. Fraternal struggle for a little piece of mirror. False eyelashes and mascara. Complicity and mutual adoration. This happens on those evenings when my father isn't home, when he's in the suburbs or the provinces, nails and hammers, going about his construction worker's business, and we're free, my mother and I, to go to the Paradis Perdu.

I offer roses to the customers there. I go between the tables selling roses. Tight trousers and silk shirt, hair falling onto my forehead and neck, I earn my living at the Paradis Perdu. No more school.

Every night, Jean-Ephrem de la Tour gives my mother a pass for the promenade gallery. She loves being there among the damp bodies crowded around her, she watches the show so intensely that it hurts her eyes, as if she were looking too long at the sun. Sometimes the warmth of a hand brushes her too closely, slips onto her, settles on her hip, burns her, makes her limp as a melting candle. She frees herself gently, smoothes the pleats of her black taffeta skirt and says: "Hands off."

Very quickly, she turns back to the show, all trembling and wet.

The greatest marvel of the evening is unquestionably Jean-Ephrem de la Tour, with plumes on his head and his quivering wings unfurled. He moves and dances. His tall body vibrates and sways. He is radiant; a thousand stars at once, all the way to the back of the house, pierce my heart, while I prick my fingers on the roses' thorns.

No echo lingers in the deserted auditorium. It's all over. Backstage, calm is gradually restored.

He is quiet, rested, after the shower water has gushed over his exhausted body. It seems to me that he's thinner. What had to happen is happening right now. Jean-Ephrem de la Tour invites me to his place. With my father at home and my mother keeping him company, I'm as free as the dark air of the nights, where I so love being just now.

ROSE-ALBA ALMEVIDA

After the festivities at the Paradis Perdu there is the conjugal vigil in the lodge on rue Cochin. Bare-chested, Pedro Almevida, my husband, is lifting weights. He won't fight with me until his biceps are just right.

He puts his shirt back on and sits astride a chair, facing me. He lists his grievances in a monotonous voice. He leaves nothing out and I get bored listening to him, I'm like an accused person waiting to hear the expected sentence. What's different now is that I don't love him any more and he doesn't love me. The Paradis Perdu has come between us, like a continent of perverse wonders where I am happy and where he will never set foot.

"My wife is a thief!"

And he mentions the vacation money that I took to buy myself a dress from Marie-Christine a thousand years ago.

"My wife is a bad mother!"

And he talks about Miguel who is turning out badly and who sells roses at the music hall.

"My wife is a slut!"

And he keeps harping on about my mane of hair that was sacrificed to offend him.

"My wife is a whore!"

And he says that he knows all about it, about the promenade gallery and the Paradis Perdu.

"You aren't my wife any more and I'm not your husband."

And he takes me so forcibly that I bleed like I did the first time.

JEAN-EPHREM DE LA TOUR

It's engraved in Gothic letters on my performer's card. It's written in capital letters on the program of the Paradis Perdu. Jean-Ephrem de la Tour, star dancer. It would be unwise for anyone to try to trace all the names and surnames that have been lost along the way, as far back as the early records of the children's aid department.

Miguel Almevida. Little brother, oh, little brother of the poor. Not yet born. Not puny. Slim in the extreme. With great empty eyes and curls falling onto his forehead.

He's at my place. Advancing cautiously, leaving trails behind him on the thick carpet, like someone strolling along the soft sand of a beach.

Little by little he sees everything. His eyes veined with yellow and green fill with the strangeness of the place. Small gilt chairs, walls hung with crimson velvet, shelves of leather-bound books, concert grand piano, deep sofas, Chinese screen, huge mirrors waiting only for the slightest smile, the most secret tear in the shadow of eyelashes.

He thinks it surpasses the Paradis Perdu itself in magnificence. He is no longer moving at all. He's like an acrobat stopped short on his wire, in great danger of death. He looks at the brass barre on the wall, the pouffes on the floor, the subdued lamplight, the low tables covered with strange objects of gold and silver.

I extend the tour a little farther. I take him to see the first bedroom, the whirlpool bath that fills it completely, the second bedroom with the huge bed sitting on a platform, the white muslin canopy that falls like a bridal veil.

He listens and looks. He sits on the floor as if he'd fallen there. Frozen in place, knees pulled up to his chin, arms hugging his knees. The look in his eyes is that of a freshly killed hare.

Knowing perfectly well that he's had more than enough, I continue nonetheless to show him around my loft.

"Take a good look, Little Beast, look very closely at this wonderful loft that is mine, learn to call it by that strange name you've never heard before. Repeat it after me: loft, loft, loft. It's awesome, as you might say. You can see Paris by night through the big windows streaming with rain. Here, come closer. Take a good look. Lean out a little. It's no small matter, the seventh floor. Careful, don't get dizzy. It's shiny and shimmery down there on the pavement, from the rain. All those cars are heading somewhere, that's certain, each person with an idea in his head, an appointment, verifiable or fictitious, wipers beating against the windshield like a heart through tears. Watch out, you're liable to skid behind the Sacré-Coeur that stands there like a huge white cake. Twisted cars. Ambulances, police and firemen, screaming sirens. Soon we'll have to take stock of the night that is ending and decide between the dead and the living, while dawn falls over the city like the silver drizzle of rain."

I offer him champagne. In a barely audible voice, he asks for a Coke.

I tell him that his mother is very beautiful but that it won't last. "Once she's old, you'll have to throw her away and stop clinging to her like a sickly child." I laugh so hard I can barely hear what he says.

He protests with all his might, though he's already doubting the truth of his own words. "My mother will always be beautiful, she'll never be old, she'll always be beautiful. And as for me, I don't cling to anything or anybody." He's on his feet and looks like a lost child in a train station. He says that he wants to go.

"All right, Little Beast, go. It's raining and you'll get soaked. It's your choice if you want a scolding from your mother before daybreak."

His quick steps in the direction of the door. A little farther and he'll be outside.

I hold him back. Show him the full-length portrait painted by a perverse artist. "Take a good look at that portrait. It's me, with my feathers unfolded, nailed to the wall by my wings, like an owl on the door of a barn. Take a good look at my face at the moment of my ruin. It's the face I show sometimes to anyone who can bear it. Take advantage of it. My moment of truth won't return for a long time."

Suddenly he throws himself at me like a furious cat. He pounds my chest with punches that reverberate in my ribs. I smell his scent, the odour of a frightened and furious beast. I free myself and breathe deeply. My fatigue is immeasurable. I tell him to leave. He gets his breath back and delivers a sentence that doesn't seem to belong to him.

"I don't want you to be alive, or dead either. I would like you to not exist."

Miguel Almevida walks away down the deserted street, in the rain. No doubt he's afraid of the darkness and the emptiness around him, above all afraid of me. But until the end of the world he won't be able to stop himself from doing what he has to do in order to be afraid.

MIGUEL ALMEVIDA

I run in the rain. My shoes are full of water. My hair drips onto my neck. Loft, loft, loft — a strange word in my mouth, like a soft caramel that's been chewed and chewed again. Just one word, one small word that I've learned tonight and that means everything: the gilt chairs, the velvet walls. Jean-Ephrem de la Tour in his loft, like a Negro king in his castle all red and black. His noxious heart rendered visible on his entire ravaged body. The painter who did that is cursed, that's certain.

I run away. I go home, all alone in the exhausting night. I live in a rat hole, according to my mother. I sleep on a folding bed, right on the floor. I know the linoleum by heart, seeing it from so close, with its green leaves, its pink flowers, its worn spots, and its slightest cracks. But before I sleep I must appear before my parents.

Now the day is coming from every part of the city at once, grey and hazy. It pierces me more than the night itself, it wraps me in anguish from head to toe.

ROSE-ALBA ALMEVIDA

The garbage fire in the cellar. The firemen who arrive as I throw the first bucket of water onto the flames of the foul-smelling mound. A rat, two rats break away from it. I wish I could die. To die from having let the garbage accumulate, to die from not being allowed to let it pile up without being immediately punished by fire like a witch at the stake. To die of disgust, quite simply. It's as good as cancer or a heart that gives out. Killing me. My white hands, my scented body. I couldn't care less about the filth that this building secretes every day, like stinking crap.

In chorus, tenants and owners squawk at my door. "Madame Almevida! Madame Almevida! There's a fire! Do something!"

I'd like to throw the lot of them into a common grave to

rot in silence, in the darkness of the earth, until their bones are stripped clean.

All day I have time only to sew, hunched over my machine which fills the house with its deafening racket. Driving me crazy. I work for thieves who exploit seamstresses working from home. It might last and then again it might not. One day I'll denounce them. For the time being, I need the money. I want a fur coat and I'll have it. I'll wear it to the Paradis Perdu. That's where I'm happiest, among creatures from a dream, adorned to the hilt, flung into the furnace alive, to the sound of thunderous music.

The promenade delights me more than anything else in the world. Its friendly darkness, its animal warmth against my hip, its delightful crowd of mature and knowledgeable men lying in wait in the shadows.

"Madame Almevida! Madame Almevida! You're dreaming! For heaven's sake wake up! The place is full of smoke. I'm suffocating. My eyes are burning. Do something!"

"Fire's under control. The firemen are sure. Go home."

Pedro Almevida, my husband, gently shoos them out of the lodge, shoves them almost tenderly, leads them to the stairs in the dark, flicks the switch. Five a.m. in November. They aren't a pretty sight in the bright light, the tenants and owners together. You old pile of brightly coloured bathrobes, I don't like you, I never have and I never will. I'll go to the Paradis Perdu and take a break from all of you and from life in general.

At last we're alone. I take off my pink satin dressing gown. Before I get into bed, I accuse my husband of throwing his cigarette onto the garbage in the cellar. He shrugs, says I'm crazy. I think he's laughing in my face. I look for my son. I find him asleep, as usual, on his little camp bed between the buffet and the table. I'll never know when he came home. Too much bedlam tonight to know what's really going on in my house.

MIGUEL ALMEVIDA

Quiet nights in the fifth arrondissement. My father left the house right after he tried to strangle my mother. She was probably screaming too loudly before she blacked out, and he was afraid of annoying the owners and tenants, who would agree to call the police.

He lit a cigarette and left, smoking — for Spain, he said. Taking none of the necessary things, no jacket, no pants, no razor, no shirt, no clean underwear, no baggage, nothing, hands in his pockets, cigarette stuck in his mouth, red-faced though, like someone who's not in his normal state. His heart was beating so hard you could hear it in the kitchen until he left through the front door.

Sitting on the floor, half-choked, my mother came back to life, with the marks of my father's fingers around her neck.

"All he had to do was not look under the bed where I hide my things. All he had to do was not see my fur coat in its golden cardboard box. But who could have told him about Monsieur Athanase?" my mother finally managed to say, between two fits of choking.

The coat lies on the floor, sprawled like a great dead animal.

Rose-Alba Almevida, half-undressed and torn apart and trembling, drags herself over to the coat, strokes it gently as if she were petting a cat. "This coat cost me a lot." Then come some incoherent words interrupted by sobs, about the promenade gallery and the encounters that take place. "He told me I was as lovely as a picture and he took me to the furrier right after we left the four-star *hôtel de passe* on the quay."

Something terrible went on inside my father's head, as if the red cape that's waved before a bull had been waved right in front of my father's narrow brain, as if thin banderillas had been planted in his heart, and my father came very close to murdering my mother, the short breath of murder up against my father's furious face. He couldn't tolerate that, the thought of murder. He went away, taking nothing. Maybe he's hoping to find what he wants back in Spain — their old life, intact and pure, my mother with her long black hair, smiling at him. Me, still unborn. Her, innocent of me and of him. Content to wear her bridal crown perfectly straight on her raven hair arranged in an extravagant chignon. Her long veil falling to the floor in cascades of transparent white. If only the blond prostitute who's taken my mother's place on rue Cochin in Paris would disappear forever. What my father couldn't do I'll do myself one day. The murder of Rose-Alba Almevida will take place. I, the son, cover my face with my hands and weep. Dishonour is upon our house, posted at the entrance like a quarantine notice. Already contaminated by dishonour here in my rat's hole, I love my mother more than anything in the world. I forgive her for everything.

ROSE-ALBA ALMEVIDA

The marks on my throat are changing colour, from red to violet, from violet to blue, from blue to a dirty yellowish green. I wrap a silk scarf around my neck. I hide my wound and my fury behind the silk that was given to me by the man from the promenade gallery. I'm hibernating in my lodge. I'll stay there as long as that cruel necklace, a gift from Pedro Almevida, my husband, stays around my neck.

My son looks at me with eyes filled with alarm. He puts ice cubes in a transparent plastic bag around my neck. He speaks softly so as not to rouse the last scene, still alive, lurking in the four corners of the darkened kitchen. I can't tolerate any light. Or the lodge, open to everyone. I've pulled the curtain over the glass door that opens onto the landing. A few calls for help come to me, I'm lethargic, they fall around my bed like blunt darts.

"Stairs not done for days, polish, polish, I'm expecting a delivery, stairs caked with dirt, Lafayette, Lafayette, delivery, delivery, urgent, urgent . . ."

I hear distinctly the voice of the blond student with the rough moustache who shouts: "Marquise, come out! We want you on the stairs lively and affable, as usual!" He repeats: "On the stairs! The stairs, Marquise!" His loud laugh rings out from the bottom of the stairwell to the top.

I plug my ears, I close my eyes, I imagine diamonds and gold, fine pearls and blue sapphires to hide my wound, heavy necklaces that sparkle around my neck like a hundred flaming suns when I open my lynx coat partway. And I fall asleep. Sleep and dreams intermingled. My son takes advantage of my sleep to fly away to the Paradis Perdu. I shall join him there when I'm healed.

Money has no odour, they say. But I can smell it as soon as it's inside the house, in the blue box under the bed, its odour as pungent as strong Spanish tobacco, reassuring and comforting. And now I can sense the absence of money, it's like breathing emptiness, a trough in the air that I fall into. Vertigo. My husband's pay has disappeared along with him. Alone with my son. My sewing machine takes off like a galloping horse. "It will kill you, my girl," my mother would say. "The entire marriage bed is yours, my darling," my father would say, "stretch out there full length, full width, like a cat in the sun." Thus encouraged by my father, I fall asleep so calmly that the entire earth, with its gnashing, its trials and tribulations and its terrors, turns against my ear and I can't hear it breathing its warm oppressive breath. The crazy planet that I live on. The blessed promenade where I collapse.

JEAN-EPHREM DE LA TOUR

"Your mother's a whore, Little Beast, your mother's a whore. It was to be expected. I know everything. Monsieur Athanase told me everything. There's no reason to lose your head and drop me like an old sock. You son of a whore, you're never here when I need you. But here you are at last with your arms full of roses, your idiotic eyes showing just enough fear to please me. Where were you yesterday? And the day before? Do you mean to tell me you were taking care of Rose-Alba Almevida, as if she were a martyr under the absent gaze of God? She'll get over the conjugal marks on her magnificent neck, the neck of a Roman matron. And did I have to be on my own twice, without you, facing a ferocious audience on gala evenings? I didn't lift my leg high enough, got a cramp in my right thigh, lost the beat. Tremendous panic all through my body. Beak open, wings folded. Flap, flap, flap. Without you in the front row I break down. I go to pieces. I melt under the lights like a candle on an altar. Little Beast, I like to see you, to be seen by you, when I dance. I want you there, paying attention, holding on to your seat, marvelling at me, endlessly. Nothing else exists, including your mother. I like you to torment yourself over me."

MIGUEL ALMEVIDA

He insulted my mother. He called her the most terrible name that you can possibly call a woman.

I shouted: "And what about you? What about you? Did you never have a mother?"

"Never!" he replied, his great laugh revealing his white teeth, stretching his cheeks to his ears. "Never! Never!" he said again forcefully.

It calmed me a little to know that he's never known a

mother and it helped me understand the insult that's always on the tip of his tongue, all ready to say, as soon as a conversation turns to mothers in general. And then, very quickly, my indignation slipped through my fingers like sand and I knew that he had good reason to complain about me.

He speaks more and more softly, at the very edge of dream and waking. About shortened breath, about gleaming black skin gone dull all at once, about shame and disaster, about my unforgivable absence.

I think that in his unhappiness, he luxuriates in sad words in order to dazzle me with sadness and to make me a prisoner of my bedazzlement like a blind owl flung into the light.

Is it possible that one day I'll be totally blind and a prisoner of Jean-Ephrem de la Tour? For the time being, I just have to promise that I'll always be there when he does his act.

I draped his big towel over his shoulders and led him, dripping sweat and still elated from his own lamentations, to the shower. Before he disappeared under the rushing water, he said in a powerful voice:

"Tell your mother that Monsieur Athanase will be waiting for her at the promenade as soon as she's recovered from her husband's insults."

He emerges from the shower, streaming wet from head to toe. I bring him a dry towel, big and wide, roughly textured the way he likes it. I get ready to rub him down like a horse after a gallop. Very gradually I'm getting used to his black nakedness.

ROSE-ALBA ALMEVIDA

No more being waited on hand and foot, no more bandages around my neck, no more contrite manner or indignant heart. I'm convalescing. I'm visibly regaining my strength. I

long to go back to the Paradis Perdu. I return to the promenade gallery where Monsieur Athanase is waiting for me.
The man who wrung my neck will pay what he must. Once,
only once with Monsieur Athanase, such a beautiful lynx coat
as a bonus, but it isn't enough for my hunger and my thirst,
my anger and my indignation. There will be a long series of
encounters with Monsieur Athanase. In a four-star hotel.
Along the Seine.

In the darkness of the room, Monsieur Athanase prefers no
light at all, I could swear that the *bateaux-mouches* enter the
dark air here, brushing against me like seaweed as they pass by
in the night. He puffs like an ox long before I spread my legs.
He's crazy about me. I'm crazy about what he does to me, what
he teaches me to do. We'll go to hell, the two of us. Together
or separately. It doesn't matter. In any case, Monsieur Athanase
won't be forever. He's too hairy and he smells of cologne.

The true demon in this world is Jean-Ephrem de la Tour.

Monsieur Athanase is going to America. He gave me a
gold ring with a small blue stone that sparkles with a thousand
fires. It reassures him about my faithfulness during his absence
and it dispels his fears about the true generosity of his pathetic
little soul. I wear my ring on the fourth finger of my left hand,
like a bride. I ask forgiveness of no one, not God, not Pedro
Almevida, my husband.

When Monsieur Athanase returns from America, if he
returns, I'll tell him about the apartment I dream of, bright
and vast, with an unobstructed view of the Eiffel Tower.

MIGUEL ALMEVIDA

He looks at me as if he were turning me over and over in
his fingers. His gaze on me, prying and incorruptible. He

adds up my virtues and my flaws: "Back too bent, rib cage too narrow, legs magnificent, legs of a girl, with no hair or knobby kneecaps."

I tell him I've always wanted to be a girl and that I was persecuted on account of it.

He replies: "You would not seek me out had you not already found me. It was Christ who said that, along with some other incomparable things. Remember, for one brief moment in your mother's belly you were both boy and girl, before the preposterous choice to be only a boy. Remember how good it was, remember how sweet it was, a tiny girl without fingers or feet, a teeming mass of cells, the tiny sex of a girl, sealed like an envelope."

I can't understand what he's saying and I think I'm crying. He gets a dress for me from his big closet, a gorgeous dress that's just my size, and high boots that fit me perfectly, and elegant lingerie, everything makes me so happy I could die. He has just bought it all for me. I undress right away. My boy's clothes fall to the floor around me. Briefly, he sees me naked.

For a long time I study myself in the mirror that covers one whole wall in the bedroom of Jean-Ephrem de la Tour. What I see surprises me, but I also recognize my true reflection in the mirror, haughty and innocent. I smile tenderly and my image replies, tender and smiling too, the image, the image, the beautiful image of me, Miguel Almevida.

He pulls me away from my contemplation, takes me out of my reflection in the mirror in a way, forces me to be real, to stand opposite him in the middle of the room, sharp and alive, changed into a girl and proud of it.

He offers me champagne. I learn how to drink, while my nose prickles and my eyes fill with tears. He talks to me about my hair, which is like silk, increasingly long and silky.

"Little Beast, thou art Little Beast and upon this Little Beast shall I build my happiness."

He laughs hysterically with delight. He pulls himself up abruptly, comes over to me and strokes my hair for a long time, absentmindedly, no doubt meditating in silence upon his imminent fierceness.

Jean-Ephrem de la Tour is entertaining visitors. I serve champagne and, with a lock of hair over one eye, act as his maid in my brand-new dress.

With their backpacks, leather jackets, and worn jeans I barely recognize the performers from the Paradis Perdu, without makeup or fake jewels, just as they are, pale and dishevelled.

Jean-Ephrem de la Tour says that he's never let down either a lady or a gentleman. He laughs. He struts. He's vulgar. A lout. He selects a pale redheaded girl for himself and takes her into the bedroom with the canopy bed. He asks me not to leave, to be his witness, to wait there against the bedroom door until everything is done and well done between the redheaded girl and him.

I race away as if there were a mob at my heels. My heart sickened. My gorgeous dress wet with tears.

ROSE-ALBA ALMEVIDA

I dream about a little gilt chair with a red velvet seat, a little gilt chair just for me, Rosa, Rosie, Rosita Almevida. When I'm sitting on my shining chair, the frills of my skirt spilling over on all sides, I shall dominate the entire world and no one will be able to bring me down from my pedestal. When I dream like that it sometimes happens that I go beyond the permitted limits of dreaming, that I see too much, in mass and in number, that I imagine a whole string of little gilt chairs standing against the flaking walls of my hovel, like so many gleaming nuggets. I am enthroned in gold and red velvet. It's my beloved son in whom I've placed all my indulgences who is urging me towards these extremes of daydreaming. Has he not described for me ecstatically, repeatedly, the splendours of Jean-Ephrem de la Tour's loft?

I must see it all with my own eyes — the furniture and the silver cutlery, the books bound in tawny leather, the carpet, curly like a bison, the pure gold and the crimson velvet, the immense bed and its white gauze, false candour and light mist. One night will no doubt be sufficient for me to know everything about the black angel of the Paradis Perdu, all his secrets save for the mystery that exists between him and my son. I tremble because Jean-Ephrem de la Tour is black with green hair and I am white with hair dyed yellow like wheat. I tremble because my son adores that man who torments him, in the way that flagellants adore God during Holy Week processions in Seville.

He came home very late last night, half-suffocated in the muffled dawn, his tears running onto his neck, his girl's dress all crumpled, his girl's legs visible below his girl's dress. Barely wakened from a heavy sleep, I saw it all in a fog. My son with his overlong hair, his heartbreaking tears because of a redheaded girl, he said. And I, I knew that it was because of Jean-Ephrem de la Tour. I hated that man, my son's torturer, and, at the same time, I wanted to sleep with him so as to go deeper into humiliation and be ruined along with my son.

Now that Monsieur Athanase isn't there, I'm terribly bored at the promenade. The men who brush against me in the shadows hardly deserve to live. More than ever I want Jean-Ephrem de la Tour to be crucified by his wings, then dropped onto the stage like a great black butterfly, his wings beating. The orchestra will play a shuddering tune then and

I shall hear it from far beneath the earth when I'm nothing but ashes and dust.

Tonight, there's no performance at the Paradis Perdu. My son is sleeping like a sick child. I'll go to Jean-Ephrem de la Tour's place. I'll surprise him at home. I'll soak up the overly sweet air of his loft. I'll inhale American cigarettes, black skin, the deep carpet, the huge bed, the books dressed in fragrant leather. I'll be like a retriever with an extremely keen nose who is let loose in public. Perhaps I'll learn where Jean-Ephrem de la Tour keeps all that money he throws out his windows. I'll bask in red velvet and white muslin. I'll sleep with that very black man in a canopy bed. And maybe in return he'll give me the little gilt chair with the red velvet seat that I dream of.

MIGUEL ALMEVIDA

Her flowered muslin dress brushes against me as she goes by. Her agitated breath passes over my narrow camp bed on the floor in the kitchen where I pretend I'm asleep. Exasperating, the scent of sun-soaked geranium lingers in the room after she's shut the front door behind her. I listen to the dwindling sound of her footsteps on the sidewalk. I get up and dress. Knowing nothing about my mother's rendezvous. Wanting more than anything in the world to know nothing about what she's doing so late in the dark. I convince myself that Monsieur Athanase is back from America. Very quickly I stop thinking about my mother and abandon her to her fate, the fate of a fallen woman on the run in the night. Only one thing is necessary. To get that well and truly into my head. To reconcile with Jean-Ephrem de la Tour who offended me greatly with a passing girl, redheaded and pale as a sparrow's egg.

Once I'm outside, the familiar streets move along beneath my feet, like conveyor belts in the blue-grey of the night, illuminated here and there by the yellow glow of streetlamps. Rue Cochin, rue de Pontoise, boulevard Saint-Germain. Place Maubert. The black entrance to the Métro. To dive into it. The long journey to the end of night. Departures and arrivals. The wait on the deserted platforms. The open air. The Butte. Its hills and staircases. Sit at a café terrace. Wait for the time to pass, let it slip by in the distance without me. To be in this deserted café as if I weren't there. Go over the things that are vague in my heart. Drink coffee, one after another.

Now they're bringing in the tables and chairs. Obliged to get up and leave. Fear every footstep that brings me closer to Jean-Ephrem de la Tour. It's the first time. Me, all alone in the night, going to him though he doesn't expect me. Repeat his name like a prayer, Jean-Ephrem, Jean-Ephrem, stretch his false surname like a long thread of melted cheese that grows longer, de la Tour, de la Tour . . . Laugh at his theatrical nobility. Forgive him for the red-haired girl. Adore him like a god who is devastating and cruel. Hell and paradise for a child with nothing better to do.

I have the key. I go inside as if I were at home. Everything is in order. The red walls, the heavy curtains, the closed piano. You can almost hear the air in the room as it moves slowly, in rhythm with a calm invisible breathing, without even a hint of mist on the big mirror. Nothing is happening here. The ardent nocturnal life is somewhere else. Imagine that absent life. Feel it as it gradually makes its way into my heart like a foreign woman of whom one must be wary. Look at the two closed doors in the red wall. Desire more than anything in the world that these doors stay closed forever. Want to wall them in with stones, like tombs.

It won't be long now. The air is thick all around me. I must learn the things I'll need to know for all eternity. I've looked at the wall in front of me so hard it finally opens, so slowly that I die by inches.

My mother is a fury. Her muslin dress swollen with anger, Rose-Alba Almevida, more radiant than the crimson walls, a flame glowing red, walks out of the room that has the canopy bed, straightens her puffed sleeves, passes by without seeing me, slams the door, and goes out onto the street.

He follows behind her, towering, lanky, says that he's impotent and that it's my fault. "You're never here when I need you, you little piece of trash."

I answer him so softly that no one but me can hear what I say, so softly I am at the very edge of absolute silence. "I'm going to kill myself."

LETTER FROM JEAN-EPHREM DE LA TOUR TO MIGUEL ALMEVIDA

My child, my sister, Little Beast, little spouse whom I see in my dream, little piece of flotsam destined for the fire of heaven, tiny lost thing. I must bid you adieu. Note carefully, by the way, that strange word "adieu." I've obviously read too many books that are beyond me. Remembered whatever words aren't ordinary. Adieu, then. I must tend to my affairs. For a long time I played an angel in the theatre and a beast in bed, with fleeting companions. I've been kicked out of the Paradis Perdu. Now I must swallow the unbreathable air of this world, without thinking about it, and slip away. Towards other climes. Enigmas don't have such a hard life. Soon you'll know everything.

But where shall I send this letter? Needless to say, not in care of your mother, that beautiful victim. I'll look for you everywhere. You'll never know it most likely. I'm writing just for myself. No stamp or postman. I'll look for you in the streets. I'll keep the secret of you to myself, like a hidden treasure.

Without breaking any silence, I am yours,
Jean-Ephrem de la Tour

MIGUEL ALMEVIDA

Which of them, my mother or Jean-Ephrem, having betrayed me equally, pushes me gently towards the Seine?

I lean over as far as I can to smell the bland odour of the water.

Behind the grey clouds the day is slowly breaking. On the riverbank, a clochard lies on his cardboard, rolled up in his blanket, yells at the top of his lungs in his dreams, shouting that it will be a beautiful day.

From looking so hard at the slow and monotonous Seine, I grow weary and listen to the booming, rusty voice of the clochard who proclaims the beauty of the day and calls to me in secret.

In no time I dash up to the Quai de la Tournelle and shake myself like a dog coming out of the water.

The day is dawning on all sides at once. I must flee without further delay. One last stop at the lodge to get my things. One last look at my sleeping mother. Her party dress in a heap on the chair. She who offered herself and was refused is sleeping like a baby gorged with milk. And I, her offended son, am leaving her at this moment forever.

Soon the silence of the sleeping house will be broken. Footsteps everywhere, on the stairs, the landings, doors opening and closing, voices greeting or grumbling. Hurry, before it's too late. Hurry. The unlivable time in which I exist is becoming thinner, like worn fabric. So tired. My legs give way under me. To leave my mother without further delay. The keys there, hanging on the wall! Madame Guillou's key, cold and shiny between my fingers. Madame Guillou on vacation in the south. Take advantage of her empty apartment. I enter her place like a thief. Go directly to the bedroom. Collapse on the bed on my stomach, my face in the pillow. Risk choking because of the tears. Fall asleep in Madame Guillou's bed.

MADAME GUILLOU

They should all be kicked out. Loathsome people. The father, the mother, the son. Drive them out of the house without delay. The father, on the run who knows where, the mother, in desperate straits screaming from door to door, "Have you seen my son, Miguel?" and he, he, the little hypocrite who stayed in my apartment while I was away, he, the child I once loved, the serpent that I warmed in my bosom. Found his list when I came home from my vacation, sitting prominently next to the telephone on my night table where he'd forgotten it. It said:

Before leaving:
- *buy package of Lustigru egg noodles and just leave half*
- *put a quarter litre of water in Evian bottle*
- *close all shutters*
- *tune radio back to France Musique*
- *buy Fruit d'or sunflower oil margarine*

The perfect crime. All traces wiped clean. Now he is sinking deeper into the savage night as though nothing were amiss and no one the wiser. That child ate and drank in my house, he slept in my sheets. If I ever catch him. He, he, the affectionate little youngster I used to love.

ROSE-ALBA ALMEVIDA

A voice can be heard in the fifth arrondissement, an endless moaning and wailing, it is Rose-Alba Almevida, weeping for her son who has disappeared, refusing consolation because he's been gone for five days now.

"God of my childhood, give me back my son and I'll become a virgin again forever, beneath the habit and the veil as you want me to be, for eternity, amid the lighted altar candles, the swaying sanctuary lamps, the chubby-faced cherubs and rapturous madonnas."

At the same time, there are the outcries of Madame Guillou who's come back from her vacation. Wrinkles in her sheets, a strange odour in her bed, too much order throughout the apartment. And particularly that list left next to the telephone, written by Miguel Almevida, that she sticks under my nose.

Madame Guillou repeats "forcible entry," "breach of trust." Her upper lip curls up over her little green teeth, as if she were about to nip with a poisonous bite.

And I, I, his mother, the first to be betrayed, the first to be trampled on, I am foaming with rage. Light has been shed on every mystery. My son is a runaway, my son is a squatter, my son is a hoodlum. I'm going back to the Paradis Perdu. That will teach the child that I brought into this world for my damnation and his.

MIGUEL ALMEVIDA

On the run from my mother's, can't go back to Madame Guillou's, no fixed address, I've been wandering from street to street since this morning. Windbreaker creased, shirt soiled, shoes worn down, I drag my muddy soles. As inattentive as in school, mind blank, ravenous, I am going I know not where to lose myself once and for all. And nothing more need be said.

The grey street, the grey sidewalk, the white stripes at intersections, the rotten gutter, the red lights, the green lights. I know only what I need to know about the city in order to advance, step by step.

For a while now garish lights have been reflected on the street. I walk through puddles of colour — red, green, blue, yellow. The air thickens, filled with obscene invitations from the clubs lined along the sidewalk. Voices come to me, muffled and hoarse. Pleasure is offered to me from door to door by barkers in richly coloured uniforms.

Who then has brought me here? Dragging me by the hand, pushing me by the shoulders, bringing me to this place where I'd sworn I would never return?

The scent of the wet air reminds me of the scent of his big body streaming under the shower.

If I don't watch out, Jean-Ephrem de la Tour's massive apartment building will rise before me like a blind fortress against the black sky.

My footsteps, without resonance or echo, resemble those of cats lost in the night.

No, no, I didn't want that.

JEAN-EPHREM DE LA TOUR

One tiny lamp, at the end of a long cord, stands in the middle of the room. All that is left of the light is there on the floor and I'm on the floor as well, looking as if I'm using a camp-fire for light. All around me, the carpet like a wasteland. Here and there, spots left bare and brown where the furniture has been taken away.

All the treasures that were here have been removed — furniture, books, trinkets. Even my bed, covered with white muslin. The life that I lived here, flashy and mad, has been carried off and taken far away. I expect that I'll be taken too.

Movers came with a truck. They left a void around me. Now I'm sitting cross-legged in the middle of my devastated loft. I'm eating a ham sandwich and picking up the crumbs as they fall to the carpet.

My big body, kicked out of the Paradis Perdu for obscure reasons, scrutinizes itself in the low muted glimmer. My hands on my knees look dead, one beside the other. My face frozen like a stone. My bare feet displaying the calluses of the skilled dancer. I persist in this implacable examination. I pretend to look over my badly lit body for a trace of some unknown sin that might be the cause of everything.

No defeat then. Real life is quite simply elsewhere. Instead of real life I'll have a look at what it's like elsewhere. Plenty of boredom most likely, and disgust, which is worse than bore- dom. All of that before the arrival of soothing habit and recovered laughter.

The rain has left long spurts of scattered drops on the glass. I press my face against it but it doesn't cool me. On the other side of the world, the city in mist. Its damp breath- ing. I watch for the long car that's supposed to come for me at any moment.

From my position it's impossible to see the small silhou- ette hugging the walls, advancing along the sidewalk towards me, slow and light as a shadow.

MIGUEL ALMEVIDA

He is standing in the doorway looking furiously at me, as if I shouldn't exist before him.

"Where have you come from at this hour of the night, Little Beast?"

I look at him too, at this man who, dead or alive, was made to be seen by the greatest number of people on stage in a theatre.

People emerge from the elevator, scatter on the landing, and laugh very loudly. Hurriedly, Jean-Ephrem de la Tour shows me into his loft.

A single lamp, standing on the floor, throws light onto the black carpet. There are no other lamps anywhere. Jean-Ephrem de la Tour's loft no longer glows, vast and deep as far as the eye can see. Every corner now is full of darkness. So empty as to discourage you from living. Our enormous shadows on the wall no longer look like anyone. Is it here that everything will end? We don't know what to do with our eyes, mouths, ears, with our hands that hang down on either side of our bodies. It's a question of knowing who will be the first to break the silence. He, the embodiment of my ruin? Me, so overjoyed by him that it could kill me? Now each of us facing the other, each in his skin as in a fragile shelter.

It is he who moves first. He paces the room, barefoot, holding his shoes, then throwing them violently at the brass barre left behind on the wall.

He turns back to me. "I don't have much time. You'll have to leave in a hurry."

He sits back down on the floor and puts on his shoes, slowly, like a child tying laces for the first time.

He talks so softly that it's like a breath, just barely perceptible against my ear. "I'm expecting someone."

It doesn't surprise me that he is expecting someone, nervous as he is. If it's my mother I'll kill him, and my mother too. I'll be handcuffed and taken to court. I enunciate clearly, as if I had a part in a play and weren't fully there: "I hope it isn't my mother."

He laughs and he says that it's not. He takes his shoes off

again and starts doing exercises at the barre. It reminds me of the Paradis Perdu and I want to cry. He puts his shoes back on and looks out the window. He talks with his back to me, still looking out the window.

He seems to be speaking to someone invisible, someone floating between heaven and earth, right there at the level of the seventh floor. Jean-Ephrem de la Tour's breath leaves condensation on the streaming wet window.

"I've been confiscated. Do you know what that means, confiscated? They took away everything that was here. The furniture and knickknacks. Even the gold chain from my neck and the bracelet from my wrist."

I wish I could console Jean-Ephrem de la Tour, take him out of his unhappiness. I murmur, just in case, as if I know what I'm talking about: "Didn't you pay your rent?"

That makes him laugh and he turns towards me, animated and happy as if he were going to start dancing again. "I like you, Little Beast, you make me laugh. But I don't have much time left to look after you just now. Didn't pay my rent, as you say. Didn't pay. Anything. Debts everywhere. A mob is after me. I have to go away."

"Take me with you." I say this as if the words had escaped from me by themselves, without my wanting, without my even opening my mouth, a little like blood on the surface of the skin, barely touched by the air as it passes.

"Little Beast, you're dreaming. And me, I was made for living, for living without reins and without scruples, do you understand?" His dazzling teeth so close to my face, his breath on my cheek. His gaze fixed in a strange squint, like a wolf's.

I look at him as long as I can, wanting desperately never to lose sight of him. I tell him he looks like his portrait and that it drives me to despair.

He turns away. He stands at the window again. The bad weather exasperates him. He complains about the fog and the height of the building not letting him see what's going on in the street. Says again that they're waiting for him and that he ought to go down right away. He unplugs the little lamp on the floor and tucks it under his arm to take away. "It's all I have left. Better bring it along."

I hear him breathing in the dark as my heart fills the room with rapid, muffled beating. His shadow against my shadow in the dark room.

JEAN-EPHREM DE LA TOUR

Nothing to say. Nothing to explain. Keep my distance. Let him mind his own business. Let me mind my own. Tell him again to go away while a vague glimmer enters the room through the open window. I believe he's shivering in the mist that sweeps in here as if we were at the seaside. I'd rather he insult me and cry openly. At one stroke I'd be rid of the patient and furious expectation of my punishment.

I hear his voice that's come from I know not where, across the grey and empty room: "I would so much have liked to be a girl and to marry you."

I talk to him about a wedding gown, white and billowy and falling to the floor. I tell him that his love of clothes will spell his ruin. I recite to him the hallowed formula of marriage. I insist on the bride's obligation to share everything with her husband, for better and for worse, till death do them part.

He answers so quietly that I guess rather than hear what he says. "Yes, yes, I want all that, I want to marry you."

Night lies slack over all the city. And yet it grows brighter and brighter in this empty room where I'm shut away with Miguel Almevida. From looking in the dark so much I'm able to see as if it were daylight. A little while longer and I'll have his dazed face before me, staring at me. That must be avoided at all costs. Talk in the darkness of my lowered eyelids. Give in to theatrical lines worthy of the Paradis Perdu. Admit that I'm going on a trip to the sun and the sea, in the company of a very mature and very rich lady. Then move on in sheer fantasy.

"As for my pitiful heart, which is as old as a hundred-year-old Chinese egg, I leave it to you as a token. Do what you want with it. All my sins are there. I have only one thing in mind at present, to start life again as if nothing had happened. Go, Little Beast. Go, I beg you, go."

For another moment he stands there before me, ready to flee, motionless and mute, while the blood inside him rushes and stirs as if for a sudden death.

I tell him again to go. "Go now, Little Beast. Go. They're waiting for me."

He has the misfortune of being unable to leave. I push him towards the door. I bid him adieu, tenderly, like in a novel.

MIGUEL ALMEVIDA

Not at my mother's or at Madame Guillou's or at Jean-Ephrem de la Tour's. There's no place where I can sleep and eat, laugh or cry, in peace. Driven away from everywhere. I go down onto the deserted riverbank. Day is breaking in the grey sky. There's no clochard to declare that the day will be beautiful.

I am heavy, so heavy, like a woman carrying a child on her back. Jean-Ephrem de la Tour, my husband. I shall deliver him from his evil. I shall take responsibility for his burden, fasten it to me like a big stone to drown me.

After looking for a long time at the Seine lapping at my

feet, I begin to see images half-dreamed in the shuddering water. The Spain of my parents, with its white houses, its silvery olive trees, its green vines all in a row, undone by the invasive water when I bend over it. Someone sacred I don't yet know is preparing a suit of light for me, in secret, in the midst of the waves and grey ripples, for when I'll have arrived among the dead.

MADAME GUILLOU

Those people are impossible. The son has drowned himself in the Seine, the mother is screaming so loudly you can hear her in the street; as for the father, rumour has it that he prowls the city in the hope of getting his wife back and erasing all dishonour from his house.